BADD MOJO

A BADD BROTHERS NOVEL

Jasinda Wilder

BADD MOJO

ONE

Canaan

WHO KNEW A BAR FULL OF THURSDAY NIGHT PATRONS could be closed in less than five minutes? But that's what just happened when Rachel Kingsley arrived to confront Tate about her pregnancy.

As Rachel paced and ranted about immaturity and irresponsibility and ruined lives, the four of us just kind of stood there and listened. Her rage was a palpable thing, a physical force. As she railed on, my mind went back in time, remembering her when we were just kids.

She *hated* Corin and me.

She hated this bar.

She hated our family name, and everything about

us. Why? I wasn't sure. I only knew that she'd always hated the Badd brothers. She'd barely tolerated her daughters, Tate and Aerie, hanging out with us when we were kids, and that was only because the girls had actually run away together the one time their mother had tried to force them to stop seeing us. At age thirteen, they'd stolen their mother's credit card, forged her signature, and had gotten as far as Portland, Oregon before they'd been hauled back in custody by an FBI agent Rachel was friends with. They had been grounded for a month, but the blow-out screaming match the three of them had had about the whole scenario had convinced Rachel that it was probably safest to just let the girls see us—under watchful supervision.

These rules had meant that the only time we saw them was either around Dad or Rachel, or in a public place, like the mall or at school. No private studying, no hanging out when there weren't other adults around. Not that Rachel's fears hadn't been somewhat justified, as Corin and I had both lost our virginity very young and had begun pursuing girls with a focus so singular it was only matched by our dedication to music. So, given the reputation we'd earned by the time we were sixteen, I can definitely understand Rachel's concerns. We were horndogs, and with Dad being the way he was—working open to close every single day and half-drunk by ten most nights—we had little to zero supervision. Meaning… we ran roughshod over Ketchikan, banging any girl that would let us into her pants.

Rachel had been worried for the virtue of her daughters. I get it, I do.

Bast wasn't any better…and neither were Zane, or Brock, or Bax. The only two who didn't earn reputations as lady-killer man-whores were Luce and Xavier, and being the babies of the family, they were young and had other interests. So, again, I understand the distaste a prim and pretentious woman like Rachel would develop for us. Her daughters were gorgeous, and outgoing, and smart, and popular, and talented… she wanted them to have a future, and letting them get tangled up with us Badd boys seemed, to her, the death knell of their potential. We'd just ruin them, Rachel assumed.

That part is bullshit.

Corin and I had plans. We had no intention of sticking around Ketchikan for our whole lives. We were gonna be rock stars, and tour the world, and make millions of dollars, and buy mansions in Beverly Hills. Knocking up girls had no place in those plans, and so we were always very careful.

Which is why Corin's mistake with Tate is so damn confusing to me. This whole year, being back in Ketchikan to help run the bar, it was meant to be a temporary hiatus for us, nothing more. We'd intended to develop our own label and release our own music during that time, but the plan had always been to get back out on the road as soon as we could.

I still had no intention of settling down in Ketchikan permanently, not anytime soon, at least.

I loved touring. I loved the craziness and the chaos, the solitude of the time on the road, the lights and the noise and the crowds...I was born for it. I wouldn't mind having Ketchikan as my home base, as my private refuge when I needed time away from it all, but to just...stay here?

Yeah...nope.

But with Tate being pregnant, things had become complicated.

Honestly, I'm pissed at him. That'll have to wait, though.

Right now, Rachel's anger took precedence.

"...I just don't understand how you could let this happen, Tate! I thought you knew better! You've assured me up and down since the time you were sixteen that you'd never let this happen. 'I won't be having any babies until I'm ready'—those were your exact words, verbatim, less than six months ago." Rachel stopped pacing, breathing hard, shaking her head. "I just...I don't even know what to say."

"You seem to have plenty to say," Tate said.

"Your modeling career is over, Tate. Over. Even successful supermodels don't go back to mainstream full-time modeling after having a baby. That's a major shift in career paths for a model. Even if you do everything right, stay in shape, watch your diet, get your body back as quickly as possible after birth, you won't be the same. Things won't be the same. And...how are you going to raise a baby? What do you know of parenting? Of real responsibility? And what...you're going to do it alone? I'm busier than ever—you know that. I've opened a talent management office, as you know, so it's not like I'll have time play Grandma so you can go gallivanting off modeling like you're used to." She snorted, gesturing derisively at Corin. "You think *he's* going to stick around? You think *he's* going hang around playing daddy with a baby he never wanted with a girl who was never anything but an easy piece of ass for him?"

Corin took a single aggressive, stomping step toward Rachel, his voice deadly quiet. "You know *nothing* about me, Rachel. You know nothing about us or about our relationship...you don't even know anything about your own daughter." Another step, his voice still pitched low with fury. "How *dare* you— how fucking *dare* you assume that about me, much less about your own daughter? You assume she would let herself be that, what you called her? An easy piece of ass? You think that about your own daughter?"

Tate stepped up beside him. "He's right. You have no right." She clung to his arm with both hands, and it was obvious she was only barely controlling her own anger. "You are so far out of line I don't even—I can't even…" she trailed off, at a loss to encapsulate her emotions.

"Oh stop with the poor insulted us routine," Rachel sneered. "You know I'm right."

Tate hissed. "No, actually, you're wrong on just about every level there is. God, you're fucking impossible, Mom!"

"Oh? Wrong about what?" Rachel crossed her arms over her chest and quirked an eyebrow. "This I'd like to hear."

"About me, about Corin. About us, like he said. This may have been unexpected—" she lifted the pregnancy test she was holding in one hand, "—but it's not…Corin isn't going to just abandon me. We're *together*."

"Oh, you're *together*," Rachel said, sarcastic. "How nice. My mind is changed."

"We're in love, Mom."

Rachel touched her chest with a dramatic flourish. "Oh, you're in *love*! My, my, my—everything is fixed, now!" She shook her head again, rolling her eyes. "And what about your career? What about *his*?" She glanced at me and Corin. "I heard you two boys were doing a little music thing…this affects that somewhat, doesn't it?"

"You're being a bitch, Mom," Aerie said, standing beside me.

Rachel didn't even glance Aerie's way. "You stay out of this. I'll get to you next, missy." To Tate, then: "Being in love is very nice for the two of you. It won't last, but at least you have that going for you at the moment. It still doesn't change the fact that your modeling career is ruined."

"I NEVER WANTED TO BE A MODEL!" Tate shouted. "You forced me into that. I never wanted it! I'm glad it's over!"

Rachel blinked, shocked. "I didn't force you into anything—stop being so damn dramatic."

"For the record, it's not a little music thing," I felt compelled to add. "We were signed with a major label, and we were in the middle of a world tour when our father died unexpectedly. We came back home to be with our family."

"Your *family*," Rachel sneered. "A bunch of lazy, itinerant, philandering, swaggering brutes and thugs and hoodlums."

Brock and Bast were both behind the bar, quietly listening and watching and letting the four of us handle own drama—they'd closed down the bar early when Rachel had started ranting, so now we were alone in the dining room; Mara, Dru, and Claire had vanished to give us privacy, and Lucian and Zane had retreated into the kitchen.

Hearing Rachel's last statement, Bast swaggered out from behind the bar, his size-fifteen steel-toed boots clomping like thunder on the hardwood floors. He stomped over, slid in between Rachel and Corin and Tate, crossing his massive, tattooed arms over his thick chest, his expression fiery; Bast was intimidating when he was in a *good* mood...when he was angry? Well, let's just say I wouldn't want to be on the receiving end.

He stared Rachel down for a long moment. When he spoke, his voice was tight and cold. "Listen up, bitch. This is *our* bar you're standing in. You don't get to stand there actin' all high and mighty, insultin' me and my brothers. I got no quarrel with you. I get you looking out for your daughters. I get you being pissed that Tate's come up pregnant. I even get you being upset she got knocked up by a Badd...god knows none of us are saints. But you want to have this conversation with them under my roof, you will keep a civil tongue in your fuckin' pretentious-ass head, you understand me? You wanna keep insulting me and mine—and that includes Tate and Aerie by the way—you can take your ass out of here."

To her credit, Rachel faced Bast without flinching, although she did go as pale as a sheet. "You—you can't talk to me like that, you big ugly brute," she snarled, blustering.

Dru appeared out of thin air, putting her face into Rachel's. "He's too much of a gentleman to outright threaten you, and he certainly wouldn't put a hand on you." Dru's hand shot out and latched onto Rachel's, pinching the web of her hand between forefinger and thumb—a pressure point, apparently, since Rachel squeaked in pain and went utterly still. "Make no mistake, Rachel Kingsley—I can and will literally *throw* you out of this bar, and you'll land straight on your face. You do *not* get to talk to any of us like that, especially not my husband." She let go, and Rachel staggered backward on her Louboutins, rubbing her hand.

"You're all barbarians." She glared daggers at Dru…from a safe distance. "Touch me again, and I'll sue you." She gestured at all of us. "I'm here to collect my daughters and take them home where I can deal with them and the mess they've made of their lives. I don't need any of *you* people sticking your nose in my business."

Bast chuckled, a deep rumble. "Yeah, well, then you shouldn't have stormed into the middle of a busy bar on a Thursday night and started screaming like a crazy woman."

"I was not screaming like a crazy woman!" Rachel protested.

"I had to apologize to my customers for the embarrassment and disruption, not to mention the fact that I then also had to close several hours early, which is losing me thousands of dollars." He pinned her with a hard glare, stabbing a finger in her direction. "So yeah, crazy woman."

Rachel huffed. "That's not my problem."

"It's about to be," Dru snarled. "I'll *make* it your problem."

"More threats," Rachel said. "How shocking."

Lucian appeared from the kitchen, then, standing to one side with his hands in his back pockets, casual and calm and giving off an air of grandfatherly disapproval. "This is getting out of hand." He glided to stand behind Rachel, gesturing at the front door with one hand. "You need to leave."

"I'm not—you can't—"

Lucian's voice snapped like a whip. "*Now.*"

The command in his voice was so sharp and authoritative that her feet were carrying her to the door before Rachel even realized it. She stumbled to a halt, and Lucian remained behind her, arm extended to prevent her from retreating back into the dining room.

"Now you wait just one moment, I'm not leav-ing—" Rachel started.

"You *are*," Luce interrupted. "You aren't wel-come here, Mrs. Kingsley." This was phrased with the utmost politeness, but his voice was colder than ice. "Now…or ever."

Rachel pointed at Tate and Aerie, and then snapped her fingers as she headed for the door. "Let's go, girls."

Aerie and Tate exchanged looks, and then Aerie moved to stand beside Tate, and I stood beside her, so we were all four of us in a row, arms around each other's waists.

"I don't think so, Mom," Tate said.

"You're coming home with me, Tate." Rachel jabbed a finger at the floor. "Right *now*."

Tate shook her head. "I said no."

"I can get you in to see Dr. Vickers. He'll have this little oops of yours taken care of quickly, pain-lessly, and easily." Rachel tried a different tactic. "I can help."

Tate pressed her hands over her belly. "Dr. Vickers? At the women's clinic, you mean?" She shook her head, backing up. "Like…an *abortion*?"

"It's the most logical solution, Tate." She even managed to sound sympathetic.

"Fuck you, Mom," Tate snarled. "That's not an option."

"Fuck no, it's not an option," Corin said. "Please leave, Rachel."

"You're making a mistake!" Rachel shouted. "*He's* a mistake. This whole thing is a mistake."

"I'm not going to ask again, Mrs. Kingsley." Lucian stepped directly into her line of vision. "Leave now, or the police will be involved."

"I'm here for my daughter!" Rachel said. "I'm not leaving without her. You're making a mistake, Tate."

Tate let out a breath, hesitated, then crossed the room to stand by her mother; Lucian stepped aside, but didn't go far. "Mom, listen." Her voice was quiet, calm, almost loving. "I know you mean well. I really do. I'm sorry we had to leave like we did, I'm sorry we quit modeling when that's what you wanted for us—" Rachel tried to cut in, but Tate spoke over her. "No—*no*! Mom, please hear me: I *never* wanted to be a model. I went along with it because I was sixteen and didn't know any better than to think you really did know best for us. I'm an adult now, and I can legally make my own decisions. If you want to help, then back off, be emotionally supportive, stop being so combative and crazy and difficult, and just...be my *mom*. I don't need you to manage me or my life anymore, and I haven't for a long time. To be honest, I resent your interference. That's why I'm *here*."

"Tate, you can't know—"

"Shut *up*, Mom!" Tate snapped. "I'm here because this is where I want to be. I'm with Corin because he's who I want to be with. I know you've never approved of them—you seem to hate all of them, as a matter of fact, and I've never understood why. They're good men, all of them. They're kind and intelligent and successful, and they're loyal—and Corin...he's...he's...he's talented and funny and kind, and he understands me like no one ever has or ever will. I *love* him, Mom. This isn't sudden—I mean, yeah, it is, but it's also not. We've known each other our whole lives. Now we're adults and it just makes sense. I don't need your approval. I don't need your help."

"Tate—" Rachel whispered.

"No. Just...don't. I love you, Mom. I know everything you've done has been with our best interests at heart—please believe me when I say I really truly do understand that. But you're...you need to let go a little. Let us live our own lives. Stop micromanaging everything." Tate guided her mother to the door. "I'm never going back to modeling. Never. I'm done, permanently. I don't know what I'll do, but it won't be that."

"So you'll be a…a *housewife*?" Rachel asked this with a maximum amount of derision placed on the term.

"Maybe! And if that's what I choose, then there won't be a damn thing you can do about it."

"So you're…you're just done with me?" Rachel sounded pathetic, now. Petulant.

Tate groaned. "God, you're so dramatic. No, Mom. I'm not *done* with you, I'm just done with you trying to micromanage every aspect of my life, trying to tell me what to do, or where to go, or how to live, or what I do with my life, or who I'm going to be with." She was physically guiding Rachel out of the building. "If you want to be in my life—speaking only for myself right now—you have to get a grip on yourself. You can't just barge into someone's place of business and start screaming obscenities at people. It's embarrassing, and I won't stand for it. I also won't let you speak negatively about the man I love or his family. So…again, if you want to be part of my life, you'll have to be nice. To me, Corin, Sebastian and everyone else. I'm not playing games anymore, Mom. *I'm* not a child, and *you* need to stop acting like one."

Rachel sighed, a long, dramatic exhalation. "Fine. Have it your way, then. But don't come running to me when your life falls apart."

"Can't you just support me, Mom?" Tate's voice

quavered, then, and she exhaled sharply, steadying herself. "You don't have to agree with my decisions, but at least act like you love me and support me anyway. Is that really so much to ask?"

"You're throwing your life away, Tater-Tot." Rachel cupped Tate's face, smiling sadly; her manner was rife with condescension. "I know you think you want this, but I promise…you *don't*. I'm just trying to protect you from yourself."

Tate knocked her mother's hand away. "You don't get to call me that." She backed away. "Bye, Mom."

And then Tate turned her back on her mother. She had tears in her eyes, but her shoulders were back and her head was high, and she gratefully returned to the shelter of Corin's side.

Rachel paused in the doorway, holding the door open with one hand, glancing back at Aerie. "And you, Aerie?"

Aerie, standing next to me, leaning against my side with one hand on my chest, head leaning on my bicep, just shook her head. "She spoke for both of us regarding your behavior and how you treat us," Aerie said. "And I have nothing else to say to you right now."

"Fine." Rachel sighed. "I'll be leaving Ketchikan on Saturday morning. I'm staying with Grandma and Grandpa until then. I'll see you there?"

"Probably not," Aerie said. "Not after this."

"I just—"

"*Bye*, Mom," Aerie said, with a sarcastic wave.

Yet another angry huff, and then Rachel Kingsley was finally gone.

As the door closed behind her, a long, tense silence filled the bar.

"Wow, she's kind of like the Great Dragon of the East or something, isn't she?" Xavier said, from the doorway to the kitchen.

Tate laughed. "She means well, but her delivery lacks...tact, you could say."

Corin snorted. "Babe, I'm sorry, but...your mom's a cunt."

Aerie whacked him. "Nobody calls our mom a cunt except us," she said. "But she *was* acting like a cunt—and speaking as woman, I don't use that term lightly, especially about my mother."

Tate rubbed Corin's chest where Aerie had slapped him. "Like I said, she really does mean well."

Brock, who hadn't said a word the entire time, nor moved from his place behind the bar, yanked a bottle of whiskey from a shelf behind the bar. "That was fucking intense, and I need a drink."

The door leading to the apartment stairs opened, and Zane appeared with Jax in his arm, the little guy staring backward over his dad's shoulder as Zane approached the bar. "Is the crazy lady gone?" he asked in a whisper-shout. "Ooh, whiskey. Yes please."

As if his words had summoned them, the rest of the gang all reappeared from wherever they'd gone.

"Do it up for everyone," Bast said to Brock, lining up a row of shot glasses. "Except for Tate, since she's apparently carrying the newest member of the Badd family." He said this with a wink at Tate. "Luce, Xavier, you can have one too, just this once, but keep it on the DL, yeah?"

"Of all the times to not be able to drink," Tate moaned. "Because I seriously need one right now."

Aerie laughed. "I'll do yours for you, sis."

Tate glanced from person to person as Brock poured shots. "I'm sorry about that, everyone. She's always been a little fired up about everything, but that was excessive even for her."

Lucian and Xavier joined the crew at the bar, and Xavier sat on a stool while Lucian stood beside him.

Corin took his shot glass as Brock passed them out, and when everyone had theirs, except Tate, who had a shot glass filled with soda water, he lifted his into the air. "So, this wasn't how I thought the announcement would go, but…" He laughed, gesturing with his shot glass. "Tate's pregnant, ya'll!"

There was a chorus of congratulations from everyone, and we all did our shots. Tate slammed her glass onto the bar with an irritated huff. "Soda water.

It's bullshit."

"You have to think of the baby," Zane said. "Gotta take care of little baby Badd."

Tate glared at him. "I literally *just* found out, Zane. Like, literally not even five minutes before my mom showed up. I haven't exactly had time to process this."

"Oh." Zane glanced at Corin. "So, Corin, buddy. Need to borrow my copy of *The Expectant Father*?"

"A little soon for jokes, Zane," Corin said.

"Who's joking? I read that shit three times while Mara was pregnant."

"Watch your language around the baby, Zane," Mara chided.

Everyone seemed totally cool with this whole thing. They were all like, hey, Tate's pregnant. Cool! The more the merrier.

But I wasn't so copacetic with the whole thing. At all.

And nobody seemed to notice, or care.

Finally, I couldn't handle the whole scene anymore. "Fuck this," I snarled. "This is bullshit."

I stormed out of the bar, ignoring everyone's stares and murmurs.

TWO

Aerie

Everyone stared after Canaan as he stomped out through the kitchen, and then the door to the alley squealed open and slammed closed.

Tate glanced at Corin. "What crawled up his ass and died?"

Corin shrugged and shook his head. "For once, I have no clue." He glanced over at me for help. "He's usually the more levelheaded one. I don't know if I've ever seen him have an outburst like that."

"I'll go talk to him." I headed for the kitchen, and then paused, glancing at Brock, who was leaning against the service bar. "Can I have a couple beers? Might help break the ice a little."

Brock reached into a refrigerator under the counter opposite the bar, pulled out two bottles of local pale ale, popped the tops, and handed them to me. "Just make sure you bring the bottles back in—they're technically not allowed outside."

"I will."

I took the bottles and stopped at the fryer station on the way to the back door—Xavier had a habit of always making more fries and chicken tenders than he needed, because someone was always popping in to steal some. I tossed some fries and tenders into a cup and nudged the alley door open with my hip. The brothers always parked the Silverado they shared in the mouth of the alley to prevent anyone from parking there, and so the alley was quiet. Canaan was in the bed of the truck, the tailgate open. He was lying down on the tailgate, legs hanging over the edge, kicking his feet, hands under his head, staring up at the stars. He lifted his head and glanced at me, and then rested his head in his hands again.

"I don't wanna talk about it," he grumbled as I hopped up onto the tailgate beside him.

"I haven't even said anything yet."

I rested the cold, sweating bottom of beer bottle on his forehead, and he just glanced at me in amused irritation. "Really, Aerie?"

I just shrugged, propped my own bottle between

my thighs to free up my other hand, and touched a French fry to his lips. "Really, really," I said in a terrible Scottish accent, attempting to sound like Shrek.

He snorted. "You suck at accents." He snapped his teeth around the fry and chomped the rest into his mouth, taking the beer bottle and sitting up.

"Yeah, but it's fun."

Together, in silence, we ate the food, sipped beer, and didn't say a word.

Eventually, Canaan hissed in frustration. "You're really not going to ask?"

"I followed you out here with food and beer, Canaan." I leaned into him and nudged his side with my elbow, playfully, affectionately. "Obviously your tantrum is why I'm out here. So…do I really need to ask you, 'Hey Canaan, what are you so pissy about all of a sudden?'"

He huffed another laugh. "I think you did just actually ask, though."

"No, I said what I wasn't going to say, which is different."

"In literal terms, yes, it's different. In practical terms, not so much." He punctuated this by tipping his beer bottle up in a long swig.

I tapped the underside of the bottle so it spilled down his shirt, making him sputter and laugh. "Don't be a dick."

He wiped his mouth and smeared at his shirt with one hand, shaking his head. "You're impossible."

I shrugged, tilting my head to one side with a coy, demure smile. "What can I say? It's a gift."

Canaan just shoved a handful of fries into his mouth, finished them, and then cut his eyes at me. "Fine, I'll bite." He finished his beer, set it on the lip of the bed, and lay down. "Tate being pregnant fucks everything up for everyone, and I'm pissed off."

"You're not pregnant, and you didn't get her pregnant," I said. "I know you guys are twins and all, but it's not really your problem, is it?"

He actually laughed at me as he sat back up. "Aerie. You're not serious, are you?"

I stared at him. "I mean...yeah?"

He shook his head. "How's Corin going to go back on tour when Tate is pregnant, or when the baby comes?"

I frowned. "Back on tour?"

Canaan's answering frown was puzzled. "Um, yeah, back on tour. This year in Ketchikan isn't per-manent. Or, at least, it wasn't supposed to be. It was meant to be one year, which is almost up. The plan was we'd spend the year here, help the brothers with the business, build up our own record label and all that, and start over as a new band. Go back on tour. Come back here to record and all that, use Ketchikan as our home base, but…" He shrugged. "That was the plan."

"And Tate being pregnant throws a big ol' monkey wrench into those plans."

"Exactly."

I lay back on the bed this time. "I hadn't thought about it that way."

"Thought about what?" Canaan asked, lying beside me.

"Everything, I guess." Now that I had a moment away from all the drama that had started the moment Tate announced her pregnancy, I began to process what had just happened. I started to freak out. "Shit, shit, shit, shit."

Canaan eyed me sideways. "Now *you're* having a meltdown?"

"I haven't had time to process it, yet. Tate is *pregnant*. Tate has no plans of ever being a model again." I rubbed my face with both hands. "I—that throws a monkey wrench into *my* plans."

"Tate is pregnant."

"Tate is pregnant," I echoed him, as if repeating the phrase could force a deeper understanding of the reality upon me. "My twin sister is going to have a baby."

"My twin brother is going to be a father."

"Tate is going to be a mommy." I sat up, my heart

palpitating. "Canaan, what the fuck are we going to do? If Tate doesn't want to be a model, if she wants to stay here and just be a mother, or if she has some other plans, what do *I* do? We made our name in the fashion industry as a single entity, as Tate and Aerie, Aerie and Tate, the twin models. The next Mary-Kate and Ashley. If Tate is out, where does that leave me?"

"That's what I'm saying!" Canaan yelled. "Cor and I have been in a band our whole lives—ever since we first discovered music when were four years old. I had an old, out-of-tune, missing-strings guitar of Dad's and Corin had a bucket and some sticks. We even wrote our own songs. We've been doing this as a unit since…since before I could even piss into the adult-height urinals. Without Corin, I don't what *I'm* going to do. I mean, can a pregnant woman go on tour? What if she doesn't want to? What if…what if *he* doesn't want to tour with me anymore? This fucks up everything. That's what I'm pissed about, Aerie."

I laughed bitterly. "Yeah, well, now I am too."

A long silence stretched between us, then.

"Canaan?"

"Yeah."

"What about us?" I asked this in a quiet voice.

We both sat up at the same time.

"What do you mean, what about us?" He sounded wary.

"Us, hanging out together." That wasn't the only way I'd meant that, but it was obvious from his wary reaction that he wasn't ready for the *other* conversation.

"I mean, I don't know." He sighed. "I don't know. These past few weeks have been…different, and fun, and challenging, and I love it. I just…"

"It was never meant to take the place of you and Corin?" I suggested.

He nodded. "Yeah, I guess." He shot a quick glance at me. "Which doesn't mean I think any less of the music and you and I make together, Aerie. I mean that."

"I know."

"It's just…Bishop's Pawn was…we were *good*. Corin and I can do some incredible stuff together. And me, as a musician—I don't know how to put it… but in some ways it feels like my identity as a musician is sort tied in with Corin. Which becomes a problem, now that he and Tate are…like, super serious or whatever."

I laughed. "They're gonna have a baby together…I sure as fuck hope they're *serious or whatever*."

I left it at that, my eyes on his, and I was intentionally leaving a giant gaping opening for Canaan to talk about us, as a couple. But he didn't. He was the first to look away, and I know he caught the intent behind the silence that followed, but he ignored it.

Yeah, he wasn't ready.

Which…I understood. It's not like I was sitting here expecting a ring or a declaration of love. But I'd like to know where we stand. What we are. What he wants from me besides the obvious. I mean, not that I'm in any way complaining about him wanting me for the obvious, since I want him for the obvious just as much.

But…I want more than that.

I want *him* to want more than that. I want him to pursue *the more* with me. I don't want to be the aggressor, the pursuer. I'm not super hung up on traditional gender roles in a relationship—not at all. I'll ask a guy out, I'll pay for meals, I'll be the first to make a move to bring things into the bedroom, and I won't think twice about any of that. The issue is, I've gotten used to doing that stuff. It's become habit, to the point that I've started hating letting guys do things for me.

Don't ask me out. Don't pay for me. Don't make the first move. It's safer if I do it. I'm less likely to get shot down that way. I mean, I doubt there are many men who would turn me down for a date, and even fewer who would turn me down if I made it clear I wanted things to move to the bedroom—that's not arrogance, it's just reality. And yeah, a lot of guys are pretty happy to let me pay for my own shit on dates. I don't think less of men for any of that, either.

But all those men…

They're not Canaan.

They were never serious.

It's never been…*real*, I guess.

But this is *Canaan*.

Sex with Canaan has been better than I'd even fantasized, better than I expected, and better, honestly, than any sex I've ever had. It's just superior in every way. His body fits with mine perfectly. His cock fills me just right, not so big it hurts, but just big enough to stretch and burn and ache and throb when he's inside me. He kisses me like it's the first time, every time. He has a wicked talented tongue, and is not only willing but eager to use it on me. He's mostly dominant in the bedroom, but totally willing to let me take the lead when the mood strikes and, being a musician, he's got great rhythm.

I want a deeper emotional component to our relationship.

There, I said it.

I'm terrified of going after that, though, because if I make the first move and he shoots me down, I'll be wrecked. I tried that once, and the result is my deepest, darkest secret.

And fuck no, I'm not going into that. Not with

Canaan, not with anyone, not ever. Not even Tate knows.

"Aerie?" Canaan's voice snapped me out of my thoughts.

"Hmmm?"

"I lost you there for a minute," he said.

"Oh…just thinking."

"About what?"

I shrugged. "A lot of stuff."

He eyed me. "That sounds like a blow-off."

I sighed. "Yeah, a little bit of one."

He chuckled. "That's a first—never heard any-one admit to blowing me off before."

"It's not that I don't want to tell you what I'm thinking, it's just that…a lot of it is stuff I'm not ready to talk about at all. A lot of stuff I'm still working through, I guess."

He nodded. "I get that."

We both glanced up as Corin came out through the kitchen.

"Cane, I think we should—"

Canaan cut in. "Nope. Not ready to talk about it with you, bro."

Corin stopped short. "Dude, what's your—"

Canaan hopped off the truck's tailgate and rounded the back end, walking away. "Don't push it, Cor. I'm not ready, okay? I just…I need a bit of time."

Canaan rounded the corner and vanished, and I hopped off to follow him.

Corin grabbed my arm, stopping me. "Hey, what the hell is going on with him?"

I sighed. "I feel like if I get into it with you, I'll be betraying Canaan's trust. He's your brother, Corin—he'll talk when he's ready to talk, okay?"

"He talked to you about whatever he's pissed about though?"

"Well…yeah. A little."

Corin paced away, hands laced on the top of his head. "I—we've had fights before, obviously, I mean—we're twins, we quarrel. But this just…it feels different."

"That's because it *is* different, Corin." I tried to smile at him, but I knew it was coming off sad and pitying.

"I don't get it."

I frowned at him. "Come on, Cor—you really don't have *any* idea why your twin brother could possibly be pissed off right now?"

He turned back to me. "I mean, I know this is unexpected, but—"

I backed away from him. "I have to go, Corin."

"But—"

"He's your twin, he'll come around. Just…give him time."

"Yeah…yeah. You're right." He turned away, tossing a wave as he reentered the kitchen. "Go."

I followed Canaan and found him in their studio, his electric guitar plugged in, headphones on his ears, his fingers flying, eyes closed. He was standing with one foot propped up on the amp, glossy brown hair loose around his shoulders, head down and bobbing rhythmically. I closed the door quietly and snuck into the studio to sit on a stool, watching him, wishing I could hear what he was playing.

He played a minute or two more, and then his hands went still on the strings, head still bowed as the last note faded in his headphones. He opened his eyes, saw me, and smiled. He tugged the headphones off his ears and let them hang on his neck.

"Hey."

I tossed my hair. "Hey. Long time no see."

He snorted. "Funny." He gestured at the rack of instruments. "There's a ukulele over there. Wanna jam?"

I slid off the stool and eased the uke out of the rack, pulled the stool closer to Canaan's. I played a few chords, testing the tuning, adjusted the pegs a touch, and then glanced at Canaan, waiting for him to lead us off. He hooked a toe around another stool and tugged it over to himself and perched on it, settling his guitar on his knee. A moment or two of fiddling with the tuning, twisting knobs, reaching out a toe to tap one of the pedals on the floor near the amp, and then he shifted and wiggled, let out a breath—I recognized these movements as his giveaways for preparing to play.

He plucked a single string with his pick, and a long low note filled the studio; he held the note, sliding his finger up and down on the fretboard to make the note quaver. Another moment, and then he tilted the guitar toward the amp to create feedback, sliding his finger down the fretboard so the note howled up the register before he switched to a different string, a different note, which he then drew out once more.

I heard my part in my head, a quick looping series of chords that would circle around Canaan's melody. I hunched over the ukulele and strummed the first chord, went immediately into the second, strummed there a few times in a quick rhythm, and went back to the first chord, then the second. I strummed but the next time I did this, it was in a lower key, and Canaan provided a harmonic counterpoint as he peeled out another long quavering high hum. We didn't have to talk about it, we didn't consult. This was improv, and I'm at my best when I'm improvising. I feel the music, hear the next part in my head...I can almost taste the notes as they flow through me, almost see them; I've always wished I could have synesthesia, the ability to see sound as colors. As Canaan ran with his riff—hammering on from note to note in slow, sliding progressions—I continued my looping series of chords, dropping my register when he went up, going up when he went down, my ukulele creating a skirling counterpoint to his guitar's slow wail.

There was still something missing, though. What was it?

Ah, there it was—I felt it, and since we were alone and just jamming, I went with it, let it out.

I started humming, a low note at the bottom of my vocal range, soft, quiet. And then, as we kept playing and our counterpoint harmony increased in intensity, his notes coming faster together, my chords skirling faster and faster around his, I let my voice creep higher and higher, louder and louder, from a hum to a vocalization, from a vocalization to a wail. It built and it built, until Canaan wasn't just hammering on from note to note but shredding now, and my fingers were flying on the fretboard, strumming as fast as I could, holding a long high howling wail. I was rocking on the stool as I held the note, strumming hard, fingers aching as I danced from chord to chord in an absolute frenzy, faster than I've ever played.

We held the frenzy, carried it to its absolute maximum, and then Canaan glanced at me, nodding once, twice, and a third time—on the third nod, we both silenced our instruments.

And just stared at each other, stunned at what we'd just done.

"Holy shit, Aerie."

"Uh, yeah."

"That was…" He shook his head, at a loss for an accurate description of his feelings.

"It felt like sex," I blurted.

"Exactly." He stared hard at me. "But not just any sex."

"Really crazy intense sex," I added, "where it's so good you're just sort of stunned stupid at the end."

His gaze didn't waver from mine. "So, in other words, like every time we have sex?"

"Jamming together felt like fucking, for you?" I held his gaze in turn.

"Yeah, it kind of did." He tilted his head side to side. "But…more intense, in some ways."

"How?"

"Music is…it's deeply, intensely personal. For me, at least. Playing like that with you, it…it felt like sharing something unique."

"You jam with Corin all the time," I said, trying to not let this conversation go where it felt like he was taking it; I didn't want it to go there because I doubted he was going to say what I wanted to hear, and I didn't want to feel the hurt and disappointment I knew was waiting for me on the other side.

"Yeah, but that's different. He's my brother and my twin, and you of all people know how that's different, Aerie."

"Yeah, but—"

"With you, it was…cathartic, and…exhilarating. With him it's just comfortable and familiar." He broke the stare, glancing down as he idly fiddled with his whammy bar. "With you it's…I went to a different place, mentally, emotionally."

"I did too."

He glanced up at me again. "Aerie, I—" he broke off, sighing in frustration, his eyes searching mine. I could see a billion different thoughts and emotions rippling across his expression, none of which he seemed capable of verbalizing.

"Don't, Canaan," I said, my voice low, almost a whisper. "Not right now."

"Don't what?"

I plucked a string. "Don't go there. Not yet."

"Why not? I thought you'd want—"

I interrupted him. "I do, but not now. With everything that's going with Corin and my sister, plus my mom, I just…it'd be too much."

"I don't want you to think I'm not—that I don't—"

"Canaan." I reached out and put my finger to his

lips, silencing him. "Shush, okay? Play about it, if you need to get it out right now. We'll talk…just later."

It was odd; that I was the one avoiding the conversation he was stumbling into. But…it was obvious to me that he hadn't really thought this through; that he hadn't come to grips with his feelings. He still needed time. And, honestly, so did I. Yes, I wanted more with him, but I wanted it to happen in a way that would set us up for long-term success. Stumbling into things blindly would just create more trouble.

Best to stick to having earthshaking sex mostly devoid of intense emotional connection. I mean, don't get me wrong, there was a very real and very undeniable bond between Canaan and me. There were very real emotions in our sexual relationship. But it was all…subsurface, so to speak. Unexplored. Unspoken. Buried deep.

Truth be told, I was afraid.

Of Canaan. Of the connection. Of us. Of *us* not panning out.

See…down deep, in my heart of hearts, I'm a romantic. But I'm always the pragmatic one between Tate and me, the less outwardly emotional one. The thinker and planner versus Tate's reactionary, put everything out there, seat of her pants personality. Tate is fiery and fierce and not just a little crazy, and a lot impulsive—obviously, seeing as she's pregnant. Me? I

tend to stay in my head more than I should. I over-
think things. I keep my emotions pinned down inside
me.

It's weird, though. Because Tate is emotional and
crazy, but when it comes to the deep stuff, she doesn't
ever deal with it. I may be outwardly emotional in a
crisis or something, but I still deal with my shit. I cry
when I need to cry. Tate lets it all build up until she
has this epic blowup, whereas I tend to blow up in the
moment. After Tate has her explosion, she's done and
over it, whereas my explosion is just the start of me
spending hours, if not days, running the situation in
my head over and over and over again.

It's complicated, is what I'm saying.

I'm emotional, but I'm also not.

God, boys are right—we are complicated.

Canaan was watching me as all this flitted
through my head, my finger still on his lips, our eyes
locked, searching each other.

"Okay." He nodded, sighing. "Fine. Talk later,
play now." He grabbed my finger and playfully bit
down on my fingernail.

Which was hot…providing a nice little
distraction.

"Canaan, it's not that I—"

He put his finger on my lips. "Now who's trying
to talk about things? I thought you wanted to jam

instead of jabber?"

I grabbed his hand, keeping my eyes on his and, with excessively over the top eroticism, slid his finger into my mouth. I pursed my lips around his digit, and we mimicked oral sex.

"Goddammit, Aerie…"

I licked his fingertip before letting him take his finger back. "What?" I asked, playing coy.

"Now I'm horny."

"We literally just fucked, Canaan. Like, less than an hour ago."

"And when you suck on my finger like that, it makes me horny all over again."

"It does?" I asked, pretending innocence. "And why would that be, do you think?"

"Because you sucking on my finger makes me want you to suck on my cock, Aerie, that's why."

"Oh." I set the ukulele aside. "I see."

"You see?" He played a little riff, absentmindedly noodling. "What is it you see, Aerie?"

"I don't know, Canaan. What is it you think I see?" I stood up, prowling toward him.

He stood up, backing away from me toward the door to the studio, and I followed him; his guitar's cord was long and curly, like an old-school telephone cord, long enough that he could walk across the entire studio and lock the front door so no one could interrupt us. He eyed me as I stalked toward him, communicating my arousal in the spark of my eyes and the sultry sway of my hips.

His casual noodling turned into him playing a song, which took me a moment to recognize as "Closer" by Nine Inch Nails. We shared a grin at his choice of song as I stopped inches from him.

"I think you see that when you look at me like that, you make my cock so hard it hurts." He tilted his guitar away from his body.

I dropped my gaze to his zipper, which was straining, bulging. "I see." I sank to my knees, staring up at him. "You know what I see?"

He kept playing "Closer."

"What do you see?"

"A painfully hard cock in desperate need of a good sucking."

"Is that so?"

"Do you know the words to that song you're playing, Canaan?"

"Sure. It was one of the first songs I learned how to play and sing at the same time, just because it was so dirty and I was thirteen."

"I'd love to hear you sing it to me, then." I licked my lips as I teased him, tracing the zipper with my fingernail. "Serenade me while I suck your cock."

"For real?"

I flicked open the fly of his jeans and slowly lowered the zipper. "Do I look like I'm joking?"

He tightened the strap of his guitar so it was higher up and tight against his body. "Holy shit, Aerie."

I tugged his tight black jeans down his thighs and then his underwear. "That's not how the song goes, Canaan."

"Okay, okay, um…" He breathed out a shuddery breath as I palmed his length. "'You let me violate you…'"

He sang the intro as I fisted his length a few times, and then, when he started the first verse, I took him into my mouth, swirling my tongue around the plump head.

"Mmmm—" This was a sound of surprise from me as I backed away. "You taste like latex and semen."

He was strumming, in between verse and chorus. "I'm…sorry?"

"You have alcohol upstairs?" I asked.

He nodded. "Sure. Some vodka, I think."

"Then I'll just have to rinse the taste out of my mouth with some vodka while you return the favor."

"Sounds—ohhhhh *shit*—sounds good…"

The *oh shit* was because I had, without warning, returned his thick, straining cock to my mouth, taking him as deep as I could all at once. He was game, though, and kept playing and singing. The fact that he was struggling to keep his thoughts together, struggling to remain coherent as I went down on him honestly only heightened the intensity of his performance of the song. He was pausing now and then to suck in sharp breaths, letting them out in long gusty sighs before going back to singing, and occasionally he'd stutter over the lyrics, or stumble as he devolved into groaning.

I was watching him, watching his face as I pumped his cock at the base, watching his expression shift with his emotions. Canaan was normally pretty hard to read since, like me, he tended to keep his emotions off of his face. Now though, I could read him easily.

I mean, obviously the primary thing he was feeling was pleasure, seeing as I had my mouth around his cock. But beyond that was a myriad of other emotions. He kept playing, his eyes closed as he sang the second verse, and then he started the chorus and his eyes snapped open, and his gaze was intense, fierce, hungry, and each word of that chorus he was singing directly to me, for me, meaning each and every word.

You know the song—turn it on and listen to it, and picture this:

Me, on my knees. My hands around Canaan's long thick perfect cock, stroking him slowly as I wrapped my mouth around the tip, tongue circling.

Imagine Canaan, a guitar in his hands, fingers playing that low, snarling, erotic, driving riff, staring down at me, singing those beautifully raw and delightfully dirty lyrics to me, but you have to hear his voice, rough and straining, gasping here and there as I took him deeper and sucked harder, the raw power of his voice compelling in its vulnerable intensity.

Picture him, tattoos on his arms shifting as he played, lip ring glinting as he sang, septum moving with the rhythm of his head as he nodded to the beat. Picture him staring down at me, willing me to hear in him singing more than just the words. Chocolate-mocha puppy-dog eyes piercing and hot, long brown hair thick and glossy and loose.

Picture me, both hands fisted around his cock, stroking faster and faster beneath my mouth, then letting go to claw my fingernails down his hairy, muscular thighs. Picture me, taking him into my throat and backing away again and again, eyes turned up to watch him as I slid the upper few inches between my lips, over and over again, sucking, cheeks hollowing.

Canaan was growling the lyrics, the final chorus, as I brought him closer and closer, until he was gasping and his hips were driving and he was stuttering over the final repetition of the chorus.

"Aerie…" he breathed.

And then he came.

I pumped him slowly through his orgasm, cheeks hollowing, throat working as I swallowed his cum. Canaan was holding back, wanting to fuck my mouth, but stopping himself. I wondered if I should tell him, sometime, that I secretly want him to stop holding back, to give me his wild side, his rough and uncouth and dirty side. Oh, we get plenty dirty together, but he's always considerate, to a degree. As nasty as we can be together, there's an element of restraint to the way he fucks me.

And I want that edge gone.

But I don't know how to tell him that.

I've been trying to communicate that without words, in the way I am with him.

But...he hasn't picked up on it.

I need to just tell him.

God, there seems to be a running theme here, doesn't there?

THREE

Canaan

Aᴇʀɪᴇ Kɪɴɢsʟᴇʏ ɪs ғᴜᴄᴋɪɴɢ ᴄᴏᴍᴘʟɪᴄᴀᴛᴇᴅ. I ᴍᴇᴀɴ, ᴀʟʟ chicks are confusing, but Aerie? Sometimes she gets me so mixed up I don't know whether I'm coming or going. I know she's on edge about our relationship, about what our relationship is. Is it just sex, or something else? It's not *just* sex, and it never has been. But she's…shit, not closed off, because it's easy to tell when she's upset, but it's not always easy to figure out what she's upset *about*. Did I do something wrong? Am I leading her on? Is it nothing to do with me? Is it everything to do with Corin and Tate, which affects her as much as it does me? There are so many factors, and I don't know how to parse any of them.

I know I like her, a fucking lot. I know sex with her is very literally life-changing. As in, I don't think I could ever fuck another woman without comparing her to Aerie, and that comparison would always leave the other woman coming up seriously short.

But does that equate to…

Love?

Shit, it's hard to even think about that. Love? Am I in love with Aerie? I don't know—I don't think so. But what if I am, and I just don't recognize the symptoms? I don't know how to be in love. Being in love means, like, I have to put her first in my life, and I'm not ready for that kind of responsibility. That's a fucking lot, man, a person all wound up and tangled in and woven into my entire life?

But if there were anyone who could be that, it would be Aerie.

If I can see that as being possible with her, doesn't it mean that this is what it is?

I see her looking at me strangely, sometimes. Waiting, expectant. Is she waiting for me to tell her I love her? I tried to talk about our relationship, and she shut it down. She wanted nothing to do with that conversation. Which is another confusing thing, because don't all chicks always want to talk about the state of relationships? Okay, shut up, I know—that's a gross generalization and unfair and chauvinistic of me to even think that. Right?

I'm an ass.

But it *is* weird that she seems to be waiting for something from me, but when I try to instigate a conversation to get at what she wants and what she's expecting and what we are, she avoids it.

She didn't just shut down the conversation—she shunted us away from talking altogether and into sex. And not just sex, but a blowjob.

I love getting BJs. I mean, duh, I'm a dude—I'll never turn down a BJ, like ever. But I'm also a thousand percent aware that her giving me a blowjob doesn't provide sexual gratification for her in any way. Sure, maybe she might get a thrill out of it, might enjoy in an arousing sort of way my visceral response to what she's doing to me—god knows she can suck me senseless and leave me gibbering and incoherent by the time she's finished. But her going down on me when I tried to bring up our relationship, especially after Tate and Corin's…*announcement*…and the blow-up with Rachel, and the whole *but Daddy I love him* thing. Yes, I know, it was her mom, not her dad, but the movie trope is *but Daddy I love him*—

Yeah…that was classic avoidance via sexual distraction.

I benefitted from it—case in point, I'm currently incapable of speech, because Aerie blew me so good my brain isn't firing on all cylinders just yet. My mind is spinning and stuttering and wobbling, and wandering.

Aerie is still on her knees in front of me, staring up at me, probably wondering what's going through my head. My jeans are still around my knees, and my guitar is still humming through the amp. She's got a droplet of cum dribbling down from the corner of her mouth. Her hair, long and blonde and loose around her shoulders, is a cascade of sunshine, and her eyes are soft and green with hints of amber in streaks around the edges of her irises. She's wearing work clothes: tight faded blue jeans and a black Badd's Bar & Grill T-shirt, with a pair of well-worn sneakers. No makeup—or minimal makeup, at least—just a pair of small diamond studs in her ears, fingers bare of rings, no tattoos, just her flawless skin.

She's so beautiful that when I look at her I sometimes forget what I'm saying, what I'm doing. Like right now, I am still brainless from the orgasm she sucked out of me, and stunned silly at how fucking gorgeous Aerie is.

I push off the door, pull myself together, and let my guitar sling around behind my back, then bend to lift her to her feet. I keep my eyes on hers as she rises to stand in front of me, tension crackling between us. I want to bear down with all the questions I have, but

I don't. She's chosen to avoid, so I let her avoid. Also, I'm not ready any more than she is.

Instead, I lifted my thumb and smeared away the droplet on her cheek; Aerie smirked, licking the drop off of my thumb with an erotic swipe of her tongue.

I backed away from her, unlocked the front door, set my guitar in the rack, and shut off the amp. Taking her hand, I led her to the stairs.

"Come on," I growled.

"Where are we going?"

"For what I want to do to you, we need to be behind closed doors."

She trotted after me eagerly, holding my hand as we ascended the stairs. "I like the sound of this."

"You should."

"What are you going to do to me, Canaan?" This was murmured low, her voice buzzing with curiosity and arousal.

I ignored her question until we got the hallway, where I hesitated. Cor and I shared a bedroom still, and I knew Tate and Cor would need some time alone too, after everything that had gone down. I was mad at him, but he was still my twin and my best friend, and I'd always look out for him. I glanced at the other doors, Baxter's, and Lucian's. Luce obviously would need his room, but Bax was gone indefinitely—at least, he still hadn't mentioned to any of us when he and Evangeline were coming home, and someone spoke to Bax every other day, if not every day.

I grabbed the doorknob to Bax's room and shoved the door open.

"Isn't this Baxter's room?" Aerie asked, as we entered.

"Yeah."

"We can't just use his room."

I'd never actually been in here before: growing up with seven brothers, we learned early on the value of respecting each other's personal space. The unspoken rule was you don't mess with your brother's shit. You stay out of his room, and out of his business; if he feels like sharing, he'll share; a closed door means keep out.

But this was…extenuating circumstances, you might say.

So, I was a bit surprised at what I found in his room: bookshelves. He'd shoved his bed and dresser together along one wall, had a seaman's chest under the window, and the other entire wall beside the closet was occupied with two side by side bookshelves, each so stuffed with books that he had them stacked two deep in places, with more lying sideways on top.

Look, Bax is my bro, and I love him, and I know he's a smart guy, smarter than most people give him credit for, but I still never quite took him for the

bookish type. But then, if he wasn't working, working out, or at a fight, he was in his room, the door
cracked open as a signal that he was available if needed. None of us have ever been into TV, since Dad
never got cable in the apartment over the bar where
we all grew up, and we just never got into the habit
of watching TV. We're all too busy, have too many
other more important interests. So, no TV, he's not
in school, no video games…what does he do in here
during his off time? Read, clearly. I feel kind of judgy
for being so surprised.

Aerie glanced at me after she'd taken in the bedroom, surprise on her face, and I just laughed.

"I know, right?" I said. "Who knew?"

Aerie meandered past me to the full bed, which
was neatly made and covered in a flannel blanket,
with a fuzzy throw folded across the back end. The
room was impeccable, with few personal effects other
than the books.

"Are you sure it's okay we're in here?" Aerie
asked me.

I shrugged. "He's not here, and hasn't been here
in almost two months, and I'm not sure when he will
be here. Bed space and privacy are limited, so I say we
take what we can get."

She sat down on the edge of the bed, gazing
up at me. "So. You mentioned needing privacy for

something or other?"

I locked the door behind me. "Something or other…yeah." I prowled slowly toward her. "I'd originally planned to just rip your clothes off, go down on you until you start screaming, and then fuck you until we're both stupid."

She reached for the hem of her shirt. "I like the sound of that."

"But I'm thinking I have another idea." I stopped her from peeling her shirt off.

"Oh? What's that, Canaan?"

This could backfire. It was totally impetuous. I was going with what my emotions were telling me— there's a fuck of a lot more to this thing between us than just sex, and we may not be ready to confront all of that, but I still owe it to her and to myself to communicate somehow that I recognize the *"more"* that is floating unspoken between us.

I stood in front of her, staring down at her, trying to decide how far I was going to take this.

"Say something, Cane. You're making me nervous." She was relaxed, though, her knees parted, hands on her thighs, just watching me. Only the way her lovely amber-green eyes were constantly flitting and searching mine gave away her nerves.

"You trust me, Aerie?"

"Of course."

"Don't just say that to say it." I turned away, opened Bax's closet, and slid a necktie off a hanger, and a pocket square from the breast pocket of a suit coat, and a red bandana from a shelf. "You really mean it? You really trust me?"

She eyed the striped, brightly colored tie dangling from my fingers, and her nostrils flared, her eyes widening. In answer, she stood up and held out her hands, wrists together. Her chin lifted defiantly, confidently.

I pinioned her wrists together in my hand. "That's my girl."

"I am, you know."

"You are what?"

"Your girl."

I lowered her wrists and leaned in to kiss her, slowly, softly. "I know," I whispered.

"You're not tying me up?" she asked, sounding disappointed.

"Not this time around." I led her away from the bed to the middle of the room and stood behind her. "I want to do...*this*, first."

I refolded the pocket square in half, so it was a rectangle, and placed it over her eyes. I lifted her fingers to her face, prompting her to hold the silk in place. I wrapped the tie around her head, pinning the pocket square in place as I knotted the ends of the tie tightly behind her head.

"Can you see?" I asked.

"No."

"Good." I fiddled with the positioning of the tie and the square. "Not too tight?"

"It's perfect."

"And you're okay with this?"

"More than okay," she answered.

Her skin was pebbled with goose bumps, and her nipples were poking through the fabric of her bra and T-shirt.

"You'll tell me if it's too much, right?" I asked, touching my lips to her temple.

"Of course."

Now that she was blindfolded, I was going to play with her a bit.

I backed away. "Stay still."

"What are you doing, Canaan?" Her voice was an excited whisper.

I circled around in front of her, moving as quietly as I could. She was swiveling her head this way and that, trying to sense my presence.

"Canaan?"

I tiptoed closer; her nostrils flared, scenting me. I leaned close, touching my lips to hers in a ghosting tease. Aerie pursed her lips, expecting the kiss, but I slid my mouth along her cheek instead, to her

cheekbone, down to the corner of her jaw just beneath her ear. Up, then, kissing around the shell of her
ear; she tilted her head toward me, offering herself to
me. I breathed on her ear gently, a huff of warm air.

"Are you wet, Aerie?"

She nodded.

"Are you sure?"

She nodded again.

"Show me."

"Wh-what?"

"Show me how wet you are." I tangled my fingers with hers and guided our hands to her zipper. "I
wanna hear how wet you are. I wanna smell and taste
how wet you are for me, baby."

I slid open the button fly, and then slowly lowered her zipper. Aerie's hand dropped away, anticipating my touch. I breathed a laugh in her ear, and
then moved to stand behind her, chin on her shoulder,
hands sliding over her belly and up to her diaphragm,
teasing her with my touch, purposefully avoiding her
sensitive, erogenous zones.

"Oh no—no, I want *you* to show me."

She tilted her head back and twisted it toward
mine, lips brushing my temple. "I've never been this
wet in my life, Cane…"

"Good. Show me."

She dipped her fingers under the elastic of her

panties, down to the juncture of her thighs. She hesitated and then leaned back against me for support as she shifted her legs apart. I watched over her shoulder as her hand moved inside her underwear, a finger or two slipping into her channel. I heard the slick squelch of her fingers inside her, and then she withdrew them.

"Hear that?" Aerie murmured. "I'm all juicy."

I reached out and grabbed her wrist, bringing her hand to my face. I sniffed her glistening fingers. "You smell like something I want to taste."

She traced the seam of my lips with her middle finger, and then slid her finger into my mouth, and I licked it clean of her tangy, musky, female essence.

"I want you to taste me," she breathed, beginning to shimmy out of her pants.

"Ah-ah-ah," I said, imprisoning her hands with mine to stop her. "Not yet."

"Canaan, you're making me crazy."

"Good." I nipped her earlobe. "Trust me."

"Okay. What next, then?"

"Touch yourself again."

"With all my clothes still on?"

"For now."

"Canaan, I don't know if you understand how sex works, honey," she teased. "We both have to be naked to do it."

I huffed a laugh. "You underestimate me, then, my dear. Maybe someday I'll prove to you we can fuck fully clothed." I slid my hand along her belly again, daring upward. "In public, maybe, even. You game for that?"

"You get me worked up enough, I just might be."

"Challenge accepted," I breathed, marking a line with my thumb just beneath the underwire of her bra. "Now, Aerie...I want to watch you make yourself come."

Her fingers dove under her panties again, down between her thighs, and I watched her hand move as she dipped a finger inside herself, drew it out, dragging her wetness around her clit, moaning softly at the touch of her fingers. She began to circle, then, slowly.

"Oh...god—Cane, *please* touch me. Play with my tits. Something—*anything*, just put your hands on me."

"I will, babe, don't you worry about that."

You'd think, after a month and a half of nonstop, several times a day, numerous times per session of Aerie and me fucking that we'd have exhausted the ways we could turn each other on, make each other desperate and crazy. Yet...every time, every *single* time...it got hotter, crazier, and more desperate.

A little voice in the back of my head rather

unhelpfully pointed out that this fact may very well be how people can be married to the same person for decades, how they could have sex with the same person for all those years and never get tired of it, never need something different or new.

Nope, nope, nope—not going there just yet.

I watched Aerie's circling finger, obscured by her panties, and felt a rush of need, deep-seated, fiery, fierce, and demanding—I *needed* to see her. Touch her. Feel her. I denied myself, letting memory and imagination fill in for me for a moment or two longer. Denying myself made this all the more erotic for both of us.

She began to moan, and her finger circled faster, and I finally let myself cup her breast over her bra, strumming across her erect nipple with my thumb. Her spine arched, pressing her breast into my hand, begging for more. My other hand, then, danced across her stomach up to her other breast, both of them cupped in my hands. I pinched her nipples over the fabric, squeezing them until she whimpered in protest, and then I released them.

"God, Canaan, I'm getting close."

"Good, baby. Bring yourself there. Don't stop. Let me hear you—we're alone, the whole apartment is empty. So just let go." I whispered this in her ear, caressing her tits over the slippery fabric, pressing myself up against her, grinding into her butt, teasing us both. "Feel how hard my cock is? Just from watching you touch yourself like this."

"I want it…"

"I know."

"Take my clothes off, *please*? I want to be naked with you."

I peeled the hem of her shirt up over her boobs, just beneath her chin, and then unhooked her bra and let the cups sag. "How's that?"

"More…more!"

"Are you close?"

"So close."

I palmed her cheek and tilted her face to mine, briefly yet intensely kissing her, tasting her mouth, demanding her tongue; her fingers flew around her clit, and I tugged a bra cup down to bare her breast, flicking her nipple with my fingernail.

"Oh—oh—oh fuck, Canaan, I'm there, god, I'm there!"

She leaned back against me, hips pivoting, legs bowing, bending, head hanging on her neck, mouth open, whimpers escaping her lips as she ground herself into her own fingers, faster and faster and faster, and I bared her other breast and rolled both nipples between thumb and forefinger in time with the rhythm of her touch.

A soft, breathless scream, then, as she came, knees dipping as the orgasm washed over her.

I scooped her up in my arms and laid her on the bed. "Keep touching yourself," I instructed. "Keep coming, honey."

"Oh…god, I don't know if I can."

"Try."

I tugged her jeans off, bringing her panties with them, and her knees immediately drew up, heels together, baring her pussy to me, her fingers dipping in again, dragging more essence over her clit, and then she began tentatively touching herself all over again, slowly. Careful to not dislodge the makeshift blindfold, I eased her T-shirt off, and then her bra, leaving her naked.

"I don't wanna touch myself anymore, Cane," she breathed. "I want *you* to touch me."

I knelt on the bed, kissing the inside of her knee. "Like that?"

"More, god—*more!*"

"Greedy, aren't you?" I murmured against her skin.

"Fuck yes. I need you, Cane."

I dragged my lips up her thigh, teasing, kissing, licking, nipping, closer and closer to her core, and then just as I reached it, I began all over again at her opposite knee, kissing and teasing my way up.

"Quit teasing me, goddammit," Aerie snarled, fingers moving faster now as she neared her second orgasm.

"No, I don't think I will." I nipped the velvety soft silk of the inside of her thigh, so close to her core my jaw brushed her hand as she touched her clit. "You like this."

"Fuck yes, I do. But I want your mouth, Cane… *please*."

"You have my mouth," I teased.

She growled, a feral sound of irritation. "You know what I mean, damn you."

"Getting a bit vulgar, aren't you?" I murmured.

She just moaned in response, her spine arching off the bed as she fingered herself closer and closer to climax. Watching her near the edge, I knew my need to touch her, taste her, wouldn't be denied much longer.

I nudged my middle finger against her opening, and she gasped.

"Oh fuck, please, please touch me. Please."

I slid my finger inside her curling it upward and inward, hunting for that secret place inside her that drove her so wild. I'd only hit it a few times, and she'd absolutely lost her mind every single time.

"Like this?"

"Yeah…god, yes, right there…"

Her fingers were circling madly now, crazily, flying around her clit so fast they were a blur. I watched her carefully, gently and slowly massaging that spot inside her, hearing her cry out with increasing intensity, until I knew she was at the very edge.

At the very last second, I nudged her hand away, buried my face against her pussy, and the taste of her intimate essence filled my mouth. She yelped in surprise, and then both hands tangled in my hair, piling it on top of my head like I did with hers, and she clutched me against herself as I devoured her, holding nothing back, my finger inside her, adding a second, squelching them in and out under my chin, my tongue flying. She screamed, then arched totally off the bed, spasming against me.

"HOLY SHIT HOLY SHIT HOLY SHIT!" she gasped, flopping down onto the bed as her climax passed through her. "Holy shit, Canaan." She reached up to peel off the blindfold, and I stopped her.

"Oh no, I'm not done with you yet, babe." I pinioned her hands, crawling up her body to hover over her. "That's just the start."

"Just...just the start?" she squeaked. "Oh—oh god. I like the sound of this."

"Wanna know what's next? I bet you can't guess."

She pressed her wrists together and offered them

to me. "You tie me up and have your filthy way with me?"

"Hmmm, tempting, but no." I kissed her, quickly.

"What's next, then?"

I moved off the bed to stand beside it, helping her sit up and pivot so she was sitting on the edge again. I folded the bandana and pressed it into her hands. "Now you blindfold me, without taking yours off."

"Ummmm, okay?"

Her hands reached out, searching, and I took one of her hands, leading it to my shoulder. She shifted forward on the bed, exploring my body with her hands, and then she stood up, using me to pull herself upright. Touching my face with the tips of her fingers like a blind woman, she gently found my eyes, and then placed the fabric over my eyes, leaning against me to tie it behind my head.

"There, how's that?" she asked.

"Good. Can't see a thing."

She remained leaning against me, touching kisses to my cheekbone, my forehead, my cheek, the corner of my mouth. "Now what?"

"Now get me naked."

"This is crazy, Canaan—we're both blindfolded now."

"Exactly. It's all about feel now, sweetheart."

"You're rather crafty, aren't you, Mr. Badd?"

"Why yes I am, Miss Kingsley."

She went slowly, beginning with my shirt, peeling it up and over my head. Her fingers trailed down my chest, sliding over the ridges of my abs. Without sight, I had no way of knowing where her hands were going next, heightening the anticipation. Once my shirt was off, she spent a moment exploring my upper body with her hands, roaming over my shoulders, down my back, up my abs, palming my pecs, into my hair. Then I felt her move, felt her hands sliding down the backs of my legs, to my shoes, which she untied; I toed the shoes off and she peeled off my socks, and then I felt her hands roaming upward once more. To the fly of my jeans. I hissed in surprise and then moaned in pleasure as she pressed her lips against my stomach, kneeling in front of me, kissing across my abs, up to my diaphragm, and then back down, kissing and kissing and kissing as she unbuttoned the fly and lowered the zipper. Her hands hooked into the waist of my jeans and boxers at the same time, tugging them down as her mouth continued its slow, loving exploration, delving downward as she gradually removed my jeans and underwear. My heart was racing, my mouth was dry, and I was shaky—an intense physical reaction to something as simple as her mouth kissing my body.

She's gone down on me on numerous occasions

but somehow these trailing, dancing, exploratory kisses were leaving an intense and permanent brand on me, on my skin, on my heart.

I couldn't see where she was kissing next, that was part of it.

She was teasing me, dragging the garments down past my groin, kissing around my cock, down my thighs, kissing my belly mere inches from my cock, so close that her cheek brushed me, and then away. Her hands cupped my ass, clutching and caressing, and her lips continued to tease me, until I was breathing hard and groaning in need.

"Shit, Aerie. You're driving me crazy."

"Tit for tat, Cane."

"I'll tat your tit," I said, just for something to say in return.

"Ah, no, thanks. No titty tattoos for this girl."

"No?"

"No."

"Not even a little tiny one, like on the underside or something? I'm the only one who'd even know it was there."

"Nope. I'm tattoo free and have every intention of staying that way, thanks." She laughed, breathing on my stomach. "Titty-tat. I tot I saw a titty-tat."

I laughed with her, and then barked in surprise when she abruptly took my cock into her mouth, going deep without warning. I'd been so hard for so long it was a very short trip to the edge, needing a single stroke of her mouth over my erection, her tongue flicking and circling.

I reached down and hauled her to feet. "Oh no… no, no, no. You do that and you'll mess up my plan." I pulled her up against me, exploring her naked body with my hands. "Besides, you already did that. I want something else, now."

"And that would be what, now that we're both blindfolded and naked?"

I slid my foot across the floor, seeking the edge of the bed, and I found it. I moved past her to sit on it, and then reached out to find her, and my hand brushed against skin. Further exploration told me I had her thigh, and then I found her hips and twisted her in place so she was standing between my knees. I pulled her closer, cupping her ass, mirroring her from moments ago, kissing her belly and then up between her breasts. I latched my mouth onto one nipple, and then the other, and she whimpered, pressing her core against me.

"Canaan, I need you," Aerie murmured, reaching down to cup my head, holding me against her breasts as I laved her nipples, one after the other. "Please, I need you."

She bent, then, palms on my cheeks, and her

mouth stuttered over my cheek, found my lips, and her kiss was desperate, delirious, wild, passionate. Demanding. No more games, this kiss said.

Breaking away from her kiss momentarily, I cheated, just a little: I lifted my blindfold just long enough to peek in Bax's bedside table drawer, relieved when I found a pile of condoms. I took one, replaced my blindfold. Reached up to bring her back down, resuming the kiss.

She pressed into me, whimpering into my mouth in desperation. "Cane…"

I flopped backward to the bed, bringing her down on top of me. She eagerly straddled me, sliding her bare pussy over my hard cock, teasing me.

"Tell me you have one," she murmured.

I groped, found her hand, and pressed the condom into it. "You do it."

"This could be tricky, blindfolded."

"Makes it all the more fun."

"Hold still," Aerie ordered.

"I won't move a muscle," I promised.

She remained straddling me, and slid down my body in an erotic tease, lips trailing, stuttering, dancing in jumping kisses from chest to stomach to hips, and then she had her hands on me, stroking me with one hand in slow twists. She paused, and I heard foil rip, and then she gripped me in one hand and I felt her roll the condom onto me, using both hands in a hand-over-hand movement that drove me wild.

Then, as slowly as she'd descended, Aerie moved back up, the tips of her breasts tracing hot, silky lines across my skin, her damp core dragging. Her hands scoured my body, circling my chest before delving into my hair, and then her mouth was on mine as she hovered over my erection. I reached up between her thighs, found her slit wet and waiting, traced the opening, using my other hand to guide my cock to her entrance. I notched myself inside her, just the very tip of the head at first, wanting to take this slowly.

She had other plans.

The moment she felt me inside her, Aerie sank down on me without breaking the kiss, her palms on my cheeks, crying out as I filled her. "Oh god, Canaan—fuck, you feel so good." Her forehead touched mine as she finally paused the kiss to gasp, her ass flush against my thighs. "Touch me, kiss me, fuck me."

"You're like a dirty poet," I murmured, palming her hips. "I like it."

"Dirty poetry, huh? I like that idea. Maybe I'll write you a dirty poem someday."

"How about this—you write me a dirty poem, and read it to me while I'm fucking you fully clothed, in public."

She giggled, and her walls pulsed around me with her laughter. "God, that's an amazing idea. Let's do it!"

"For real?"

"Fuck yeah, for real." She kissed me again, slowly lifting her hips to draw me out, hovering when I was still just barely inside her. "I'm not kidding, Canaan. I want to do that."

"You seriously do?"

"I seriously do." She gasped as she sank down on me again, driving me into her. "You make me crazy. You make me want to...you make me want to do crazy things I'd never do with anyone else, things I'd never even consider with anyone else. I don't know what it is about you, but you just..."

I slid my hands all over her skin, exploring her soft flesh, my hands carving from shoulders to waist, hips to thighs, up her stomach to caress her tits. Again and again, I explored her body in an endless circuit of touches, and she rose and fell on me, drawing me out and impaling herself on me over and over and over in slow, deliberate movements. Unhurried, relishing the feel of us connecting, gasping each time I drove into her tight wet hot slit. I groaned with her, and we continued like that, me touching her, Aerie holding the pace of her strokes to a maddeningly slow glide.

Finally, I could take no more. I gripped her hips

in my hands and tugged her down onto me, thrusting up with my hips. "I want it to last forever, but at the same time I want more, right now."

"God, me too." She bent over me, touched her lips to mine. "You can't stop time, can you, Canaan? So we can have this moment just like this, for as long as we want it?"

"Wish I could, sweet thing. Wish I could."

She couldn't keep the pace slow anymore, either. When I pulled her down onto me, she whimpered, leaning back, bracing her hands on my chest. She held there for a moment, my cock buried deep inside her, balanced on me. I wished I could see her, naked above me, her breasts perfect teardrops, with small dark nipples and wide areolae. I wished I could see her, the way her pussy looked wrapped around my cock, her thighs braced on either side of my hips. Her trim waist, her long blonde hair cascading around her shoulders.

I didn't take the blindfold off, though—removing my eyesight meant I felt her all the more intensely, felt the way her slit hugged me, pulsing, throbbing around me. Her weight was a delicious presence on top of me, pressing me into the bed, her skin softer than silk.

She whimpered again, and lifted up. "I can't wait anymore, Canaan. I need to come." She sank down. "I need to feel you come."

I could only groan in response, the wild explosive delirium of feeling Aerie begin to rise and fall, faster and faster…it was too much. I couldn't speak, could only grunt and moan and sigh. I gripped her hips and thrust with her, driving into her.

Faster, and faster.

My hips slapped loudly against her ass as our bodies met, and she was crying out nonstop, now, wordless howls of crazed bliss. I felt her touching herself, the swift circling movement of her hands brushing against the joining of our bodies.

Nothing but touch, her smell, our bodies united and sliding together.

I felt her come, felt her clamp around me, heard the hoarse cry of her voice as she detonated around me. "Cane! Cane, god…Canaan!" She fell forward, wrapping her arms under my neck, burying her face against the side of my throat. "Come for me, baby… come with me, Canaan!"

Her encouragement was all it took to let go.

My hands clenched into the crease of her hips and I pulled her down, burying myself deep, and I drove into her like that, hips rolling, grinding against her. She growled, a low murmur of ecstasy as she continued to come around me, and then I was letting go, heat blasting through me, my orgasm wrenching a shout out of me.

Her lips met mine, demanding, kiss-starved, desperate, as she felt me coming. She whimpered into the kiss, her hips rolling to milk my climax, which went on and on, until I was dizzy and gasping from the force of it.

Finally, after what felt like minutes of mutual orgasm, Aerie went limp on top of me, and I buried my face in her hair, whispering…I don't even know what. Random sounds? Gibberish?

Aerie giggled, her body jiggling pleasantly. "Canaan, what are you saying?"

I laughed. "I don't even know. That was so good it fucked all the sense out of me."

She nodded. "God, wasn't it?" She rolled off me and rested her head on my chest. "I like being blindfolded with you."

I peeked, and saw that she still had hers on. I removed mine, and then hers, and her green/amber eyes met mine. "That was crazy intense."

"It was more than just intense, Canaan."

"I know," I whispered. "But we're not talking about that, are we?"

She shook her head. "No, not yet."

A long comfortable silence in which we just… snuggled, for lack of a more manly word.

And then she lifted up on an elbow, staring

down at me, her hair a messy tangle around her face. "Canaan…I have something to say to you."

I frowned up at her, tangling my fingers in her hair. "Okay?"

She sucked in a deep breath, and let it out. "I want more."

I blinked, hesitating to answer. "More, how?"

She rubbed my chest with one hand. "Just… physically. There's more to this, but like you said, we're not talking about that just yet."

I hesitated again. "Um, I mean…we have sex, like, twice a day. How much more can we have?"

She shook her head. "No, I don't mean in frequency. I mean in terms of…god, I don't even know." She flopped to her back beside me, sighing. "I don't know how to put it."

"Bluntly? Just say what you want, Aerie."

"You make me crazy. I said this already. Well… I've always been the careful, responsible one. The reserved one. I never went really boy crazy like Tate did. And…you just…you bring something out of me." She paused, thinking, then resumed. "I…at the risk of sounding weird or melodramatic…you've awoken something insatiable inside me. And I want more. More *craziness*."

"So what does that look like, Aerie?"

She shrugged again. "I don't know." Another

pause, then she glanced at me. "That's not entirely true. You're sometimes...it feels like you're being careful with me. Gentle. Like you're holding back from being as...as rough and wild, I guess, as you might otherwise want to be."

I nodded. "That's true enough."

"I don't want you to do that anymore. I don't mean rough like painful, I don't think I'd enjoy sadism or anything, but just...let go, with me. Don't be gentle. Don't be careful. Don't always be...sweet."

"I just...I guess I hold back because I don't want to scare you, or make you think I need things to be all...caveman, or whatever, all the time. I like it when it's slow and sweet."

"And so do I," she answered. "Just...not all the time. Like this—" she lifted the blindfold, "this was amazing. But I really do want you to actually tie me up and just do whatever the fuck you want to me. And I really do want to have sex in public with you, fully clothed, and read sexy poems to you. And whatever else."

"Why, Aerie? Why do want all this with me?"

She shrugged and shook her head. "I don't know. You just make me want it. I've never wanted anything like what you make me want. But I feel safe with you. I trust you. So...I'm willing to let go, willing to explore a little."

"I think that could be arranged."

She quirked an eyebrow at me. "Arranged, huh?"

"Yeah. I may be able to figure something out, eventually."

Aerie bent and snagged my T-shirt off the floor, tugging it on. "You promised me vodka. And also, I'm hungry again."

"Several orgasms will do that to you, I guess." I tugged my jeans on commando, fastened them, and we left Bax's bedroom.

Aerie rummaged in the fridge while I got out the vodka, some glasses, and an unopened bottle of tonic water in the back of a cupboard. Aerie found a block of cheddar cheese and a package of crackers, and we took our snacks and drinks to the living room where we sat and demolished the cheese and crackers and more than a couple vodka tonics, all in a companionable silence.

We'd finished the snack and were discussing whether we wanted to hunt down Aerie's iPad to watch Netflix when the door to the stairs opened and Corin and Tate entered the apartment. Which led to a long, tense, awkward silence.

Eventually, Tate shook her head, sighing. "I'm too exhausted to deal with this bullshit." She rubbed her face with both hands, and then shot a look at Aerie and me. "My first act as an official crazy pregnant lady is to claim the bedroom for Corin and me. I can't handle being apart from him right now."

"We decided to crash in Bax's room for the night, since there's no word on when or if they're coming back" I said. "We kind of assumed you guys would need the bedroom to yourselves."

"Thank you for that," Tate said, grabbing Corin's hand and leading him toward the bedroom. "Now, if you'll excuse us, I'm so completely done with this whole being awake bullshit."

Corin hesitated though, as they passed us. "Hold on, though." His eyes met mine, and being his twin, I could read the flurry of emotions there as easily as if we'd had an hour-long conversation laying it all out. "Cane, we need to—"

If I can read him, then he can read me, and I wasn't ready for that yet, so I looked away. "Give me some time first, okay?" I cut in.

Tate hauled him away. "Not now, Cor. Just…not now."

"Fuck—fine." He glanced at me over his shoulder. "We're gonna have this out, though, Cane."

I nodded. "Absolutely. Just not now."

"I just don't get what you could possibly have to be pissed off about."

"Corin!" Tate snapped. "Come on, baby. I need to sleep. This has been a hell of a day, okay? Please?"

He growled, pivoted on his heel, and vanished into the bedroom, and I watched him go. When Tate had the door closed behind them, I collapsed backward against the couch.

"How does he not get it?" I asked, irritation flooding through me.

"He's dealing with a lot right now," Aerie said, her voice gentle. "His whole life just got blown up."

"Because of stupid decisions *he* made!"

Aerie twisted, leaning close and grazing my cheek with her hand. "I know, and he has to come to grips with that, as well as the fact that he's going to be a father—which he literally *just* found out, and that whatever plans or dreams he may have had are now going to be changed in some way." She rested her head on my shoulder. "I know you're pissed, Cane, and you have every right to be, since this affects you too, but… have some compassion, huh? He's your brother."

I groaned. "Gahhhh, you're right. You're right. I'm just—"

"Trying to figure out where this leaves you?"

I nodded. "Yeah, exactly."

She stood up and hauled me to my feet. "It'll all work out, okay? For now, let's just…sleep. Okay?"

I laughed. "I'm so worked up right now I don't know if I'll be able to."

"Let's just try."

It was weirdly intimate, climbing into bed with Aerie, but not with the expectation of sex. I donned my underwear in exchange for the jeans, and we wiggled around a bit, trying to find a comfortable position...but neither of us was used to sleeping with another person, so it took us some time to figure out positions. Eventually, we settled for spooning, with her behind me, pressed up against me, her knees tucked up behind mine, her breath on my shoulder, her hand draped over my chest, her breasts flattened against my back.

And, to my surprise, I found myself falling asleep faster than I ever had before in my whole life.

FOUR

Aerie

I'VE NEVER BEEN ONE TO SLEEP IN LATE AND, AS FAR AS I know, neither are any of the Badd brothers. Tate will occasionally sleep in until maybe nine or so, but that's rare. Usually, we're both automatically up by at least seven, and usually earlier; there was always just too much we wanted to do to waste time sleeping all morning, and I figured it's probably similar with the boys. I know in the few months Corin and I have been…dating, or whatever you want to call this thing…I've never known him to sleep later than seven thirty. So, when I'm woken to voices outside the bedroom door, then peer sleepily at the red numerals of the cheap digital alarm clock and see 11:30 a.m.,

I'm shocked.

I shake Canaan. "Hey."

He mumbles, still mostly asleep. "Whazzit."

"It's eleven thirty in the morning, Cane."

"Mmmm-fmmm."

"And I think your brother is home, and about to come in."

"Hnnnn?"

"Canaan, wake up, honey."

"Nnnng."

"I don't want him to come in and find us in his bed like this."

"Fug'im. Not scared of the dumb ol' gorilla."

"I'm not *scared*, Canaan, it's just—"

The door swung open at that moment, and I instinctively tugged the blankets up to my chin, as Baxter stood hulking in the doorway, a stunningly beautiful woman of medium height with jet-black hair peering around his shoulder.

Baxter tilted his head to one side, stepped backward out of the room to glance at the hallway. "Yo, am I—this is *my* bedroom, yeah? Like, I'm not hallucinating?"

Canaan blinked awake, finally, and tossed a wave with one hand while scrubbing his eyes with the other. "Sorry, Bax. Had…um…sleeping arrangement issues, so we borrowed your bed."

I had the sheet up to my nose, now. "Um. Hi, Bax."

Baxter's eyebrow slowly arched upward. "Aerie Kingsley, all snuggled in my bed with my kid brother. How cozy."

"I'm barely two years younger than you, douche-bag. That hardly makes me your kid brother." Canaan shifted to a sitting position. "Hi, Eva. Nice to see you again."

She waved. "Hi, Canaan." Her eyes went to me. "Hi, Aerie. Nice to meet you in person."

I wiggled my fingers at her. "Hi. Um, could we maybe finish this after I'm dressed?"

Bax snorted. "Sure. Not like I need my bedroom or nothin'."

Evangeline pulled him backward by the bicep. "Honey, don't be an ogre."

"I'm not being an ogre, I just—" Evangeline must have squeezed pretty hard, because he went silent abruptly.

"Baxter." All she did was say his name, but he sighed, a sound of resignation and irritation.

"Fine, fine, fine."

Once they closed the door, I slipped out of bed and quickly dressed, while Canaan took his time, stretching, yawning, and scratching, before finally getting out of the bed.

"Canaan, come on," I huffed.

"What's the rush? It's fine. It's not a big deal."

"He sounded pretty upset, actually."

Canaan just laughed. "You've clearly never seen Baxter when he's upset then, that was...that wasn't even mild irritation." He tugged on his jeans, zipped and buttoned, and snagged his T-shirt off the floor. "Seriously. Don't stress."

"We were in his bed, in his room, without asking." I was combing my fingers through my hair in an attempt to mitigate bedhead.

"And he'll be all be like, yo, wash my sheets and maybe call and ask next time, and I'll be all like, yo, no problem, and that's that. Quit stressing, babe, for real."

We left the room, as Canaan shrugged into his shirt. Corin and Tate were nowhere to be seen and the bedroom door was opened, the bed made in Tate's signature meticulous style; Lucian was kicked back on the couch, a thick paperback in his hands, a pair of red Beats on his ears; Baxter and Evangeline were in the kitchen, leaning side by side against the counter beside the fridge, sharing a knife and a block of cheese.

I hopped up on a different section of counter, and Canaan leaned back between my thighs, accepting the cheese and knife from Baxter.

"So, I guess maybe we should have called you first," Canaan said, handing me a slice of cheese and then taking one for himself.

Baxter waved a hand, stopping Canaan. "It's not a big deal. I was just surprised, as much by the fact that Aerie was in the bed with you as that anyone was in my bed. Also not a big deal, but I *am* curious as to how all this has shaken down. I *have* been gone for a few months, and it's understandable that you might wanna borrow my bed for a night."

"More to the point, actually," Eva said, "is the fact that now that we're in Ketchikan, living arrangements need to be reexamined. Especially if it's not just me being added into the mix, but Tate and Aerie as well."

Lucian, the headphones now around his neck, glanced at us over the back of the couch. "When it was eight dudes in two three-bedroom apartments, it was a little crowded but manageable. Then it was Bast and Dru, over there, and that was fine. Then it was Zane and Mara, and that made two couples in one apartment, which was pretty tight, but then Zane and Mara moved into their warehouse apartment. But now we've got Brock and Claire, and now there's Bax and Eva, plus Canaan, Corin, Tate, and Aerie. It's becoming a housing crisis."

Baxter nodded in agreement. "If all eight of us

brothers end up with a serious girlfriend, wife, whatever, it's gonna be sixteen of us. Zane and Mara have their own place, but the rest of us are all just sort of jamming into the same two apartments. We gotta do something."

Evangeline sliced a piece of cheese and ate it, then gestured with the knife as she spoke. "Normally, this is where I'd offer to buy or renovate a building, but I'm sort of…well…there's not much I can do at the moment. I'm sort of dependent on Bax until I figure a few things out."

I glanced at her. "Doesn't your father have, like, more money than God?"

She nodded, with a heavy sigh. "Yes, he does. He's not Bill Gates or Jeff Bezos wealthy, but he has a lot of money, and it's old money, too. My family is one of those East Coast American aristocracy sort of families." She glanced up at Bax, and then continued. "But…I didn't toe the line, so…" She shrugged, as if the rest was obvious.

I frowned at her. "I'm sorry, maybe I'm not understanding. Your father disowned you?"

"That's a polite way of putting it, yes."

Baxter's expression was fierce, angry. "You guys seriously wouldn't believe it if I told you all the shit that's gone down." He bumped her with his hip. "You mind if I share, babe?"

She shrugged. "Go ahead. It's not a secret."

"Her pops doesn't like me much, and that's putting it lightly."

"It's less about you than it is me not obeying him," Evangeline put in.

"It's about the fact that your father is a controlling asshole and needs to choke on a dick."

Evangeline whacked him on the arm, but had to hide a smirk. "That's a little unnecessarily vulgar, honey."

"He's a little unnecessarily a controlling asshole." Bax swept his gaze over all of us. "She walked away. From him, from everything."

"My whole life, my father provided me with a generous allowance. The older I got, the greater the allowance, and eventually it was in my own bank account. I'd always been under the impression that this money was mine. Well, a few years ago, when Thomas first began proposing to me and Father began attempting to push me into a relationship with Thomas, I realized just how much control my father had over my life. Especially when Father and I started clashing over my choice of college major." She wrapped a lock of black hair around her finger and tugged on it. "I began skimming money out of the account Father had opened for me back when I was in high school and I shunted it into an account at a different bank. Just, you know, so I'd have a little money of my own, away from Father's control, just in case."

"Sounds smart," I said. "I take it that didn't work out as you'd planned?"

Evangeline laughed bitterly. "I rather drastically underestimated my father's willingness to control every aspect of my life, and the lengths to which he would go. He somehow discovered that other secret account, and because he's so powerful and influential, he had a word with the owner of the bank and convinced him to sign control of that account over to him, despite the fact that I'd opened it as a legal adult, under my own name, with funds that had never been attached to any kind of a legally binding contract. But...Father has his ways, and got it done. So that money, all those years of carefully and cautiously skimming and transferring, all those years of living frugally at Yale so I would use as little of Father's money as possible...all for nothing. He had control.

"When he came to get me and bring me home, after my little, um...vacation...with Baxter, he presented me with an ultimatum. He knew about the money, he had control, and he was perfectly willing to let me have it...if I married Thomas. And, oh yeah, he threatened to have Baxter detained."

"And then I went in, stormed their fancy wedding,

punched that slimy ass-hair straight in his pretty-boy mouth, and that got 'em even more riled up."

Canaan frowned. "Have him detained? Whassat mean?"

"It means he's played golf with the deputy director of the FBI every week for the last twenty years, so all he has to do is call Mr. Pritchard and mention Baxter's underground fighting, or offer to put in a word with the president for Mr. Pritchard's bid for NSA director...and bam, a couple of special agents show up, and Baxter is in jail."

"Your dad can just 'put in a word with the president'?" Canaan asked, putting heavy emphasis on the last phrase. "Like, the POTUS?"

"Like the POTUS, yes," Eva answered. "Like I said, Father is very, very influential. He doesn't hold a position in the government anymore, but he knows everyone on the Hill and in Washington. And I do mean everyone. He has standing lunch dates with the speaker, golfs with the D-D of the FBI, he was roommates at Yale with the majority whip..." she trailed off, shrugging.

"Damn," Canaan drawled. "And you made this guy your enemy, Bax?"

"'I ask you to judge me by the enemies I have made,'" Lucian said. "FDR."

"That's a nice quote, bro, but what are we gonna

do if our brother gets arrested by the FBI? He hasn't exactly been quiet about his underground fighting, not to mention the gambling that surrounds it." Canaan pointed at Baxter. "Sounds to me like you've got a tiger by the tail, Bax."

"Would he really send the FBI after Baxter when you've very obviously made your choice to go your own way?" I asked. "That seems kind of petty, if you ask me. I can kind of understand using that threat to try to keep you in line, but to carry it out after you made your choice?"

Eva shrugged. "That's part of the reason we've been laying low the last couple months. I doubt my father will ever forgive me, but he might be willing to just let me go without trying to make further trouble out of spite. He's controlling and manipulative, but he's never struck me as spiteful."

"Thomas would, though," Baxter added. "Thomas is a dick."

"This is true. But Thomas doesn't have the ear of the FBI, and Father does." She sighed. "You embarrassed them all, though, and you took me away from them, which ruined their plans."

"What do you mean, he ruined their plans by taking you away?" I asked.

She laughed. "Oh, well...Father has been grooming Thomas for the political career I was never interested in. Essentially, he's the son Father always wanted. Not only was I a girl, I had my own ideas and plans and, in his mind, I was meant to be a quiet compliant girl, meant only to help him play his game his way. He intended me to marry Thomas for political gain. See, you can't be a serious politician hoping to play in the big leagues and be unmarried—you need a wife. She has to be the perfect accessory, she has to fit an image, further your brand. I was that, for Thomas. The trophy wife, the smiling, party-hosting, perfect-figure, perfect-dress-wearing political tool."

Canaan snorted. "Maybe I'm dumb at politics, but I don't get what that has to do with your father."

"Everything. Father is Thomas's mentor. Father controls Thomas just as much as he controls me, but in a far more subtle way, and I don't think Thomas really realizes it. Father has kept the best of his connections for himself, only allowing Thomas the contacts he wants to give him when he wants Thomas to have them. He'll introduce Thomas to a particular senator when it suits Father's machinations. He's a spider with an enormous web, and Thomas is just a strand in that web. Of course, his real plan is to plant Thomas in the Oval Office, which would place Father as Thomas's chief advisor, and thus one of the most powerful men in the country, beyond even where he is now. And I was always meant to be Thomas's wife, and that's an integral role in the whole game. There's no real power in being first lady, but there is huge power in the optics of it all."

Eva sighed, waving her hand. "In refusing to play their game, I'm forcing them to figure out a plan B for Thomas's arm candy trophy wife, and I think Father had always banked on being able to manipulate me into going along with it."

I was somewhat dumbfounded. "Is this, like, real life, or is it an episode of *Scandal*?"

Eva laughed. "Aerie, you have no idea. It's enough to give me a headache."

"For real, though," Canaan said, "they wanted you to be the eventual first lady? Like, your boy Thomas really has a shot at being the actual president?"

Eva nodded. "Unfortunately, yes. He's smart enough to fill the role, but he's easily manipulated enough that Father can make sure the real power stays with him. Thomas does have the looks and the charisma to pull it off, that's the scary thing. He's good at politics, too. If you can look past the fact that he's a philandering, womanizing, arrogant asshole, he's actually quite a remarkable person."

"So...he's just like the rest of Washington?" I asked.

Eva laughed. "There are good people there,

people who truly do want to serve, to help the country. But…yes, Thomas will fit right in with a certain crowd."

Baxter waved both hands, shutting the conversation down. "How did we end up on this topic? We were supposed to be talking about living arrangements."

Lucian tossed his headphones onto the couch. "We're short on options. I'd be fine sharing a room with Xavier, but I'm not sure that'd be a good idea for him. He kind of needs his space. Not sure what other options we have other than people finding their own places."

"No, Xavier needs his own room." Baxter looked down at Eva. "We can get our own place."

She glanced down at her feet. "I left everything behind, Bax. Literally, everything. Including school. I also have zero work experience, and I do mean zero. I only started washing my own clothes, doing my own dishes, and things like sweeping and vacuuming after I moved out for college. I'm…" She let out a frustrated breath. "I'm just not sure how much help I'm going to be in terms of getting our own place. I have no money and no job."

Baxter curled his arm around her shoulders and pulled her against him. "Don't worry about that, okay? I've got some money saved, so I can put a down payment on a place near here. It won't be the Ritz, but it'll be home."

"And I'm still going to be dependent on a man." She wiped her face with both hands. "I'm sorry, this probably isn't the best time to be having this conversation, is it?"

"It's a perfect time," Baxter said. "You're among family now, babe. We don't judge around here. What we do is figure shit out and help each other."

"I'm the definition of a spoiled rich girl, Bax! What am I supposed to do? I can barely care for myself. I used my father's money to pay for my life." Eva shook her head, hair bouncing, and I think I detected a tear running down her cheek, which she quickly brushed away. "Sorry, sorry, I just…I've been thinking about this nonstop, all those hours on the bike. And I just…it kind of hurts to realize I'm basically useless as a person."

"Useless as a person?" Baxter sounded pissed. "Eva, honey, you're not—"

"Ketchikan is a tourist town," Lucian cut in. "We get steady traffic year-round."

"Luce, buddy, what's your point?" Baxter asked.

"I thought I remembered hearing you were majoring in art, which was problem for your dad." He addressed this to Eva.

She nodded, sniffling. "Yeah, but—"

"What kind of art do you do?"

She shrugged. "Painting, mostly. I was experimenting with mixed media, before all this happened."

Lucian tapped the back of the couch with a fingertip, eying her speculatively. "No nice way to ask this, but…are you any good?"

Eva sniffed a laugh. "Well, I had a private study program with the head of the Fine Arts program at Yale, and he's one of the most prestigious artists and critics in the world, so…I guess I'm okay."

I stared at Evangeline. "Wait, let me get this straight. You turned down a marriage with a rich, good-looking, highly powerful and influential man who might someday be the president, you walked away from your entire family, you walked away from your comfortable, cushy life paid for by your father, you walked away from your inheritance, and you walked away from a paid-for private study arts degree from Yale University…all to be with Baxter?"

She stared back at me, and then looked up at Baxter in a way that could only be described as one of absolutely besotted, mad, crazy love. "Yeah, I did. Seems like a lot, when you put it that way. But…none of that meant anything to me, not if I couldn't be with Bax. I certainly didn't want to be with Thomas, no matter what perks may have come with that relationship."

"Mercedes-Benzes and vacation houses won't make you happy," Bax said.

Eva laughed. "Honey, I got a Mercedes for my sixteenth birthday, and my own condo in Manhattan at eighteen, just for when I wanted to go shopping on Fifth Avenue. If I'd married Thomas, I'd have a garage full of Rolls Royces and Bugattis, and private estates in the Caribbean. Thomas is already independently worth far more than Father, and he's barely thirty." She shook her head. "But you're right."

"That's amazing," I said. "That you two found love like that with each other."

"Amazing doesn't begin to describe it," Eva said, gazing up at Bax. A pause, and then she glanced at Lucian. "What was your point with those questions, Lucian?"

He lifted a shoulder. "Oh, well...just that I know several people around town who do well selling their art. Cafes and bars will display your stuff, and there are a couple of independent art galleries that do rotating artist features. It may not be the same as having your work displayed at a fashionable gallery in Manhattan, but if you work at producing art, you can make a decent living."

Eva stared at him. "I...really?"

He nodded. "Bringing home local art is a big thing for tourists. Keep your canvasses on the smaller side and they'll often take it home with them right then and there. If you offer to ship it for them, they'll buy the bigger frames too."

"My plan was always to try and make it in the New York art scene," Eva said. "I had the connections, and my professor always said that when I was ready to start displaying my work, he could help me get in touch with some influential people. I just wanted to finish my degree first."

"If a tourist sees a piece of art that moves them, they're not going to stop and ask if the artist has a degree before they buy it. If it moves them, they buy." He fiddled with his headphones. "Make meaningful, moving art, and people will buy it. And, like I said, I know a few people, too."

The conversation moved on from there back to Baxter and Eva's plans to find somewhere to live, but I stopped hearing anything they were saying. I kept seeing the look on Eva's face as she gazed up at Bax. She gave up her whole life to be with Bax.

Amazing doesn't begin to describe it, she'd said.

I stole a glance at Canaan, and our eyes met.

His expression was…complicated. Hard to read. Deep.

And I wondered if he was having similar thoughts.

Why was it so hard to come out and tell him I wanted a love like that?

Oh, yeah...I remember now. I tried that once, and got my heart broken. I don't think even Tate knew all the details of that particular situation, nor how serious things had gotten, or how fast. No one knew. But then, that was the whole point of that relationship—the excitement, the forbidden, the daring, the exhilaration. It had been a secret.

I had been the secret.

I wasn't supposed to fall in love, and neither was he. But I did, and I thought he had too.

I thought things were different than they were.

It turned out that I was wrong...very, *very* wrong.

I have to tell Canaan about this.

My heart cracked and twisted at the thought, and my stomach dropped out. I *couldn't* tell him...I just couldn't. I've never told anyone.

If I want to bring honesty and truth to our relationship...I *have* to.

I've been trying my damnedest to keep the memories of the past suppressed. I've tried to not think about it, to pretend it's not me who experienced it all. I've tried to keep the pain of it from tainting my relationship with Canaan, but...

I can't keep pretending.

I want more.

I want *love*.

I want Canaan to love me, and I want to love him

back. I want what Eva and Baxter have, but I'm terrified, because I have deep, dark secret.

And it's eating away at me.

It's poisoning my relationship with Canaan, and preventing me from going after what I really want.

I don't know what to do.

It's festering inside me, an infected wound in my soul.

But I can't keep pretending I *don't* want more. I can't keep doing this stupid dance with Canaan, acting like what we have is purely physical when we both know it's not. He wants more too, but he's just as scared as me. Maybe he has his own secret. I don't know. I just know…

I have to tell him.

I feel my stomach welling up, my throat closing, hot acid burning bitter in my mouth. Tears sting my eyes.

This is why I don't think about this, why I don't go here, emotionally—it makes me physically ill.

"I'm sorry," I blurted out. "I'm sorry. I—I have to go. I—I need to get out of here. I need—I need air." I fled, stumbling out of the kitchen toward the stairs.

I felt everyone looking at me, surprised, confused. I felt the questions no one asked.

I left, and I found myself on the docks, sailboats on my left, the masts bobbing in the wet cold wind that just kicked up. The sky is gray and heavy overhead, the air chilly, with a wet cold wind blowing. I don't know how long I walked along the docks, but I knew Cane was behind me. I felt him.

Eventually, I stumbled to a stop. My feet ached, burned, throbbed—I had run out barefoot.

"Aerie, babe, what the fuck?" Canaan was out of breath when he caught up with me.

I collapsed forward onto the dock, sobbing, shaking my head, unable to form words.

"Aerie?" He was beside me, his arm over me. "Talk to me, babe. You're scaring me."

I sat up, turning my tear-stained face to Canaan's. "There's something I need to tell you."

FIVE

Canaan

THIS WAS SCARING THE FUCK OUT OF ME. AERIE WASN'T the type of girl to freak out like this. Tate, sure—Tate was prone to unexpected outbursts, but they were like tropical thunderstorms, gone as fast as they came. Aerie? She just didn't explode. She was measured, fairly even-keeled. If her feelings got hurt, she got angry, if she was sad, she cried—she emoted normally, whereas Tate tended to bury those kinds of things until everything just popped suddenly. Aerie didn't keep things in.

So this was crazy.

I couldn't make sense of what just happened. I didn't know what to do, except sit on the dock beside her. My initial reaction, when she said she had to tell me something, was raw panic: she was pregnant. What else could cause such a freak-out in someone as even-tempered as Aerie? But then I looked closer, at her eyes, at her face...I saw pain. Agony.

"Aerie...god, what's going on?"

She shook her head. "I...I can't. I can't. I can't." She was rocking back and forth, sitting on the damp dock, barefoot; it had begun to drizzle, and her fine blonde hair was dampening and sticking to her face.

"Honey, you're worrying me. I don't understand what's going on."

"I have to tell you, but I can't. I can't." She was staring out at the bay, unseeing, a haunted expression on her face.

"Tell me what?"

She just shook her head.

I pulled her to her feet. "Aerie, honey, it's raining. We need to get inside."

She finally looked at me once more, tears trickling down her cheeks. "Okay."

I led her back down the road to the studio and we sat down on the couch near the guitar racks. We kept a few throw blankets down here, because this was Alaska and it got chilly sometimes. I unfolded a blanket and wrapped it around Aerie's shoulders. She didn't want to be too close to me—I tried to pull her onto my lap, but she just shook her head and slid over to the middle of the couch, the blanket draped around her, head hanging, sniffling, tears falling steadily.

I gave her a while, letting her work through it on her own, occasionally touching her back, or stroking her hair.

Eventually, she sucked in a deep breath, sat back, rubbed her eyes, and then rested her head on the couch, gazing at me sideways. "Okay. I've been trying to talk myself out of this, but I can't. I need to…I need to get this out. To someone. To you."

"Aerie, whatever it is, it's going to be okay." I took her hand, twined our fingers together. "You can tell me anything."

Keeping the blanket wrapped around her, she got up, shuffled to the guitar rack, took the ukulele, and returned to the couch, propping her feet up and wrapping the blanket around her so only her hands could be seen gripping the instrument. She plucked a slow, mournful melody.

"Playing helps me think. It calms me," she said, as if I of all people would need an explanation.

"Preaching to the choir, babe."

"I know." She plucked and strummed for another minute or two, staring at the ceiling, obviously deep in thought. Then, slowly, she began to talk. "Just after high school, right when we were really starting to blow up, we were mostly working in the Manhattan area. We hadn't started traveling yet. We didn't have any set plans, but Mom was definitely working us toward modeling and the whole social media thing. I was into it more than Tate. It's easy to see that now, looking back, but then it didn't even occur to me that we could want different things. You know? Of course you do." She hesitated, and then continued. "Tate was boy crazy. She's always been boy crazy. I...I played the scene with her, went on dates here and there, went to parties with her and hung out with guys, but I never took it anywhere." She glanced at me, meaningfully.

I let out a breath. "Aerie, honey, don't try to spare my feelings by mincing words, okay? I'm a big boy. Just tell it like it is."

She nodded, and her gaze went back to middle distance, staring into nothingness as she gathered her thoughts, still strumming idly. "So, as I said, I played the game and all that, but I rarely slept with any of the guys I met."

That's not quite how I remembered things, but as I thought about it I had to admit that most of the stories of their sexual exploits had been about Tate, while Aerie had always hinted at things, but she'd rarely been outright about the details.

"Okay," I said. "I'm following so far."

"I *did* sleep with guys occasionally, but not as

often as I allowed you and others to assume." She sucked in a deep breath and let it out, her hand stilling on the strings. "And, like I said, I dated, but never seriously. I just wasn't that interested. No one ever seemed to catch my interest."

I wanted her to get to the point, but I kept quiet and listened, knowing whatever this was, it was serious, and she needed to get it out in her own way, in her own time.

She kept going. "Then I met Lex."

The name rang a bell. "Lex?"

She nodded, her hand tightening on the neck of the uke. "Lex Landon." She said this as if it was admission.

"Lex Landon, the lead singer of Ghostmother?"

"Lex Landon, lead singer of Ghostmother—Lex Landon, who did a run on a Broadway show—Lex Landon who was and still is the lead in *Blood Brothers*."

Blood Brothers was a TV show set and filmed in NYC, a fictional show about paramedics, shot with handhelds like a war documentary, that often told true stories from real EMS calls.

Lex Landon was a true-blue superstar, already famous from a triple-platinum, Grammy-winning rock band, who then became even more famous from a handful of supporting roles in movies wherein he stole the scenes from the more famous leads, and then did a turn in an original Broadway musical that won a Tony, and was now leading a TV show which had racked up four Emmys in as many years. A golden boy with the Midas touch.

He was also thirty-something.

"When…when was this, again?" I asked, feeling a little queasy.

She didn't answer right away. When she did, it was in a very quiet, very uneasy voice. "I was just barely eighteen, and he was thirty, almost thirty-one."

"Aerie. Come on."

She stared hard at me. "I thought you said it was going to be okay, don't mince words, I could tell you anything?"

I hissed. "Fuck, you're right, I'm sorry. I just feel like he should have known better."

She laughed, an intensely bitter sound. "I haven't even told you what happened, Cane."

I nodded, slumping lower on the couch. "Go ahead, babe. I'm listening. No judgments here, I promise."

"Oh, just wait. You'll judge, and you'll have every right." She let the silence stretch for a while, and then resumed her story. "Tate and I were at a party. Lots of famous people, lots of networking, lots of posing with celebrities and acting like we had the world in the palms of our hands. Which, to be honest, we kind of did. I'd just taken a selfie with Clooney, who's just darling by the way, and stepped out onto the rooftop deck for some air. Lex was out there, smoking a joint by himself. He offered it to me, and I took a hit or two with him, and we got to talking. Innocent enough. But…he was Lex Landon! I mean, I don't get star struck easily, but he was someone I really, really liked and looked up to. I loved Ghostmother, and I thought he was a fantastic actor, and god, he was so fucking gorgeous. So I was a little giddy. It was fun. We talked on the roof for an hour or two, and then we went back to the party and went our separate ways. That was it. But we kept meeting at parties. Like, it was weird. He was at every party I went to for a month straight. Finally, I confronted him about it, and we laughed. I was like, dude, Lex, you're stalking me, you super-creep. It was funny, because he was the famous one and I wasn't.

"So, finally, he asked if I wanted to meet for coffee. Also innocent enough, and why the hell wouldn't I want to have coffee with Lex Landon? Coffee that day became coffee every week." She looked at me then, a hard, meaningful glance. "I suppose I should point out that absolutely no one knows about this, including Tate. Me and Lex, and that's it, and I seriously doubt Lex has ever told anyone either."

I frowned. "Not even Tate knows about this?"

"Not even Tate." She ran a finger along a string on the uke, continuing. "We started hanging out. It was weird, and we both knew it. But we had so much fun together, just talking about everything. It was innocent enough, I thought. Just talk, always in public—that was it. Have a cup of coffee together, talk for an hour or two, and that was it. But it consumed me. *He* consumed me. I thought about him, fantasized, daydreamed. It was…bad. Teenage infatuation, I know that now, but then…it felt like love. I was in love, I knew it, I knew it down to my bones."

"I don't know if you can so easily dismiss that kind of intense attraction or whatever as nothing but teenaged infatuation," I said. "I've had that, and it feels very, very real in the moment."

She sucked in a shuddery breath. "God—thank god you get it."

"It's so fucking intense, you know? Like, it feels so real, so genuine, so all-encompassing. It's *everything*. All the more so because it's so new, the first time you've ever felt anything like that."

She nodded. "So that's what I was feeling. I thought about Lex, all the time. All we ever got was an hour over coffee, usually when he was either on the way to a shoot, or on a break from it. It was easy to keep it from Tate because she'd been taking an art class that I decided to skip out on, so I had that hour free to myself every week. And I just…I never told Tate about it. I was jealous, maybe. Scared she'd steal him from me, or make fun of me? I don't know. Maybe I thought she'd pop the bubble, like…ruin it for me or something. I just didn't want to share it—share *him*. He was *my* secret famous friend. See, it was secret for him, too. He never said it, but it was obvious, even then. He was always there first, in a ball cap and big sunglasses, sitting in a back corner of this particular coffee shop we always went to. It was our spot. This went on for…months."

Another pause, in which she was clearly gathering courage for the next part of the story, which I could sense the shape of, in that tense, waiting silence.

"We were sitting together having coffee. He had a double espresso with little bit of foam, and I had a vanilla latte. It was just past three in the afternoon. A sunny, beautiful day. I remember it…very vividly. The tension had been building for months, and neither of us talked about it. Then, suddenly, he interrupted me. 'I can't do this anymore,' he'd said, in this gruff, scary voice. 'Do what anymore,' I asked. 'See me,' he said. He couldn't see me anymore, it was too hard. So I freaked out and got up and left.

"We never saw each other on the street, never walked in or out together, we only ever sat at that hidden little table in the back of the coffee shop, where no one could see us. Well, when I walked out, he chased me. Grabbed me. Spun me around and gave me one of those little envelopes they give you at hotels, with a keycard in it. It was for a local hotel, just a couple blocks away. Little boutique hotel, kind of out of the way. The kind of place he could go and pay them to keep quiet and not ask or answer questions about him. It had the room number on it, in black Sharpie—533." She paused again, strummed a chord, and quieted the strings. "He told me he was going to that room, right then. He'd be there in fifteen minutes. He didn't tell me to meet him there, didn't say anything else, just handed me the keycard and told me he'd be there in fifteen minutes. And then he walked away.

"I knew exactly what he was doing, leaving it up to me to decide what to do. Well…I went. I knew it was…weird, at the very least. I knew no one would approve, least of all Mom or Tate. I knew if the press got wind of it, it would blow up and be bad for both of us. I knew all this, and I went anyway."

I didn't know what to say. I didn't even know exactly how I felt about it. So…I just kept quiet, and let her talk.

After another long silence, she kept going. "I went up to room 533 at this upscale boutique hotel, and as soon as the door closed behind me, he was all over me." Her eyes went to mine. "And don't think

I was a victim in it—I wasn't. I wanted it, I wanted him, and I went into that room knowing exactly what would happen. And it did."

I didn't like this at all.

I didn't like the bitter knot of acid in my stomach, or the way my heart hammered and twisted. I didn't like the jealousy smashing through me like lightning. I didn't like the anger I felt toward Aerie for doing that, and I didn't like the anger I felt at him...I didn't like anything about this. My teeth ground in my jaw, painfully. I kept still, kept quiet, and kept listening.

"Like meeting for coffee, I went back to room 533, at that hotel, at the same time almost every single day for several weeks. It was...incredible. I'm sorry, I really am, I hate saying this to you of all people, but it just was. I won't go into details, but...it was just...it was amazing. And he was thirty-one, and I was eighteen.

"I was in love." She shook her head, blinking hard against the tears that fell again. "I just...I *knew*, in my heart, all the way down, I knew that I loved him, and that he loved me, and we should stop being secretive about it. He could take me to premieres and the Oscars and I'd be his girlfriend...I had it all planned out."

The pain on her face, in her voice...sliced me to the bone. It was so palpable, still so fresh, but all the more potent after being stoppered up inside her for so long.

"God, Aerie."

She shook her head. "Ohhhh buddy…just you wait. This is where it starts to get *really* interesting."

"Shit."

"Shit is right."

Aerie was still composed, but just barely, and I knew that once she got to the really "interesting" part, she was going to completely lose it.

Aerie held off the tears, and kept going. "So. Weeks of this, me and Lex having our secret trysts. I was still going to parties, hanging out with boys, going on dates, all the things I was always doing. I wasn't sleeping with anyone else, and I think even Tate started to get suspicious, but I'd always gone through dry spells where I just wasn't into sleeping with anyone—I've been that way since we lost our virginity at sixteen. So that's how I played it. She'd taken another art class in that same time bracket, and his shooting schedule was always the same, so our meetings were regular. I never even had his phone number, and he never had mine. I just met him in room 533 at two p.m., and we'd sleep together, talk a little, and then he'd get dressed and leave first, and I'd leave second, a few minutes later. We never talked about it, it was just the way things were."

She was blinking a lot, and her voice was tight, and I could tell we were coming to the heart of the matter; I touched her ankle, squeezed—she was sitting a ways away from me on the couch, clearly needing space to get the story out.

"Well, one night Tate and I were at another big, high profile party with lots of famous people. We were doing our thing, hanging out, talking, and taking selfies. I was near the entrance of the ballroom where the party was happening, talking to some random person. Well…the doors opened, and Lex came in. With a woman. They were holding hands, like they were comfortable together because they'd been together for so long." She hesitated, swallowing hard. "And…and he was wearing a wedding ring on his left hand, which he'd never worn before. I'd known he was with someone, or used to be, but there hadn't been anything in the tabloids about them lately, so I guess I assumed they'd broken up." She sighed, paused, and then continued.

"So he saw me, and I saw him, and our eyes met, and—and he just walked straight past me as if he didn't know me. It cut me to the fucking bone. I mean, I just…I knew he'd been keeping our relationship a secret from the press, because he was almost fifteen years older than me…but finding out he was fucking *married*? It was bullshit, and I was pissed, but what could I do? Confront him right then and there, at the party? I couldn't do that. Those parties were career events for Tate and me, and I didn't dare make a scene. Especially since Tate was there and had no idea about the whole thing. So I just had to swallow the hurt and acted like everything was hunky-fucking-dory."

"God, Aerie, that fuckin' sucks," I said. "What an asshole."

Another bitter, sarcastic bark of laughter. "Oh god, Cane, you have no idea."

"That's not the end of it?"

She sighed. "I wish." Aerie spent a moment trying to compose herself. "I didn't go to the hotel at all that week. I was so pissed, I just couldn't even think straight. Tate knew something was off with me, but I wouldn't talk about it, even with her. So, for a full week I stayed away."

I groaned. "You went back to him?" I asked. "Not judging, just...curious."

She smiled sadly at me. "I was hooked, Cane. It wasn't just that I wanted—*needed*, maybe—the sex. I also needed to confront him about it, and that hotel was the only way I knew how to get hold of him. So...I went. Two p.m. on a Monday afternoon, in November. It was a cold, windy day. About two weeks before Thanksgiving. I, um...I went to the hotel, used the keycard to let myself in, waited an hour, and...

and he never showed up. I went back the next day, waited for an hour, and he didn't show up again. So the next day, I went to the coffee shop, *our* coffee shop. No show. Figures he'd ghost on me, right?"

She snatched a tissue from the box, holding it in one hand while trying to breathe through the tears. A tear slid down her cheek, and then another, and she dabbed them away as they fell.

"Aerie, honey, you don't have to—"

She sounded so shaky as she spoke over me, her voice trembling. "So, um. A full month passed from the time I saw him and his wife at the party. Then six weeks had passed. I cried, and tried to tell myself it was for the best. And that was—that was when I realized some—something. I—I'd missed my period."

The blood drained out of my face, and my heart skipped several beats. "Aerie, no. Seriously…no."

She nodded, tears flooding down her face. "Seriously, yes. I waited another week to be sure, but it was undeniable at that point. I'd started to feel sick in the mornings, and my emotions were all out of whack."

"Shit. You were pregnant?"

"Yep. I took a test, and it came up positive, and I promptly threw up into the sink." She dabbed at her nose with the tissue, sniffling, sucking in a shuddery breath. "I didn't tell anyone. I didn't sleep for three days, didn't eat, and forced myself to drink water. I thought about finding him, telling him, demanding he help me…I wasn't sure what I wanted him to do."

"So…what happened? I mean…" I struggled with how to phrase my question, and came up empty.

"What happened?" She drew her knees up onto the couch, wrapping her arms around them, cocooned in the blanket. "I hunted him down. Found out where he was shooting, talked my way past security, found his trailer, and snuck in. Waited for him. All damn day, I sat in that trailer. He had good snacks in there and a fridge full of Perrier, so I helped myself. Finally, around eight that night, he came in. But…um. He—he wasn't alone."

"No shit. Seriously?"

"Seriously. Amy Thompson-Frasier was there, the actress who plays the lead opposite him. And they, um. They didn't see me at first, because they were too busy getting it on. She had his pants open and she was yanking him and he had her skirt up around her hips before they even made it into the trailer. Turns out Detective Ellen Rooney doesn't wear underwear beneath those pencil skirts."

"You have got to be kidding me."

"Wish I was, Canaan, I wish I was." She was still crying, fighting sobs. "I was on the couch with a bag of pretzels and a bottle of Perrier, and I guess that couch was where they were planning on fucking. So, yeah. They saw me. Amy screamed, Lex shouted 'what the fuck, Aerie?' and I just sat there, eating pretzels. Weirdly, I was amazingly calm. I asked for a few minutes alone with Lex, and Amy got her clothes back in order and left. I didn't know what to say, or how to start the conversation. Lex just stood there, his pants open, staring at me like I was an alien. Finally, I just said it; 'I'm pregnant.'"

"How did the cheating dickbag take that?"

She closed her eyes for a moment. "He was silent for, like, a full minute. And then he—he just looked at me, cold as ice, and said, 'so get an abortion.'"

"He didn't."

"He did. Just like that." Aerie bit her lip, eyes closed again, tears dripping off her chin. "Um. So. I left. I didn't say a word. I just left. With his bag of pretzels, actually."

I could only stare, trying to absorb this. "Aerie, you…you…"

"I Googled clinics from my phone, called one, asked how much it would be, went to a bank and withdrew cash to pay for it, and then went to the clinic that same day, within an hour of seeing him." She shuddered, sucking in a shaky breath. "I had the abortion on November twentieth. Completely alone. I took a cab home, pretended to be sick for three days.

I never told Tate, never told Mom, never told anyone. I couldn't. I was…I was…"

She broke into sobs, then, finally unable to hold them back.

"You're the first person I've ever told."

I had no idea what to say.

"I was…" she started, but had to stop and try again. "We'd been together, the day of the party—when I saw him with his wife, I mean. He and I had… after we fucked, he actually stayed in the bed with me for a while, and it…it felt nice. And I had been feeling so much for him, trying to pretend I didn't and just failing miserably. So…uh…we were in the bed together, and I put my head on his chest, and I told him I thought I was falling in love with him."

"Oh god…Aerie…" I reached for her, but she shook her head, holding out a hand to keep away.

"Don't, Canaan. Just don't." She gathered herself yet again. "As soon as I said that, he got up, dressed, and left without a single word to me. Then he showed up at that party with his wife. He knew I'd be there. Up until then he'd always made sure not to be at any party I'd go to while we were sleeping together, so he clearly knew how to make sure our social circles didn't overlap. So him showing up at that party with his wife, and the way he looked at me, making sure I saw them, it was a message. He was making it absolutely clear to me how things were."

"Goddamn, Aerie, that's savage."

"I spent a month of my life trying to get over Lex, trying to convince myself I'd never been in love with him, that it was just infatuation or lust or whatever, and I'd finally started to make some progress at getting over him, when I found out I was pregnant, and he just…he looked right into my eyes and told me to get an abortion—" She broke into a sob, covering her face with both hands.

"Holy shit."

She couldn't talk anymore, and she wouldn't let me near her. She kept holding out a hand to keep me away as she fought through her sobs. She was just… shattered.

And I couldn't do a damn thing about it.

"You got an *abortion*?" Tate's voice rang out from the stairs behind us.

SIX

Aerie

I SOBBED ALL THE HARDER AT THE SOUND OF TATE'S VOICE, at the betrayal in her tone. Canaan was on the other side of the couch from me, staring at me, probably wishing he'd never met me, probably wishing he'd never touched me. And Tate...god. What a way to find out.

"I'm sorry," I gasped. "I'm sorry, I'm sorry."

"How could you?" Tate asked, rounding the couch to crouch in front of me. She was...so angry. So hurt. "I don't understand, A. Why would you... how could you keep that from me? How could you *do* that? That was...it was a *life*! A *person*!"

"Don't you think I *know* that?" I screamed. "I've

thought about that every single day for the last three years of my life!"

"Why didn't you tell me?" Tate whispered.

"I couldn't. I just…I couldn't." I lifted my eyes to my twin's, saw tears in her eyes, trickling down her face. The hurt, the betrayal, the confusion, the anger…it was too much. "How much did you hear?"

"Enough." Tate stood up, turned away. "Too much."

"I can't tell the whole story again."

"You don't need to." Tate crossed her arms, still facing away from me. "You had a secret affair with Lex Landon, a man twelve years older than you, who was *married*—a fact you could have looked up on Wikipedia, by the way."

"Right, because you've Googled everyone *you've* ever fucked."

"That's not the point."

"Then what *is* the point, Tate? That I'm a slut because I had a forbidden, torrid affair with an older man? We could talk about the number of guys you've fucked, which I guarantee is more than anyone else in this room—"

"Watch your mouth, Aerie!" Corin snapped, having just entered the room.

"You stay out of this, Corin!" I snapped back. "This doesn't involve you."

"Guys, that's enough." Canaan stood up, moving between Tate and me. "Tate, why don't you and Corin give us a minute, okay? Everyone's upset, tempers are flaring, and we're not going to help anyone if we're all upset."

"My twin sister had a fucking abortion and didn't tell me! How am I not supposed to be upset about this?" Tate shouted. "Why don't you stay the fuck out of this too, Canaan? This is between Aerie and me."

"It's actually not, Tate," Canaan said with a touch of anger in his voice. "It's between Aerie and *me*. She was talking to *me*. *You* were eavesdropping."

"We came down the stairs and overheard her talking," Corin said, stepping toward his brother. "We weren't *eavesdropping*."

"Sure as fuck seems like it to me." Canaan crossed his arms over his chest, staring his brother down.

"You have something to say to me, Cane?" Corin demanded.

I shot to my feet, putting myself between them. "STOP! Both of you, stop. *All* of you stop. Everyone just…just…*shut the fuck up*!" I felt panic rifling through me. "You guys aren't supposed to fight. Neither are we, Tate. We're twins, you guys are twins. What the hell is happening to us?"

Corin let out a ragged sigh, running his hands over his face. "Shit. You're right, A, you're absolutely right. What *are* we doing, right now?"

I couldn't handle any more. I was still reeling with the renewed agony of having finally told my secret...to Canaan, no less, whom I was beginning to fall in love with. My sister had overheard, and now the secret was really out there, because even Corin knew, now. Everyone knew.

It was all too much. Too fucking much.

"I—I…" I turned to Canaan, clutching at his shirt. "Take me home, please."

He just stared at me. "Home? Where's home, Aerie?"

"I don't know! Fuck, I don't know! I don't have a home. Nowhere is home. This isn't, New York isn't—" I backed away, but he had my arms and wouldn't let go. "I just…I need to be alone. I need—I need…"

"Mom is at Grandma and Grandpa's, so you can't go there," Tate said. "Mom will know something's wrong after one look at you, and I *really* don't think she could handle this news right now. She'd have an actual heart attack."

Baxter and Evangeline came down the stairs, then, and I burst into tears at the sight of them. I didn't need them to see me like this, and I wondered if they'd heard my story, too, and the thought sent me into an actual panic attack. The kind of panic attack where I was hyperventilating, gasping for breath, heart palpitating, dizzy, and a flood of emotions cascading through me.

I felt soft, warm hands on my face; Evangeline was talking to me, but I couldn't hear her. Canaan was behind her, and Tate, and Corin, and Bax...

I shook my head, tried to pull away, and Eva wrapped an arm around me and guided me...I don't know where. I was disoriented, dizzy, stumbling, faint. Crying. I felt a strong arm supporting me, Canaan's arm. I clutched him, held on to him just to stay upright.

Voices.

A bed underneath me. Faint female perfume.

Silence.

Sweet, blessed silence.

A hand, stroking my hair. Braiding it. Evangeline, sitting on the bed beside me, humming softly.

I couldn't stop crying.

Canaan wasn't here, and I was glad, because I wasn't sure I could handle him right then.

Evangeline just kept fiddling with my hair, kept humming, her presence a soft, calming, soothing balm.

Eventually, my breath steadied and I got a handle on my tears; I blinked through the haze of tears and realized we were in Baxter's room.

I looked up at Evangeline, trying to get myself

under control, but I was still shaking and shuddering through the aftershocks of sobs. "Why...why are you here? Why are you doing this?"

"Sometimes we just need a friend. Not a sister, not a man, just...a friend." She finished braiding my hair, and I sat up; she took my hands in hers. "I've never really had anyone I could call a true friend. There's literally no one back East I even miss. No one has called me, or emailed me, or texted me, or asked where I was." She smiled at me. "I need a friend, and so do you. So...here I am."

"Tate and the boys are really the only people I've ever trusted or felt close to, and now things with them are all so tangled up and messy, I just...I don't even know what to do anymore." I glanced at her. "Did you hear what I was saying?"

She shrugged. "I heard some. It's none of my business, though."

"When I was eighteen, I had a secret affair with an older married man, a pretty famous one, too. He got me pregnant, and I had an abortion." It was a little easier to put into words, this time. "I kept the entire thing a secret from everyone, until just now, when I told Canaan...and my sister overheard.

"I'm falling in love with Canaan, but I don't know how to tell him, and I'm scared to be in love...I don't *want* to be in love—scared isn't the right word, actually…I'm outright *terrified*. I especially don't want to be in love with *him*. Canaan and Corin have been my best friends—and really my only friends my whole life, same for Tate. So it's…it's really complicated. But it's already complicated now, because Cane and I have slept together, and Corin and Tate are together and in love, and we almost made things even more complicated a couple months ago by mixing up partners, but we didn't, thank god, and now Tate is pregnant with Corin's baby, and everything is even *more* fucked up."

"Wow…that's…a lot," Eva replied.

"Bet you bit off more than you can chew, huh, Evangeline?"

"Call me Eva," she said, "and no, not at all." What are you going to do?"

"I have no idea." I shook my head and shrugged. "I really don't. It's tempting to just stay in here and ignore all three of them for a while." I looked around and said, "You guys need your room, though, huh?"

She shook her head. "I guess you missed part of the earlier conversation. Bax and I are going to look for an apartment in this area, and you and Canaan are taking this room. It just makes more sense."

"But…" I hesitated. "I'm not sure I'm ready to move in with Canaan. I don't even know what we are, or what he feels, or anything."

"That does complicate things."

"Yeah, exactly."

She shifted on the bed, putting her back to the wall, and I moved to sit beside her. "Why don't you want to be in love, and why not with Canaan?"

I sighed. "I want to say it's complicated, but it's not, really. I was in love with the man who got me pregnant, and he was just using me for cheap, easy sex. The moment I admitted I was falling for him, he ghosted, but not before making sure I knew he'd been married the whole time. It was an intentional knife in the back. When I found out I was pregnant, I confronted him with it, and he flat-out told me to get an abortion."

"What a jerk."

"No shit, right?" I sighed. "Maybe I wasn't ever really in love with him. I don't know. It sure as hell felt like it at the time. I've thought about this nonstop, and I realized I couldn't have really been in true love with him because I knew nothing about him. It was just sex. He hid the fact that he was married, that he was cheating on his wife, and that I was the other woman. I've always sort of…shied away from getting emotionally involved with men since then. I've…I've sort of avoided men in general, actually, except when I start to need…you know, sex. I don't know. The whole thing is fucked up. I'm fucked up."

"We're all a little fucked up about something,

Aerie. I let my dad control me my whole life. I'm a spoiled brat with zero life skills or work experience of any kind." She giggled and leaned close. "And I'm honestly worried Bax is turning me into an actual sex addict."

I giggled with her. "God, I know the feeling. There's something about these Badd brothers, I think. They have a way of turning us women into mindless sex addicts."

"You too?"

I nodded, stifling a laugh. "It's so bad. It's part of the problem, honestly. Am I crazy to think it could be love I'm feeling for Canaan? I thought I was in love with Lex Landon, and look where that got me."

Eva stared at me in surprise. "The older married man was *Lex Landon?*"

I nodded. "Yes. The one and only. Unfortunately, as a real human being, he's a piece of shit." I sighed. "At least, he was to me. I know I should have done more in terms of making sure what we had was legit, but it was young and it was so fun, secretive and forbidden and sexy. That was all part of the attraction, I realize now, looking back. But it was empty, and meaningless, and it was never going to go anywhere, and I should have been wise enough to know that. But I wasn't. And now…" I groaned. "He's a sexual predator, that's what he is. A cheater, a liar, and a total scumbag. I was an impressionable, gullible eighteen-year-old, and he took advantage of that, and then discarded me like so much garbage."

"*He's* the garbage, not *you*." Eva shook her head, visibly upset. "You were so young! God—men like that, who take advantage of girls like you were, then, they just…they make me so mad. It's so wrong, that your story is, sadly, all too common. And the fact that you're still hung up on the rejection of it all, and not just the way he victimized you? Even still you're… you're feeling the stigma of that." She shook her head. "No, stigma isn't the right word. I think the rejection hurt you worse than you realize, and you're putting that fear of rejection onto your relationship with Canaan."

I nodded, but I couldn't breathe, because her words were so, so true, and it hurt all over again. "I thought we had something, I thought—I thought maybe…I thought Lex at least *cared* about me, at least a little bit. I think I knew, deep down, that he didn't love me. But…when he ghosted on me, and then showed up with his wife…" I shrugged, unable to put it into words.

"It cut you to the core. And when he told you to abort the pregnancy, it…" she trailed off, shrugging.

"It broke something inside me, I think," I finished.

"Right, and that's totally understandable. But

here's the thing, honey. Talking about this, getting out, so it's not a secret anymore…that's the first and biggest step toward healing. You were victimized by an older man. He's a predator, nothing more, nothing less, and you were the prey. You can't blame yourself for that. He didn't reject you, he *used* you, and threw you aside when you'd served your purpose for him. That's on *him*, babe, not you."

Eva ducked her head, staring at the blanket between her crossed legs.

"I've been thinking a lot about this stuff, lately, and Bax and I have had a lot of really brutal conversations trying to keep things open and honest between us. In some ways, we didn't want to come back here and try to be a couple around all of you when we still only barely knew each other. So we took the time we needed to learn about each other. Which meant both of us opening up about a lot of things. Such as that I now have undeniable confirmation of the fact that my father never really loved me. I believe my mother loved me but only insofar as it suited Father's plans. Thomas…well…that part at least is obvious—I was only ever a means to an end for him.

"So when I came here to Ketchikan on my own and met Bax, I leaped—somewhat recklessly, I might add—into a relationship with him. But really letting him love me? That's going to be harder. We knew we had these strong emotions for each other, and we knew we had a crazily intense physical connection, but the kind of love that allows people to…to really *be together*, in terms of a healthy lifelong romance—a real *marriage*…well, that's a little different.

"It's easy to have sex, easy to say we love each other, but sometimes he wants to take care of me, and I don't want to be taken care of because that's all I've ever known, whereas for Bax, he's always been totally independent and has never had anyone to take care of, never had anyone that needed him. So… there's a disconnect there."

I blinked at her. "That's…um…are you sure you're not a relationship counselor? Because that's… it's the most self-aware statement I've ever heard."

Eva blushed and shrugged a shoulder. "Like I said, we've spent a lot of time over the past few months trying to figure out how to have a meaningful relationship. And I know to a lot of people Baxter comes across as this big, brutish, hard-headed, hard-fisted monster who thinks only about things like football and working out and whatever…but he's actually very sensitive and very thoughtful. At least, he is with me. He's also surprisingly articulate and intelligent."

I glanced around the bedroom. "When Cane and I first came in here we were somewhat surprised to see all these books," I admitted.

"So was I, my first time in here. I think he intentionally allows people to make assumptions about him. It keeps people away. He's only ever been close to his brothers, and I think he has a hard time forming relationships with anyone, male or female. I get the sense he wasn't really buddy-buddy with the guys on his football team, and I've never known anyone to call, text, email, or visit him. Except his brothers, and now me. He keeps everyone away."

"Why do you think that is?"

She tipped her head to one side. "Well, this is mostly conjecture, and it's just between you and me, right? The boys' mother died when they were very young—you've known them your whole life so I assume you know this?"

I nodded. "She died of brain cancer, I think. It hit hard and fast, took her within a matter of weeks after the diagnosis." I let out a soft breath, thinking. "We were...ten, I think? It really messed everyone up. It was so unexpected, you know? Like, Mrs. Badd was...I barely remember her, but she was just this sweet, kind, beautiful woman. She absolutely adored the boys. And then suddenly she was sick, and then Corin and Canaan told us she'd been diagnosed with brain cancer and was going to die soon, and then, bam, she was gone. It was devastating for Tate and I just because we knew her and loved her—she was like a second mom to us. For the boys?" I groaned. "There are not enough words to explain how hard it was on them—on the whole family, in fact. It messed them all up."

"Exactly," Eva said. "All of them in different ways. Their mom dying has left terrible emotional scars on all eight of them, and for Baxter it manifests itself as an inability to form relationships with anyone except his brothers, who have been the only people he's allowed to love and accept him. I understand their dad didn't take his wife's passing very well."

I laughed, a bitter sound. "How could he? Mr. Badd was always…well, Bast reminds me of him a lot, actually. Big, burly, gruff, sort of hard to read, but once you get to know him he turns out to be a sweetie, under that bear-like exterior. Mr. Badd was like that. He'd always been a fixture behind that bar, for as long as anyone in this town could remember. His dad, the boys' grandfather, had worked at the bar, ended up buying it from his former employer, built the apartment above it, and he and Mr. Badd ran it together until Grandpa Badd died in…the eighties, I think? That was when Mr. Badd changed the name to Badd's Bar and Grill, and moved his wife and Bast and Zane into the apartment. So, my point is, Mr. Badd ran the bar basically by himself until Bast was old enough to help. So anytime we'd show up to play with Canaan and Corin, Mr. Badd was back there be-hind that bar, sipping a glass of something, watching sports, shooting the shit with the regulars. But when their mom died, Mr. Badd…he shut down. Gave up. All he knew how to do was drink and work—and usu-ally both together—from open to close. Bast became the other boys' de facto parent. Doing laundry, get-ting everyone to school on time, lunches, all that. I remember it all, at least, until our Mom married Bob and moved us to Manhattan."

"So Bax's mom died, and then his dad checks out of his life…" Eva trailed off meaningfully.

"Psychologist says…abandonment issues," I said.

"Exactly." She looked at me carefully. "We all have issues. Like I said earlier, we're all messed up about something. It may not be my place to say this, but…I think you need to give Canaan a chance. You can't let past hurts and fears keep you from enjoying what could be a life-changing relationship. It's worth it, Aerie. It really is."

"What's worth it?" I asked, even though I knew what she was getting at.

"Love. I left my former life to be with Bax. Everything I know, literally, even my clothes. I am completely on my own, penniless, disowned by my family…no college, no career, no home, no friends." She held up a hand to stop my interruption. "It's terrifying, Aerie. It's utterly terrifying. What if this doesn't work out with Bax and me? What if he turns out not to be the man I think he is? What if there's something wrong with me? What if I'll never learn how to trust him, how to let him love me? What if I never find anything meaningful and worthwhile to do as a career? What if, what if, what if—I'm full of them. They run through my head all day, every day."

"And being with Baxter is worth all that?" I asked, my very doubt and skepticism rife and obvious in my voice. "No bullshit, Eva."

"No bullshit?" She met my eyes, and I couldn't help but see—and envy—the sincerity I saw there. "Absolutely. I risked everything to choose Bax, and I have no regrets. Doubts and fears that will take time to sort through, yes, but regrets? No."

"Why? How?" I whispered. "I don't get it. I mean, Bax is great, but…to leave behind everything you had, everything you've ever known, for a man you knew, what…weeks?"

She laughed. "Not even. Like I said, what I've done is…on the surface and by all accounts, it's totally nuts. Crazy, reckless, foolish…choose your word. It is absolutely all of that. But…it's *right*. I just *know* it in my blood and bones. Baxter loves me, and I love him. Not to say this is going to be easy, that there won't be times I will feel regret, but it will be worth it. I just…I know it."

A shuddering sob escaped me. "I'm envious. I don't think I'm capable of that."

"Of what?"

"Of that kind of bravery, that kind of…gamble. That kind of assurance."

"There's no reward without risk," Eva said, after a brief pause. "That's a truism I heard my father say a thousand times in reference to politics and business. I think it's true in life as well, Aerie."

"I don't doubt that, but…I just don't know if I can do it. I'm too scared."

"Of what?"

"God…*everything!* Being rejected again. I don't think I could survive it if I told Canaan I was…if I told Canaan that I'm falling for him. It would just wreck me beyond what Lex has already done to me."

"You don't think Canaan would be worth it?"

"If anyone could be, he is." I ducked my head. "But I'm too afraid to find out."

SEVEN

Canaan

AFTER EVA WHISKED AERIE AWAY AND LOCKED THE door behind them, I was left standing in the hallway alone, replaying Aerie's confession to me in my head.

God, what the fuck, though? I mean, we all do dumb shit in our lives, but…what Aerie said just completely baffles me. I don't get it, at all. I mean, how could she think a secret relationship with a famous celebrity twelve years her senior could possibly turn into a love relationship? We're all a bit stupid and naive when we're eighteen, but that's…ridiculous. And then to get pregnant by him? And have an abortion?

Jesus.

I don't even know what to think. What to feel. It's all a chaotic maelstrom in my head, and I don't know how make sense of any of it.

I hear their voices on the other side of the door, Eva's and Aerie's, and I wonder what they're talking about. Me? Us?

Is there an us?

Was there ever an us? Could there ever *be* an us between Aerie and me?

I left the hallway, because I had to get away from this whole…thing. From Aerie and her story, from how I feel about it. About her. My mind's not in a place where I know how to even begin figuring out how I feel about her story, and about her, and I don't even want to try, right now.

I headed downstairs to the studio, plugged in my guitar, turned on the amp, plugged in my head-phones, and played. But it doesn't do any good, not like it usually does.

My head just keeps…spinning.

My heart keeps aching.

Nothing makes any sense, and yet, it all makes too much sense.

It hurts.

The way she won't let us go deep, won't let us talk about what we are, what we could be…it's all tan-gled up in the whole business with Lex Landon. But there's more.

Aerie and Tate's dad left them when they were just little girls, old enough to remember and old enough to be hurt by it, but not old enough to understand. He'd already been gone a few years when Mom died, so he's only a vague recollection to me. But him leaving the girls, it's not something they ever talk about. Like, *ever.*

But look at them.

Tate was always a little boy crazy, something she'd admit herself. I won't say she was a slut, but she liked sex and wasn't shy about it, but none of the guys she was ever with were boyfriends. In fact, I don't think Tate ever really *had* a boyfriend. Just…a string of guys she hooked up with. And then she gets pregnant with Corin. The only male who has ever been a stable, consistent figure in her life.

I mean, when we went on that trip to the cabin, we all knew exactly what was going on—we were going there to have sex. I knew it, Cor knew it, and the girls both damn well knew it…yet Tate "forgets" her birth control? I'm not saying she planned it, but…it seems awful convenient. She's been desperate for a man to love her. And when Corin lets her see that he does—or that he *could*—she latches on and doesn't let go. Like I said, I'm not saying it's a ploy, just that… there are daddy issues at play here.

Then there's Aerie—responsible, thinks things through, emotionally stable…and doesn't let guys get close. Now that I've heard her story, thinking back to high school…she never really dated all that much. Not in any real sense. She'd meet for dinner or coffee, or go to the mall with a guy, but it never panned out into anything. I remember one guy who asked her out—and actually went out with her—saying she was just…cold. Nice, friendly, polite, sexy…but just…cold and closed off. Being Aerie's friend, I never saw that side of her. And the more I think about it, the more I realize that she very, very rarely showed any truly deep emotions—her stuff was all fairly surface.

The few guys I know for a fact she hooked up with in high school got sent packing within days. She just never let anyone close. Why? Her dad didn't want her, her dad walked away and never looked back, so why should any other guy be any different, right? I mean, I'm no therapist, obviously, but I've watched enough Dr. Phil to understand how that works, and it certainly applies here. And then, at the tender age of eighteen, she meets a good-looking, famous, and probably charming man who shows her what it feels like to be wanted, at least physically, and she's smitten. Infatuated. Maybe even really in love, as much as she could be when she knew literally nothing about the man.

I don't know. I just know that, according to her, the second she showed him any true feelings, *wha-BAM*, he ghosted. But he didn't just ghost; he left a knife in her back on the way out. And THEN, oh... and then, pregnant with evidence of his douchery, she goes to him and is told to get rid of it. Which she does. I mean, why wouldn't she? Eighteen, with the world in the palm of her hand, beautiful, on the rise as a model, brutally rejected by a man she thought she was in love with, a man she'd hoped would sweep her off her feet, who then had turned out to be married and just using her for her body...god, of course she's gonna have an abortion. Erase all the evidence of her mistake, and try to pretend it never happened.

God...*damn*, though.

But what does all this have to do with me? What am I supposed to do?

She won't let me close.

Physically, yes. That's easy. But if she won't talk about us, if she won't risk even trying to find out what we *could* have? Fuck. What chance is there? And do I even want that? I don't know. I don't know. I'm so mixed up.

I abruptly set down my guitar and go back upstairs, determined to face her with this. I stop, with my fist poised to knock on the door.

I heard Aerie's voice. "I don't doubt that, but...I

just don't know if I can do it. I'm too scared."

Eva's response: "Of what?"

"God…*everything!* Being rejected again. I don't think I could survive it if I told Canaan I was…if I told Canaan that I'm falling for him. It would just wreck me beyond what Lex already did to me if I got rejected again."

"You don't think Canaan would be worth it?"

A pause.

"If anyone could be, he is. But I'm too afraid to find out."

A knife, straight to my heart.

Too afraid to find out. I *could* be worth it, but she's too afraid to find out.

Meaning, in plain terms…I'm not worth the risk.

I don't cry, like ever. But I feel sick to my stomach. My eyes ache, and burn. If I'm not worth it to Aerie… then who will I ever be worth it to? Who could ever understand me like her? The answer is no one.

I don't know for sure since we haven't talked, but Corin is out of the business, I'm pretty sure. He's gonna settle down here in Ketchikan with Tate and be a dad and that's gonna be it. So where does that leave me? Nowhere. Fucking…nowhere. By myself, what do I have to offer musically? We always wrote our songs together, the music, the lyrics, everything. Our act was entirely based on *us*. Without that…?

Fuck.

I ran—actually literally ran—out of the apartment and found myself in the alley behind Badd's. I slid down to my butt, holding my head in my hands, my entire life whirling, spinning, twisting, and flying out of orbit.

So, let's recap: Aerie is too scared of rejection or whatever to be willing to be with me, and Corin is going to settle down for a quiet life in Alaska.

I admit the whole relationship with Aerie is important and scary at the same time. But right now all I can see is that I'm going to be left with a broken heart and no future.

Fuck this.

Operating on instinct, I dig my phone out of my pocket, find the contact entry I'm looking for, and dial the number. It rings a couple of times, and then he picks up.

"Canaan, what up, dude? I was just about to call you, funny enough."

"Hey, Mike. You were, huh? What about?"

"Well, uh…you know, me and the guys, we've been together as Nitro Punch for a minute, right? Like, we've been touring since the early two-thousands. We were just a bunch of kids when we first got signed, and now I'm an old fuck."

I laughed. "Mike, you're a couple years older

than me at most, buddy."

He snorted. "I'm well past thirty, bro. I just age well. All the whiskey, I guess."

"Oh. Okay, so you're old. What's that got to do with me?"

"Nice. You're not supposed to agree that I'm old, you asshole," he said with a chuckle. "Anyway, we're putting Nitro Punch on hold for a bit. We all have solo projects or other shit we're interested in right now, and I figure this is as good a time as any to put together a little project to explore the less heavy end of music, know what I mean?"

I was silent a minute. "What are you asking, Mike?"

"I know you guys got some shit going on in Alaska right now, but I'm relocating to Seattle which ain't that far from you, and I was hoping you could pop down here for a minute and jam with me. I got one other guy lined up, a strings dude. Plays, like, the mando and the dobro and all that shit, and I know you can play a few different instruments, and you may or may not know this, but I can play the keys too. So... whaddya say, buddy? Wanna get your folk on?"

I laughed, hard. "Mike, you have no idea how ironic it is that you say this."

"Ironic? Why's that?"

"Because I was calling to see if you guys were

interested in adding me to your lineup for a while. I
need a change of pace. I…I've got some shit going on
here, and I need to clear my head."

Mike grunted, and I heard what sounded like a
cap being flipped off a bottle of beer. "So," he said,
after taking a drink. "That girl you sang with—"

"Mike?" I interrupted.

"Don't ask?"

"Don't ask."

"Shit, buddy, I got women troubles enough of
my own. Come on down to Seattle. Text me when
you're at Sea-Tac and I'll pick you up and we'll go
drink ourselves stupid, play some tunes, and forget all
about our women troubles."

I'm a coward, I'm a coward, I'm a coward.

"Sounds good," I said. "I'll be down there on the
first flight I can get."

"Damn dude, I was thinking it'd be next week.
Or, like, tomorrow."

"Like I said, I'm dealing with some shit, and I
just…"

"Don't wanna deal anymore."

"Exactly."

"No worries, Cane." A pause. "So…this is just
you, then?"

"Yeah. That a problem?"

"Not at all. Better, in some ways. Your brother is

the shit, wicked talented, a great dude and all that, but I called you first because you're more what I have in mind for this particular project."

"So it all works out."

"I've got an extra room, in case you need somewhere to crash for a while."

"You're a good friend, Mike."

"Nah. I'm just not all asshole."

I laughed again, and it felt good to laugh for once, because everything else was coming apart. Or…had already fallen apart. "I'll see you in a few hours."

"Right on, Cane. Text me."

"Will do."

I went back inside and up the stairs to the apartment. Bax was on the couch, playing chess with Lucian, and getting his ass handed to him. They both shot me identical chin-jut acknowledgments as I walked past them. The door to Bax's room was still closed, and I still heard voices, but this time I didn't dare listen for fear of what else I might have heard. Instead, I went into Corin's and my room, jammed a bunch of random clothing into my go-bag, and left the room. Corin and Tate were nowhere to be seen, which was fine by me. I wasn't about to try to explain what I was doing to anyone, least of all to Corin.

Bax and Lucian saw my bag, and Lucian's eyes narrowed.

"Going somewhere?" he asked.

I nodded. "Seattle."

"Why?"

I shook my head, angling toward the door to the stairs. "Long story."

Baxter snorted. "You're a pussy."

"Fuck you, Bax."

He just laughed. "Yeah, well, when you're ready to man up, talk to me. But just so *someone* tells you: whatever you are doing right now isn't gonna work, and you're a dick for doing it."

I ignored that, heading down the stairs.

What did he know? He had this shit with Eva fall in his lap. His situation was 100 percent different from mine, and he was in zero position to try to act like he was some kind of expert at love or whatever.

This isn't me being a dick; this is me acting out of self-preservation. This is me doing what I have to do to secure my future. If she's so fucking scared of everything that she won't even give me a chance, when I've been there for her literally her whole life, when I've done everything I can short of being all like "bitch, I *love* you," then…what is there left for me to do? I need love. I ain't scared to admit it, okay? I know I'm kinda messed up too, god knows I've had enough shit in my life to be fucked up about, but…I can't put my heart out there just get it stomped all over. Rejection sucks, I get that. So why am I going to put myself out there when I heard her say in so many actual words that she's too scared to try?

I'm not.

Fuck that.

I packed up my three favorite guitars—my Fender, my Takamine acoustic, and my Gibson bass. I had a bunch of other guitars, both acoustic and electric, but I had my favorites, and I couldn't see the point in hauling all of them around. I wasn't moving, I was just…getting away.

I caught the ferry to the airport and found out I only had an hour before the next flight to Sea-Tac, so I booked it, paid to check my guitars and kept my duffel bag as my carry-on. Within an hour I was blasting down the runway, earbuds in, heavy metal grinding in my ears, heart thumping and thrumming and aching.

A tiny, insistent voice deep down told me Bax was right, that I was making a mistake, that this was a massively dickish move. I ordered a whiskey on the rocks and told that voice to go to hell.

Aerie isn't the only one who's ever been brutally rejected, and yeah, no way am I going through that again. Fuck that.

EIGHT

Aerie

AFTER A WHILE, MY CONVERSATION WITH EVA WOUND down. I needed a break from all this, from talking about it. I needed…I wasn't sure what.

Canaan.

I needed Canaan.

But I also needed a break from him, because I had no idea what to do about him. If I was around him, we'd end up screwing and that would only confuse things even more, because it was growing more and more difficult to separate sex from the confused maelstrom of my feelings for him.

I wanted to get drunk, but Tate was pregnant and couldn't drink. Maybe I could talk one or more of the others into a girls' night.

I excused myself from Baxter's room and went into the bathroom to touch up my makeup; on the way from the bathroom back to the living room, I passed Canaan and Corin's room. I went past it, initially, and then something caught my eye, and I stopped, went back. Stood in the doorway. Staring.

There was a bunk bed, and two bureaus side by side, and a closet; one of the bureaus had been rifled through, and the closet was open, hangers dangling empty. I went in, hunted through the bureau, which had open drawers—I recognized several of the T-shirts as Canaan's.

Why would...why would there be clothing missing from his room? A sick feeling shot through me, and I left the room, confused and off-balance. Eva was on the couch beside Bax, and Lucian was there as well, resetting a chessboard as Bax whispered to Eva.

They saw me entering the living room, and the whispers stopped. Eva's gaze told me she knew exactly what was going on.

"Where did he go?" I asked.

No one answered.

"Seriously, you guys. Where is he?"

"Seattle." Lucian was the first to speak. "Didn't say why."

"Where is Corin? Where is my sister?"

"They left after…all that other stuff, and I haven't seen them since," Bax said. "Just so you know, I told him he was making a mistake, and that he was a dick."

I sniffled a laugh. "Thanks, Bax."

"Hey, what are brothers for, except to call people out on their bullshit?"

I was emotionless, at the moment—the kind of numbness that happens when you're fresh off one full-blown sobfest and you're savaged all over again by something new: too much emotion, and not enough Aerie to deal with it. I stood staring at nothing, trying to come to grips with the fact that Canaan had run away from me.

What the fuck?

WHAT THE FUCK?

I shook my head. "I can't deal with this." I moved past the couch, and everyone on it.

"Where are you going, Aerie?" Eva asked.

"To the bar. I'm going to sit in the family booth and get as wasted as I possibly can."

"That's not going to bring him back," Eva said.

I laughed, bitterly, angrily. "No shit. Nor will it constitute actually dealing with the emotions of it. That's the whole point. *I cannot deal with this*. It's too much. It's all too much."

"I can go with you." Eva stood up, bending to

kiss Baxter.

"I don't want a babysitter. I'm serious. I'm planning on passing out in that booth."

"Can I make a suggestion?" Baxter said.

"What?"

"Call the girls. When shit like this happens, you call the girls. That's what family is all about." He slid a pawn forward two spaces, and then glanced at me. "For real. They'll sit and drink with you, and get your mind off of my asshole brother."

"I was thinking about doing exactly that, actually," I said. "Although I'm not sure I count as family."

Baxter sat back as Lucian stared at the board. "You count. I've known you since you were in diapers. You were there when Mom died. My brother may be stuck in his own stupid head right now, but he'll come around. May take my foot up his ass to get him there, but he'll come around."

"What if I don't want him to come around? If he's capable of this, of running away *now*? After what I just told him? Maybe that's my breaking point."

Baxter shrugged and nodded. "Sure, and that's your call. Won't make you any less family, Aerie. Your sister is having my brother's baby. You'll always be family."

My throat closed. "Goddamn you, Bax. Can't you just say something stupid and funny? I don't want to cry anymore."

He scratched his chin. "This one time, in college, there was this new guy on the team, and he was a seriously arrogant dick. He thought he was god's gift not only to women, but also to football. So me and the rest of the O-line Saran-Wrapped him to his bed, gagged him with his own dirty sock, and then each of us took giant steaming shits all over his Saran-Wrapped chest. It was awful. He not only quit the team, but left the school. Transferred to…Notre Dame, maybe? We played his team once, and he was on the opposing offense. Let's just say it was open season on douchebag. We made sure his ass got tackled *hard*. Every play, somebody would nail him so hard they heard the impact in the nosebleeds."

I snorted a laugh. "You…you *pooped* on him?"

"Straight on him. On the plastic wrap, so it wasn't like it was *on* him, but it stunk. We'd all had White Castle, so it was…god, it was the most awful smell I've ever encountered."

I couldn't help laughing. "Was he really that much of a dick?"

He rolled his eyes. "And then some. First time the team all went out for drinks together, he hit on all the players' girlfriends. Every single one. Not just harmless flirting, but outright hit on them. Coach wouldn't tolerate open fighting on the team, so we had to get him somehow. Then, on the field, he acted like he was actual football Jesus. Like he knew everything. He didn't suck, but he wasn't as amazing as he seemed to think, and yet he treated the rest of us like fuckin' rookies. Pissed us the fuck off."

"So the obvious answer is to defecate on him?" I asked, cackling.

He shrugged. "Eh, it worked, didn't it? We couldn't beat him stupid in the locker room or we'd all get cut, so we had to get creative."

I couldn't stop laughing. "Yeah, that's pretty creative," I said. "Awful, and cruel, and absolutely disgusting, but funny."

"Better?" Bax asked.

I nodded. "Better. Thanks."

"No problem. Anytime you need comedy relief, hit me up. I'm full of shit like that. Zane has some funny stories from his days in the Navy, too."

Lucian, apropos of nothing, spoke up. "I once got rolled by a prostitute."

We all stared at him.

"You...what?" Baxter twisted in place to face Lucian. "Bullshit."

"For real. What you're going to call bullshit on is the fact that I didn't hire her for sex. You won't believe me, but it's true. I hired her because I was alone in Thailand, and I got hammered. I was worried about getting sick in my sleep and choking on my vomit, so when I passed this hooker on the street on the way to my room, I handed her a wad of cash and told her in my best Thai that I wanted her to go to my hotel with me and keep from puking on myself in my sleep, and that was it. I said I had more cash that I would give her in the morning. Well, I passed out, and when I woke up I was totally naked, all my clothes were gone, my wallet was gone, my cash was gone, everything. I was still alive, and there was a trash can full of puke, so she'd done her job, but she completely rolled me."

We were all laughing.

"So what'd you do?" Baxter asked.

"Fortunately, I'm not an idiot. I never brought my passport with me, never carried anything in my wallet except enough cash for whatever I wanted to do. I never brought anything I wasn't prepared to have stolen, because I'd been mugged once and spent a month in South Africa waiting for a new passport. After that, I made sure I never brought anything ashore I couldn't lose." He chuckled quietly. "I did a walk of shame. The hotel was three blocks from the ship, so I wrapped a towel around my waist and walked back. I caught no end of shit. Especially because the moment I stepped foot on deck, someone snatched the towel. Embarrassing part was, it was a coed crew. And I'd been crushing on one of the girls."

"Lucian, buddy, you gotta tell us more stories. I always got the impression you were just this side of perfect."

Lucian shook his head, smiling. "I don't think so." He glanced at me. "My recommendation to you is to get Xavier to make you some food before you start drinking, or you'll pass out too soon and wake up hungover with too much daylight left."

"You're younger than me, Lucian—how do you know this stuff?"

He just shrugged. "The drinking age is lower in most other countries, and when everyone on the crew is drinking below deck on a transpacific haul, no one really stops to ask if you're twenty-one."

"Oh."

I made my way to the bar with Eva, and I was in luck, because Claire was already in the booth, laptop open in front of her, fingers flying on the keyboard, and Dru was on the other side, watching something on an iPad. When Eva and I showed up, there were greetings all around, a welcome for Eva from both women, and then we four sat down. I decided to head questions off before they started.

"Canaan ran away," I said, as we settled in. "So I'm here to get wasted."

Claire let out a sigh, and closed her laptop. "Well, that's work done for the day." She twisted in the booth, calling out to Brock, who was behind the bar putting clean pint glasses away. "Hey, babe? Can we get a bottle of Maker's Mark and four glasses?"

I boggled at her. "Whiskey? I was thinking I'd start slow."

Claire just shook her head. "Nope, when shit like this happens, sweetheart, you go hard and you go fast." She cupped her hands around her mouth and shouted. "XAVIER!"

Xavier appeared in the doorway of the kitchen, whisking something in a bowl. "You bellowed?"

"We need comfort food, honey. Can you hook us up?"

Xavier's eyes went from Claire to Eva to Dru, to me, settling on me. "Canaan is being difficult, I assume?"

I frowned. "How'd you know?"

He shrugged. "Process of elimination. Claire and Brock are fine, Dru and Bast are fine, and I'm assuming Eva and Baxter are fine since they just returned from an extended vacation together. Leaving you as the only one who could possibly require comfort food." He glanced at Brock who had just dropped off a brand-new bottle of Makers and four rocks glasses. "And alcohol. Wow, Canaan really messed up, didn't he?"

I sighed. "I opened up to him, and he bolted."

"Well, we all struggle with intimacy and forming healthy relationships with females, due to the fact that our mother died when we were all young. I suspect Canaan also harbors some secret rejection that has left him even more unable to form attachments. His dedication to music is total, and I also believe it serves as a stand-in for a real relationship with anyone except the seven of us." Xavier then turned abruptly and went back into the kitchen, whisking faster than ever.

We all just blinked at each other, and Brock even stopped halfway back to the service bar.

"Wow, he, um…that was…" Brock shook his head. "He's not wrong."

I massaged my temples. "We're not talking about this. I came here specifically to avoid talking about Canaan."

Claire poured whiskey into all four glasses and lifted hers in preparation for a toast. "Here's to men: sometimes getting the right one to man up and love you like you deserve requires a little bit of heartbreak first, just so you can appreciate how amazing it is when you finally get it."

I stared at her. "I'm not toasting to that."

Eva leaned close, gesturing for us to all do likewise. "Here's to the Badd brothers, and the amazing things they can do in bed."

Claire howled, Dru cackled, and I just bit my lip. "Now *that* I'll toast to!" I said.

We clinked, and drank, and that was the beginning of a day I only have vague recollections of. I know there was a lot of food, courtesy of Xavier, and I know at some point we got so loud Brock and Zane had to escort us upstairs so we didn't bother the rest of the customers, and I know at one point Tate showed up while we were trading dirty stories about men who weren't our current men, and I ignored her because I wasn't having any of that shit, and eventually she left again. Which is understandable. She was sober, we were all colossally hammered, and she and I weren't in a good place. I remember laughing my ass off with the girls, and I remember Dru trying to get me to tell her what had happened, and I may or may not have lost my mind at her, screaming incoherently, sobbing, trying to slap her…all of which she handled with more aplomb than I would have in her situation. I think I passed out, after that, or blacked out. Not sure which—I don't remember anything else.

Which, after all, was the point: get so drunk I could forget about Canaan.

I woke up and wished immediately that I hadn't. Even

my pulse was too loud, and my stomach was a pit of boiling acid, and my mouth was so dry the Mojave seemed like an oasis in comparison, and my head hurt so bad I wanted to cry. I tried to go back to sleep, but I couldn't.

So I got up, stumbled out of the bed, somehow found a bathroom, peed, and drank water straight from the faucet until my stomach rebelled, sloshing, and then shuffled back to bed. Eva was in the bed. She was wearing a sweatshirt of Baxter's, and she had an actual eye mask covering her eyes.

She must have heard me come in, because, without removing the eye mask, she pointed sloppily at the bedside table. "Tylenol. Vitamin Water Zero. Shot of whiskey. Orders from Bax."

I realized I was, yet again, in Baxter's bedroom, although I have no memory of how I got here; last I knew, I was in the apartment over the bar, sobbing on the kitchen floor, drinking a beer all the girls had insisted I probably didn't need, but which I was adamant about drinking.

I twisted the cap off the bottle of Vitamin Water, took the painkillers, and then slammed back the shot of whiskey and chased it with more water, and promptly passed back out again.

Next time I woke up, I was feeling a little less like death warmed over, and the alarm clock on the bedside table told me it was two o'clock in the afternoon.

After checking to make sure I wasn't naked—I was wearing a hoodie I recognized as Canaan's, and a pair of his gym shorts, and although the scent of him on the clothing stirred anger and hurt and confusion inside me, it also stirred emotions I didn't mind, which I also didn't dare examine too closely—I exited the bedroom, following my nose to coffee, bacon, and waffles.

Claire was on the couch, laptop on her thighs, giant headphones on her ears, and Lucian was in the kitchen, creating the smells.

He saw me first. "Ah, good. I hoped the food would bring you out." He poured me coffee and pointed at the kitchen table; I sat, gingerly, and sipped at the delicious black nectar of the gods, bringer of life, and infuser of all things that are good. "Hungover?"

I put a finger to my lips. "Sssshhhh. Not so loud. The world hurts me right now."

Lucian chuckled. "You knocked out about half that bottle by yourself, you know, and you're just a slender little thing."

I winced. "Yeah, well…your brother is a bastard, and I blame him."

Lucian didn't respond to that right away; instead,

he lifted the top of a waffle iron, forked out a thick, fluffy Belgian waffle, and set it in front of me; there was a bottle of maple syrup, a shaker of powdered sugar, and a dish of butter arranged near my plate. I fixed the waffle with all the trimmings and dug in, moaning at the goodness.

"Ohmagawd, Lucian," I moaned, my mouth full, "this is amazing. Where'd you learn to make waffles like this?"

He switched bacon from the pan to a plate covered in paper towel and set it near me, then sat down and helped himself to coffee and bacon. "I spent some time as a galley cook. Learned a few tricks." He watched me devour the waffle. "Want to hear something funny?"

I nodded. "Sure. Hit me up with humor."

"The waffles are made with mostly almond flour, the syrup is sugar-free, the powdered sugar is mostly xylitol, and the butter is organic grass-fed butter."

I stared at him. "You're kidding."

He gestured at the counter, where all the ingredients were still sitting out. "Something I've been experimenting with."

"Well...I would never have known." I held up a piece of bacon, tried a bite. "This tastes like real bacon."

He laughed. "Oh, it is. Real honest to goodness

pork bacon. No turkey or chicken nonsense here."

Claire appeared, headphones around her neck, sniffing. "Waffles? Bacon?"

Lucian laughed. "Would you like a waffle, Claire?"

"That would be fantastic, thank you, Lucian." She poured coffee for herself, killing the pot, and spent a moment making a new pot before sitting on the other side of me. "So. Aerie."

I sipped, and ate. "So, Claire." I eyed her. "Last thing I remember is being on the floor of the other apartment, crying, and trying to drink a beer."

Claire laughed. "Ohhhh god...girlfriend, you blacked out for the best part, then."

I winced, covering my face with one hand. "Oh dear god. What did I do?"

Claire snagged a piece of bacon and ate it, eyeing me speculatively. "You really don't remember?"

"Nothing past being on the floor of the kitchen."

"You chugged three beers in a row before we could stop you, and then you got this hair up your ass about needing to wear Canaan's clothes, so you booked it over here, and you started to strip before you'd even gotten inside. I had to talk you out of getting naked in front of Lucian, Baxter, and Brock, and I managed to get you into Canaan's room. You found the clothes you wanted, changed, and then you sat down in the middle of the room, crying, and sniffing the clothes. Poor Corin and Tate were super confused by the whole thing, since they'd been sleeping. Well, I managed to get you out into the living room, and you wouldn't stop crying. Just…sobbing and sobbing and sobbing, but you weren't making any sense."

"Oh god."

"Yeah, it was a lot of fun."

I sighed. "I'm sorry. I'm a mess, clearly."

"Eh, that's what we're here for, hon." Claire paused, eyeing me. "Do you remember telling us this crazy story about you and Lex Landon, and a pregnancy, and getting an abortion?"

I *thunked* my head on the table. "No. No, no, no. I didn't. Please, sweet baby Jesus, tell me I didn't."

Claire nodded, patting my shoulder. "You sure did, sweetheart. Every last sordid detail."

"Who all exactly did I tell?"

Claire made a face. "Um. Everyone?"

I lifted my head to look at her. "Everyone? Like… who is everyone?"

"Me, Brock, Dru, Bast, Baxter, and Eva. Zane and Mara weren't here, and Tate and Corin were in bed."

"Literally everyone except Zane and Mara?"

"Yes ma'am."

I groaned. "Oh my god."

Claire rubbed my shoulder again. "So…that

story. It's true?"

I nodded. "Yes, it is."

"And you told it to Canaan?" Lucian asked, setting a waffle in front of Claire and pouring more coffee into my mug.

"I told him, then promptly had a panic attack, and when I got my shit together—thanks to Eva—he was gone."

"I remember him going up to the door of Baxter's room where you were with Eva, being about to knock, and then leaving suddenly," Lucian said. "Maybe he overheard you saying something out of context."

If he'd heard me say I was too afraid to try to be with him, I could see how it would send him into a spiral—and there's no way to take that out of context. Shit, if I'd heard him say something that, I'd go into a spiral. Plus my confession…

"I guess I get why he'd run away," I said, "but it doesn't make it any easier."

Lucian turned his gaze to middle distance, leaning back in his chair, both hands wrapped around his coffee mug. "This is kind of a mess."

"Kind of a mess? *Kind of*?" I snorted a sarcastic laugh. "Lucian, this is an unqualified disaster."

Claire put her hands over mine. "So…what do you want to do?"

Abruptly, absurdly, my eyes watered, and then a tear dripped down my face. "Shit." I ducked my head to hide it. "I don't know," I whispered. "I don't know. Everything hurts, and I don't mean being hungover. He left, Claire. He *left*. I told him my deepest, darkest secret, and he turns around and checks out. I'm angry, but…I'm hurt more than anything. I told him because…because I wanted him to know. He deserved to know. Because if we…if we were going to be able to ever…" I trailed off, unable to finish.

"Why don't you take a day or two and let yourself sort of…back away from everything?" Claire suggested. "Sort through your emotions, and decide what you want. I know things with your sister are also somewhat…strained. You have a lot going on, a lot that's coming at you all at once. Take some time to process. Let things cool off, emotionally. I know from experience that it's all too easy to make snap decisions in the heat of all sorts of crazy emotions, but when you take a minute or two to step back and really think, really let yourself feel more than just the hot, crazy intense emotions, it all seems a little different."

I nodded. "I just…I don't know what to do."

She shrugged. "Go get your hair and nails done. Go shopping. I don't know you well enough to know what your hobbies are, but I'm sure you have something you love doing…do that."

"Music. I like music."

"So do music."

"A spa day and shopping sounds pretty good, too, though." I sniffled, wiping under my eyes.

"So let's get the girls together for a girls' day…" She laughed. "A *sober* girls' day, that is."

"Sounds good," I said. "Although I probably need a shower first. And my own clothing."

I hadn't been back to the B&B in a few days. I had been living out of a backpack of clothes, toiletries, and makeup. Once Mom showed up, I hadn't wanted to go back and face her, but now I had no choice. First, though, I had to get myself under control—I wasn't about to let her see me hurting like this: she'd ask questions I'm not prepared to answer.

Claire walked with me back to Grandma and Grandpa's just in time to see the tail end of another blowup between Mom and Tate; Mom stormed out the front door, letting the screen door slam loudly, stomping down the front porch steps in three-inch stilettos, her face a blank mask of anger. She pinned me with a brief, intense glare, huffed, and kept walking. I let her go, exchanging glances with Claire.

"Maybe I should go see about rounding the others up?" Claire suggested.

I nodded. "Might be a good idea. Looks like I have family drama to attend to."

Nervously, gingerly, I entered The Kingsley's Rest. Grandma and Grandpa were sitting together on the love seat, Grandpa's arm over Grandma's shoulders, their expressions nervous, tight, and anxious; Corin and Tate were sitting together on the couch, holding hands; silence reigned, thick and awkward. Tate looked up as I entered, and her expression morphed through relief, hurt, anger, and uncertainty, before she attempted to smooth her features into neutrality.

"Did I miss something?" I asked.

Grandpa snorted derisively. "Not all, sweetpea. Everything is totally normal."

"Richard, really," Grandma chided. "Sarcasm will not help the situation, dear."

"No, but it sure does feel good," Grandpa said.

"Seriously, though, what's going on?" I asked. "Mom left in a huff."

"I told them," Tate said, her voice low and small. "I told Grandma and Grandpa that I'm pregnant."

"I see. And why did this lead to a Mom-splosion?" I frowned. "She already knew, so even Mom won't blow up twice about the same thing."

Grandma sighed. "She doesn't agree with our feelings on how to best handle the situation."

Grandpa snorted again. "That woman won't tolerate anyone's decision or point of view but her own.

Never has, never will."

"Richard—"

"No, Ellen. She's my daughter, and I'm not going to ignore the way she is, or pretend she isn't that way."

I looked from Grandpa to Grandma to Tate, and then to Corin. "So...what was the argument about?"

"What *wasn't* it about?" Tate groaned. "You and me running away, Grandma and Grandpa taking us in, me being pregnant..." She threw up her hands. "It was a full-on tantrum."

"What does she want?" I asked.

"For things to go back to the way they were before we moved here," Tate answered.

I sat on the arm of the love seat next to Grandpa. "*Did* we move here? Like, permanently move here?"

Tate groaned. "Honestly, A, I don't have the energy for that particular conversation with you right now."

I waved a hand, dismissing the topic. "Fine. So what does she say regarding you being pregnant?"

"It's all tied together, for her," Tate said. "She said Grandma and Grandpa should never have allowed us to stay with them, that they should have contacted her immediately and forced us to go home with Mom, that if we were living with them, then they should have kept a closer eye on us. Apparently, to Mom, Grandma and Grandpa are directly at fault for me being pregnant."

I blinked, trying to process the logic. "Um. So… to Mom, then, you and I are still little girls? Like, we need babysitters? Like, what? Grandma and Grandpa are supposed to be our guardians? Do we need a curfew, now, too? What the hell is wrong with her?"

Tate raised both hands to slow my tirade. "Aerie, you don't have to convince *me* of this. I don't understand Mom any more than you do right now."

"She's not in control of the situation," Grandpa explained. "So…she's upset. Rachel has always liked to have every facet of her life under control. Being your mother, that control includes the two of you. So when you girls decided to take your lives and your futures in your own hands and out of hers, well… you hurt her pretty bad. It was inevitable, though, so don't feel too bad. You girls are adults, and you've *been* adults for a while. You're just now sort of catching on to the fact that being an adult sometimes means making hard decisions for yourself, decisions that may not make everyone else around you happy."

Tate sniffled. "I want to go back to being a little girl, Grandpa. Being an adult sucks." She put her face in her hands, stifling a shudder and a sob. "I didn't want this. I wanted…I don't know. I wanted a break from Mom deciding everything for us. I wanted to have some fun, I wanted to…and then we got so carried away, and now…" Tate glanced at Corin, tears sliding down her cheeks. "I'm sorry, Cor. I don't regret us, or you, or even this baby, really. I just…" She shrugged. "I don't know how I really feel. I just don't know."

Grandpa rose from the couch and moved to sit on the arm of the love seat beside Tate. "Honey, listen. I know this whole situation is confusing and upsetting. Your mother means well, and she really does want the best for you. But right now, as much as I love my daughter, and just looking at this thing as objectively as I can, you need to do what's best for *you*. You have to figure out your own life for yourself. You're pregnant, now, baby girl. That changes everything. So you're gonna have to think long and hard about what you want your life to look like, now and especially after you have that baby." He glanced at me, and then back at Tate. "Here's the hardest thing for me to say—you have to do what's best for *you*. Not Corin, much as I like him, and not Aerie, even if she is your twin. When it comes down to brass tacks, baby girl, all of us are only responsible for ourselves. You're not responsible for Corin, you're not responsible for your mom, for Aerie, for anyone. You're responsible for yourself, and for that life growing inside you."

"But I *am* responsible for Corin, Grandpa. I got us into this mess by being so…so forgetful and irresponsible. This wasn't his fault, it's mine."

"Bullshit," Grandpa spat. "Number one, there's no sense in playing the blame game. But if you're going to insist on placing blame, it was both of you—you for forgetting birth control, and him for not taking precautions whether you were on birth control or not. Reality of things is, babies can happen even when you're on birth control, even through several layers of precautions. A young couple came through here a few years ago, staying here on their honeymoon. They'd had an unexpected pregnancy, *while* she was on birth control *and* he was using protection, *and* she was only a day out of her cycle, so she shouldn't have been fertile in the first place, and she *still* got pregnant. This stuff just happens. You have sex, you run a risk of getting pregnant, no matter how you do it, unless you're having, you know…the kind of sex where—" He stopped with a gruff clearing of his throat. "Well, anyway. You get what I'm saying."

"Yeah, Grandpa, we all get what you're saying," I said, cringing. "Seriously no need for further detail."

"Right, right." He resumed his seat beside Grandma. "Point here is that passing blame around is a waste of time. It won't solve anything, and it won't help you figure out the future. Accept the way things are, and get on with what you gotta do."

"I know what you're saying, Grandpa. I get it."

Tate scrubbed her face and intertwined her fingers in Corin's, and then looked at me. "It's just hard, because Aerie and I have been making our decisions together, about each other's lives for our whole lives. I've never even thought about not taking her into account, and now, this thing, being pregnant, it…like you said, it changes everything. It already has changed everything, and I haven't even had the baby yet."

"You've got *that* right," I muttered.

Tate's gaze snapped to mine, blazing with anger. "If you've got something to say, then fucking *say* it, Aerie."

I shook my head, standing up from my place on the arm of the couch. "No, not now. You being pregnant does change everything. For you, for Corin, for me, and for Canaan. That's all I'm saying right now. But Grandpa is right—you have to do what's best for you. You, the baby, and Corin. What I want, want I *wanted*, what I thought was going to happen, none of that matters anymore. All that's left now is for you to figure what your future is going to look like, and I have to do the same for me."

"Aerie, about yesterday—" Tate started.

I held up a hand to stop her. "I'll quote you, here—I don't have the energy for that conversation." I moved toward the stairs. "You and me are going to have to sit down and have a hell of a conversation, and soon, but right now, I need to shower and change, and get some time alone to think about what I'm going to do about my own life, which is pretty messed up too, at the moment."

Tate sighed. "Aerie, I don't want things between us to be like this."

I turned back and went over to her, bent to give her a hug. "You're my twin, Tate. I love you. No matter what. It's going to be fine, okay? We will be fine. You figure out you, I'll figure out me, and when the dust settles, we'll figure out us. Twinsies for life, always, no matter what. Okay?"

She sniffled, nodding, and clung to my neck. "Love you."

I let her go, and went upstairs to shower and change.

I managed to avoid thinking about Canaan while showering, dressing, and then meeting up with Claire and the girls downtown. I managed to continue to avoid thinking about him as we shopped for new clothes, shoes, and purses, and then got our nails done and our hair blown out, and all sorts of fun girly endeavors meant to keep my mind off of Canaan and the clusterfuck that was…well, everything.

It was weird to be out with girls and doing fun girl stuff without Tate. Weird, meaning…abnormal. Disconcerting. Disorienting.

I've spent every single day of my life, my *entire* life, with Tate. All day, every day, forever. She's more than a twin, more than a sister—she's…she's like an extension of myself. You never think about your shadow, right? So she's not a shadow, which is a tempting analogy to make, here…she's so much more. She… she's *me*. A mirror image of me. I feel her. I *am* her. It's…you can't fathom it, if you're not us. So, to spend this time without her, to be doing these things, picking shoes and purses and skirts and bras without my twin…it's almost anathema.

But what hurts, what scares me, what niggles under my skin, like a pebble in my shoe…is the fact that it also feels…normal.

That's the disorienting part, the paradox, the oxymoron: it is both anathema and inconceivable and bizarre, and also a new kind of normal that feels right.

These girls, they're family. Claire, Dru, Eva, and Mara—Zane was off work this afternoon and volunteered to stay home with Jax so Mara was able to come out and join us. Let me tell you, Mara is something else. She's the kind of woman you'd imagine being woman enough to fulfill and challenge and satisfy a former Navy SEAL and man like Zane Badd.

Each of them found her own way to comfort me, to take my mind off things, to keep me relaxed and having fun.

It would only work for so long, but…like Claire said, taking the time to push the events away, to push my initial emotional reactions away long enough to look at the situation with a bit more objectivity did work wonders for me. I even managed to feel, for a few hours, that life was something like normal.

But when we got back to the apartment above Badd's to unload our haul, Tate was there, waiting for me.

"You went shopping with literally everyone except me?" Her voice quavered. "Nice. Thanks for thinking of me, A."

"Tate, I—"

"No, of course, I mean, why would I want to go shopping with the girls? It's not like I'm your sister or anything." She shot to her feet, shaking her head, hissing in anger as she paced back and forth in front of me. "Nah, screw Tate, right? Why include her? It's not like she'd need a girls' day out or anything. I mean, it's not like I'm dealing with anything stressful at all or anything."

Somehow, Claire, Dru, Eva, and Mara had all vanished, leaving Tate and I alone in the living room, facing off.

"Tate, stop."

She halted, staring at me. "What?"

"I'm sorry, I just…" I sat on the couch, keeping

my eyes on Tate. "I needed some time, Tate. There's just so much going on. Between you and me, between me and Canaan, it's all too much, and I needed some time to decompress, and honestly, that included time away from you. I'm sorry. I love you, and I know it hurt you, but I just…"

Tate nodded. "I get it. My feelings are hurt, but I get it." She sat down next to me. "So, Canaan? What's going on with you and Canaan?"

"He left, that's what."

"He…left? What do you mean, he *left*?"

I gestured at the boys' room. "He's gone. He packed his shit, took some guitars, and left. Lucian says he was going to Seattle, but no one knows where he is or what he's doing there, or when or even *if* he's coming back." I leaned back against the couch, trying not to cry. "I told him about Lex, and he ran away."

Tate was silent for a while. "Wow. I mean…Jesus. He just…*left*? I don't think Corin even knows he's gone."

"Exactly! He ran away like a scared little boy." I rubbed my eyes, refusing to cry about this. "I'm so mad at him, T! I just don't get it! I tell him something I've never told anyone, not even *you*, and he can't handle it?"

"I don't know what to say."

"Me either."

"You're mad at him, though?"

I nod. "Of course."

"*Just* mad?"

I sighed, realizing she was drawing me out into talking about it. "No, not *just* mad. I'm…everything! If there's a negative emotion, I feel it toward him. I'm hurt. I'm betrayed. I'm not just *mad*, I'm fucking furious! I *hate* him for abandoning me. I don't know… there's so much…so much anger, and hurt. I don't even have words for it all."

"Why, though? Why are you so mad and so hurt?"

"I don't need a therapist, right now, Tate," I snapped. "I need a sister."

"I beg to differ," she said, resting her head on my shoulder. "You need both. I think you're in denial."

"In denial? About what?"

"Yourself. How you feel, and what you want."

"Maybe I am, but what does that have to do with being angry and hurt?" I asked.

"Everything."

"Explain."

She sat up, pulling her legs underneath her to sit cross-legged on the couch. "You have to understand it for yourself, Aerie. If I told you, you'd just argue with me. Deny it. You'd change the subject, and come up with excuses."

I groaned, knowing she was right. Knowing

exactly what she wasn't saying, and knowing that I wasn't ready to face it. "I hate you."

"I know you're joking, but…it kind of feels like you actually do, ever since I told you I was pregnant."

"I don't hate you, Tate."

"Feels like it."

"I'm just angry at you."

"But why? I'm the one who's pregnant, not you!"

"Yeah, but you being pregnant screws up *my* plans."

She glared at me. "Really, Aerie? *Me* being pregnant screws up *your* plans?" She didn't bother hiding the anger in her voice. "Do tell, dear sister, how that works."

"We were coming back to Ketchikan *temporarily*. To get away from Mom and her controlling, domineering, momager ways. To figure out what *we* were doing next. I know you've been fed up with modeling, especially after what happened with that douchebag photographer. I get it, and I get that we needed a change of pace. We needed some downtime to plan our next move. But I thought we'd be planning *our* next move together. I thought we'd get into acting, or music, or…art, or I don't know. Whatever it was, I thought we'd be doing it together, because we're twins and we've always done everything together. Our brand, everything we've built since we were sixteen has been predicated on us as twins, as a unit. You being pregnant is a really big, giant, complicated wrench in the gears, T. Like, what now? What about us? What about our plans?"

"It doesn't have to be the end of all that, Aerie," she replied.

But even she didn't sound as if she believed herself.

"Tate, come on. At least be honest with me, okay? What are you and Corin going to do? How is this going to work for you?" I took her hand in mine. "Grandpa was right, Tate. You have to do what's best for you. Not me. Not us. *You*, and that baby, and Corin."

She sniffled, nodding. "I know, I know."

"So, what's your plan?"

She shrugged. "I don't know."

"Tate."

She looked at me miserably. "Fine! You want to know? We're going to get married, and we're gonna stay here in Ketchikan. Corin likes playing at the bar, likes the work, likes the peace and quiet, and being around family all the time. I'm going to have this baby, and I'm going to…I don't know. Take up photography again, maybe. That's what I've been thinking about, at least. That's what excites me—being behind the camera, not in front of it. Maybe I'll pick up the cello again, too—I've thought about that. I'm not ready to be a mom, but it's happening like it or not, and at least here in Ketchikan I'll have a support system around me. Grandma and Grandpa will be here, not to mention Corin's brothers and their wives and girlfriends. I was going to talk to Eva about the two of us possibly opening an art studio together. I don't know. I just know I love it here. This is home, Aerie, and I don't want to leave."

I nodded. "That's what I mean. That's not what I want, and that leaves me to figure out what I'm going to do, alone. I need to figure out what I want outside of you, outside of us as a unit."

"It's more than all of that, though, Aerie," Tate said, sighing. "It's more than what I'm going to *do*, or be, or where I live, or any of that. None of that really even matters."

"I'm lost, then."

She smiled at me. "Corin."

"Corin?"

"He's what matters, Aerie. I wouldn't care where we were, as long as I'm with him. I could make it work and be happy anywhere, as long as I have him."

"Oh my god, Tate, you're so dramatic," I said, but the insult lacked sting, because deep down, her words stirred something inside me—jealousy? Envy?

She smiled at me. "Maybe. But it's true."

"So you're totally content just being a wife and a mom? Really?"

She laughed, a bright, happy sound. "Yes! Absolutely. I love Corin with all my heart, and the thought of having my whole life ahead of me, with him in it as my best friend and my husband? It makes things like what I do for a living seem...irrelevant. We'll figure that out. I'm capable and talented, and I know I can figure out some way of making money doing something fulfilling. Modeling was never that. It never fulfilled me. It gave me a fat bank account, which is nice, and it was fun traveling the world and all that. But all of the traveling and the money has only served to reinforce how much I don't need or want any of that."

I shook my head. "See, I could not disagree any more strongly, T. I want so much more. I want to...I want to make music. I want to play in front of crowds, and sell out stadiums, and see my name on a movie soundtrack, and...I want to see more of the world. I want to walk the red carpet. I want...there's so much I want. And none of it is here, in Ketchikan. I love this place, I truly do. I appreciate the peace of it. I love having people here that I care about. Whatever I do, I'll always come back here. And I know someday, *someday*, I'll make Ketchikan home, but that's far in the future. I have too many things I want to do first, though."

She sniffled. "And that's fine, Aerie. We have to live our own lives. We're not kids, anymore. We don't have to go everywhere together, do everything together. We don't have to be Tate and Aerie, Aerie and Tate, the twins. We'll always be twins, obviously, but we can live our own lives." She met my eyes. "I think, at this point, we *have* to. I think we'd have come to this conclusion even if I hadn't gotten pregnant. That just moved the timeline up a little, I guess."

"Yeah, just a tiny bit," I said, sarcastically.

Tate and I let the silence stretch out between us.

"Where does this leave you and Canaan?" Tate asked, eventually.

I shook my head. "I don't know." I sucked in a breath and held it, trying to fend off the fresh onslaught of tears threatening and pooling behind my eyes. "God, I don't fucking know! Nowhere? How am I supposed to know where any of this leaves him and I when he's fucking *gone*?"

"The only thing I can say about that, Aerie, is that if something crazy happened and Corin were to freak out and run away, I'd be so mad the only possible option would be for me to find him and punch him in the nose, and then ask why he wouldn't just talk to me about it. I'd tell him I love him, and that being apart isn't an option."

"It's not an option?" I frowned, stood up and paced away. "Being apart isn't an option?"

Tate spoke from the couch. "It's just not a thing. Corin and I...being together, being a couple? It's more intense and more...necessary, I guess, than even you and I being twins, being connected the way we are. You and I, we didn't choose to be twins. It's always been a thing. It always will be a thing. But Cor and I? I *choose* this, Aerie. He's...he's necessary. I don't know how else to put it. I just...I can't not be with him. It's not a codependent thing, like, I *can* exist and survive on my own, I just choose not to."

"I don't know how to have that...I don't know if I even want that. I don't—" Tears sprang out, staining my cheeks, salty on my lips. "If he runs when I give him the trust I gave him in telling him that secret, then what do we have? I was trying to...I was trying to pave the way for there to be an us. I couldn't be with him, I couldn't let him be with me without knowing that about me. That secret has...it's tainted my life. That secret has ruined anything I could have had with every man I've ever known, because I couldn't talk about it, and because Lex just ruined all men for me, in so many ways."

Tate hesitated, and then spoke. "See, that's what I don't get."

"It's complicated."

"If anyone can get it, I can."

I sighed. "The way he hurt me, the way he be-trayed me…it was betrayal and abandonment and a stab in the back and salt on a wound all in one, and it made it so I just assumed every man was going to treat me the same way. I mean, shit, what reason do I have to trust any man, ever?"

"Aerie, I—"

"No, I mean, think about it, Tate. Our father left us when we were little kids, and he never looked back. He didn't want us. We didn't matter to him. We never mattered to him. And then there's Bob—"

"Bob is a dick and he doesn't count."

"I know, but he does count. He left a wife and two kids to be with Mom, and he tried to be all bud-dy-buddy with us, but…"

"He's just creepy," Tate said.

"Beyond creepy. The looks he'd give us made me sick to my stomach."

"He never did anything, but…"

"I just don't like him, and never have and never will." I shivered.

"What does Bob have to do with anything?" Tate asked.

I shrugged. "Because he's just one more man in my life who's added to my inability to believe any man could ever be…not a dick."

I felt Tate behind me. "That's not true or fair." She just stood behind me, her voice quiet, but strong. "Corin isn't like that. Bast isn't like that. Neither are Zane, or Brock, or Bax…"

"What about Cane?" I turned around, crossing my arms over my chest. "He left at the first hint of shit getting hard."

"Dick move, I grant you." Tate bumped her shoulder against mine. "Question is, what are you going to do? Only you can answer that question, Aerie."

"Helpful, Tate. Super helpful."

She laughed. "I live but to serve, swami."

Another long silence.

I finally turned to meet Tate's eyes. "Doesn't it scare you, needing Corin?"

"Absolutely." She answered without hesitation. "But it's worth it."

"How?" I asked, in a whisper. "Why?"

"I love him," she answered. "He's worth it."

"What if he leaves you? What if he decides he wants something else, someone else?"

"That's the risk, and it's one I'm willing to take. It's a gamble. He could totally decide that. I have no way of knowing with one hundred percent certainty that he won't do that to me, at some point."

"And you're still willing to give him your heart, your future? Your whole life?"

"Without question."

"Why?" I asked, because I genuinely had no answer, no understanding, no comprehension of how that could possibly work.

She shrugged, shaking her head. "He's worth it. Loving him is worth the risk. Letting him love me is worth it."

"But how can you—"

"He's not a random stranger, Aerie," Tate cut in. "He's not some bar hookup. He's not some hipster I met at a coffee shop in Greenwich Village. It's *Corin*. We played together in diapers. He knew me when I was in braces and thought Baby-Sitters Club was the height of literature. It's…it's *him*. That mitigates the risk somewhat, because I just *know* him. But this whole thing where we're in love and all that? There's no formula for it. There's no manual, no way to know. There's no secret. You just…you have to decide if the guy is worth it. You have to decide if having him in your life is enough to risk everything you have at stake."

"I don't know how to do that! How do you decide that?"

"Can you live without him? Can you let him walk away?"

I shook my head. "It hurts, Tate. It hurts so fucking bad! He left? He ran away? He couldn't…I'm not…I wasn't enough? How could he? How *could* he? I hate him so much, because I thought of anyone in this whole world, if *anyone* could understand and forgive me and love me despite…despite my secret, it would be him. But he didn't." I was crying, now, speaking through clenched teeth, anger and pain vibrating through me. "He didn't. He made it clear I'm not enough. That he doesn't care about me. That what I told him was too much for him."

"They won't admit to it, but guys get scared too, A. Guys are just as scared of being hurt, just as wary of trust as we are. Maybe he's just overwhelmed and scared, and doesn't know how to deal with it, much less admit it to you."

I had no response for that.

He's afraid? How does that lead to him going to Seattle?

My head spun. My heart ached.

I found myself outside, alone, on the docks, a cold wind blowing, tossing my hair, cutting sharp across my cheek. My thoughts swirled and wheeled, and my heart posed question after question, but I had no answers.

One thought repeated itself in my head and heart, over and over and over again—Tate's words: *can I live without him? Can I let him walk away?*

Questions of love and the future and all that

aside, I deserved more from Canaan than him just ghosting on me without a fucking word. I deserved answers. We may not have a future together, maybe neither of us was strong enough to be able to risk what it would take to have a relationship like Bax and Eva or Corin and Tate have, but I damn sure deserved more than him vanishing on me. Closure, at the least.

What did I want?

More.

I can admit that much to myself. I want more than the distrust and the fear. I want to be free of the poisonous taint Lex left on me. I want...

I want what Corin and Tate have.

I want to be worth loving, to Canaan. I want to need him. I want him to need me.

Maybe that's never going to happen. But at the very least, he owes me an explanation, and closure to whatever it was we *did* have—sexual chemistry at least, the potential for more, possibly.

I have a plan, at least, although it's not much of one—I'm going to Seattle, and I'm going to find Canaan, and I'm going to confront him. What it will get me, I don't know. But Canaan doesn't get to just run away from me and think that solves anything, or that I'm going to let him get away with bullshit like that.

NINE

Canaan

I FOUND MYSELF PLEASANTLY SURPRISED BY THE EXPERIENCE of playing with Mike and Tomas. Mike was, shockingly, an extremely talented keys player, and possessed a rich, warm voice. The songs he'd written thus far were introspective and somewhat dark in terms of lyrical content, and when you add in layers of guitar and mandolin and such on top of Mike's complex vocal style? Well…you had a really interesting sound. Mike couldn't help growling, even in a folk song, but he could also just *sing*, which made for a vocal style that could go from tortured and snarling and growling to emotive and soulful.

Tomas was a wizard with anything stringed—he

could play upright bass, cello, violin, mandolin, do-bro, lap-steel, 12-string, banjo...he was just one of those people who was created by God or the universe or whatever for one specific function, and that was to play music. Tomas didn't say much, and was awkward and weird when he did talk, but put an instrument in his hands, and he transformed into this confident master of his world. He had a slight accent, from the few times I'd heard him speak over the past three days—Scandinavian, I think, but I wasn't sure.

With me to round things out, we were able to lay tracks right off the bat. Mike had built himself a hell of a home studio in Seattle, a place where we could jam and practice and just play, but with the press of a button, we could also record. He wanted it to sound authentic, not a smooth, silky, produced thing, but rough and real. Which worked, since the three of us tended to be best once we'd been playing for a few hours, we'd hit the zone and find an element that had been missing, figure out a riff that wasn't right or a phrase that didn't work.

It was a wild, intense three days, though. We played, and we drank, and we passed out for a few hours, and then woke up and ate at a nearby diner and talked music and then went back to the studio and went back to playing, and eventually drinking and playing, and then just drinking.

Mike never asked any questions, and Tomas barely spoke, so I pretended life was totally normal, that I hadn't ghosted on everyone I knew, that I hadn't left Aerie without a word, that I wasn't suppressing everything I felt, that I wasn't in total agony, deep inside.

I channeled it all into music. I played my ass off. Every emotion, every ounce of pain and confusion and anger I felt, I put into my guitars.

In three days, we had twelve tracks, and each one was utterly inspired.

Three days. That was how long I managed to keep up the pretense that I was fine.

We cut the twelfth and best track yet, finishing at something like midnight. At which point I was a handful of shots in, and everything I'd been ignoring was gnawing away at me.

Aerie.

I had abandoned her. After what she told me, that would be the worst thing I could ever do.

How could I go back? I don't deserve to even see her again. Yet...because of Corin and Tate, I would have to.

God, Corin and Tate. My twin brother was going to be a fucking *father*. I was going to be an uncle.

A BABY. They were having a baby.

This, recording this album with Mike and

Tomas, was amazing, and fun, and I loved it, but I couldn't see myself doing this again. Playing just wasn't the same without Corin beside me. Would he and I ever play together again? We'd never tour together again, that was for damn sure. The shit of it all was, I knew, even without having talked to him about it, he would be staying in Ketchikan. I could see it in him. I could feel it. He was home. He was content. He had what he wanted. He had Tate, they had a future together. He could play at Badd's on the weekend, tend bar, love his woman, take care of his baby, and be happy. That was all he needed. He loved music, and he'd enjoyed the freedom and fun of touring, but he'd never gotten the rush from it I did. He'd said as much, before this thing with the girls ever happened.

We'd been drinking on the bus late one night, and we'd gotten talking about the road, the music, the life, and he'd admitted he liked it, but couldn't see himself doing it forever. I had felt an uncomfortable sizzle of worry at his words, but I'd been drunk and he'd been drunk and I dismissed it as drunk conversation. Now, I realize, he'd been speaking a deeper truth than either of us had realized.

Where did that leave me?

Out in the cold. Left to figure out my own life.

And what about Aerie?

My thoughts shied away from her. It hurt too much.

She was too afraid.

Of me? Of us? What was she afraid of?

"Whoa, whoa, Cane, buddy, ease up, okay?" I heard Mike's voice, felt his hands on mine.

He was prying a bottle away from me. Whiskey? An empty bottle, or almost empty, just a few slugs left in the bottom. My throat burned, and my head spun, and I realized I'd been chugging the whiskey straight out of the bottle.

"I…" I found my feet. "I need air."

Mike was at my side. "Let's get you outside then, huh?"

I was unsteady and grateful for Mike at my side, because I'd have been pinballing off the walls and the stairs to get from the studio down to the street level. Forget about it. I'd have broken bones. Mike got me down the stairs, and helped me sit on the stoop. It was a chilly, wet Seattle night, the roads gleaming wet from a recent drizzle, streetlights smearing orange stains on the blacktop, a traffic signal a block or two away cycling green-amber-red.

Mike sat beside me, dug a crushed pack of cigarettes out of his hip pocket and lit one. "Been giving you time, haven't pushed or asked, but Canaan, buddy…what the fuck is going on? We been drinking a lot last few days, I get that, but you downing three-quarters of a bottle of bourbon like that? It ain't you, man. So what gives?"

I shook my head, which set the world to reeling. "I fucked it all up, Mike."

"What was it you fucked up?"

"Her. Us. Everything. I shouldn't be here. But I was…I was upset, and scared. I know dudes shouldn't admit to being scared, but…shit, she scares me."

Mike laughed. "Ohhh, buddy. I feel you. Women have a way of scaring us, don't they? Like, they're so small and soft and confusing and they smell good and then somehow you just…you *need* her."

"But she said she was too scared. She said it. I heard her." I held my head in my hands, trying to stop the spinning. "I heard her say it, man. She said she was too scared to risk it with me."

"So you bolted?" He guessed.

I nodded sloppily. "She was too scared, which makes me feel like, what the fuck? You know? Like, I'm not worth it? There coulda been something, but she was too scared. I heard her say it, and then you called me, and…" I felt so dizzy, so sick, and I hated it. "It wasn't one of those sitcom things where I heard what she said out of context, either. No, she said…I heard her say she was too afraid to find out if I was worth it."

"Worth what?"

I shook my head. "Complicated…too complicated to explain. Basically, though…us."

"Ah. I see."

"You see. So, you see, I fucked up, because I ran away. Like a scared little puppy. Not man enough to tell her I'd heard her. To ask her why. I ran. I ran." Something heaved inside me, a rejection, a rebellion. "Oh fuck. Gon' be sick."

Mike had me off the stoop and in the street, over a sewer grate. Just in time. All that whiskey came right out of me.

It burned.

I let it burn.

"You need sleep, dude." Mike was all but carrying me, now. Or, just flat out carrying me. I wasn't sure. "You'll be all right, man. Sleep it off. Figure it out in the morning, okay?"

"Ran." It was the only word I could get out.

"I know. I've done my share of running, too. Guess we're both pussies."

"Pussy."

"Yep, you and me both."

"What's…" I was seeing the ceiling in between long, dizzy, sleepy, disoriented blinks, then seeing Mike, two-three-four of him, and walls in all directions, up and down and sideways, "…her name. The girl. You ran from her. Whass her name?"

"Leah. I lost my chance, man. She's with someone else now. I loved her, but I was scared, so I ran. When I went back to tell her, she was with someone else. Told me I'd lost my chance, that she'd loved me too, but now she had something with someone who wasn't too scared to admit how he felt, and she was over me."

"Sucks."

"Yeah. Yeah it does. A lot." He patted me on the shoulder. "If you get a chance with this girl, Cane, you take it. Take it, man. Life is too short to waste it being afraid of getting hurt. Because trust me, regret hurts a fuckuva lot worse than heartbreak."

" 'M drunk."

"You are *wayyy* beyond drunk, buddy." He patted me again. "But I got you, man. You'll be fine."

"Fuck everything."

"I know."

"You're good people, Mike. You play piano real good."

"Surprised the shit out of you with that, didn't I?"

"Uh-huh."

"It was just me and my mom growing up, and she made me take piano lessons for like, fifteen years. I hated that shit every single day, but it was important to her, so I stuck with it. Ended up in heavy metal, but now when I want to relax or whatever, I plink around on the piano. This album we're doing, it's for her, man. She's gone now, but it's for her."

"You gotta do a piano song just for her. No me, no Tomas, no guitars or any shit. Just you playing for your momma." I was so dizzy. So tired. But there was so much spinning inside me. It all hurt. "I lost my mom. She died."

"Me too, man. That shit will fuck you up *real* good."

"Real good. Hurts. Old, old, deep hurt."

He patted me yet again. "Pass out, bro. Leave this heavy shit for when you're feeling better."

" 'Kay."

Darkness. Welcoming and deep and black and thick and silent. Mercifully silent.

Oh fuck, it hurts. It hurts. Head, throat, mouth, body. Everything.

"Take this." A voice—familiar, soft, warm; a hand, feeding me little hard pills, and then the plastic rim of a bottle, something vaguely sweet and refreshing quenching the fire in my head and wetting the parched desert of my mouth and throat. "Good job.

Sleep, Canaan. Just sleep."

"I ran away." This, again. It's on repeat in my head, even as I struggle with reality and wakefulness and the drugged drowsiness of still-drunk slumber; Mike's words, echoing—*regret hurts a fuckuva lot more than heartbreak.*

"Yes, you did."

"It hurts."

"That's what the Tylenol is for, Cane."

"No—no, no, no. Heart, not head." Still so, so drunk, and hating it. "I ran."

"Go back to sleep, Cane." Who was that?

The voice was like a salve, a soothing balm on my soul. The voice of home. Of heaven. Of home, if home were heaven. Or heaven, if it were home. Something like that, something I was too blitzed and crushed to make sense of.

———————⚓———————

I woke up again, still in pain, but able to wake up all the way. There was a bottle of Gatorade and some Tylenol, which I took.

There was a backpack on the floor, near the door. Not mine. A pair of shoes. Lime green TOMS. A phone charger plugged into the wall, the white cord leading up to the dresser, where the phone lay face down—not my phone.

My head was thick and sluggish, and I couldn't make sense of what it meant. I was hot. And hungry. And thirsty. And I needed a long piss and a bucket of coffee. I was still wearing my hoodie, jeans, T-shirt, and socks—I stripped down to just the jeans and left the room, took an epic wall-hand piss, and then went in search of coffee.

My room at Mike's place was at the back of a renovated industrial warehouse, and it was a make-shift spot, the walls just framed off with two-by-fours and roughed-in drywall that hadn't been mudded yet, exposed pipes above, epoxy floor, a cheap bed frame against the wall and a third- or fourth-hand bureau, no closet, and a sliding door on a track. There was a half-bath across the hall, and that hall led out to a catwalk overlooking the living area of the apartment, couches and easy chairs and a giant TV showing ESPN high-light reels, and off on the farthest end of the apartment from where I stood on the catwalk, the kitchen, indus-trial, all stainless steel and black granite counters. Mike had admitted when I first arrived that this warehouse loft apartment was his baby, something he'd been working on for years, off and on, in between tours and recording albums. He'd done all the reno himself, built everything with his own two hands. The studio was in the same building, and he'd put that together himself too—apparently he'd bought the whole building.

Mike was on the couch, watching TV, and Tomas was on a chair, half-watching the TV and flipping through a magazine, which, as I descended the stairs, I realized wasn't in English.

Mike saw me coming down, and tossed a wave at me. "Ah, the wild beast emerges from its lair," he said in a passable Australian accent. "How ya holdin' up, buddy?"

I winced. "Alive. Barely."

"Yeah, you really outdid yourself last night." He laughed, and then wiped his face. "So, um, not sure how much you remember about last night and this morning—"

"I had weird-ass dreams," I said. "Heard this voice." I shook my head, not sure how to put the experience into words. "I dunno. It was weird."

"Yeah, about that—"

I headed past Mike toward the kitchen. "Coffee. I can't talk until I've had coffee."

Tomas grinned at Mike, and Mike just rubbed the back of his neck.

"Suit yourself," Mike said.

I reached the corner where the kitchen met the living room and the stove and fridge came into view.

And I heard a pan rattling on the range, a utensil scraping.

If Tomas and Mike were watching TV, then who was...?

I rounded the corner, and stopped.

Aerie.

Wearing black-and-white striped yoga pants, the stripes emanating from her butt in downward diagonal lines, emphasizing the lovely curve of her ass and hips. A purple tank top, bare feet. Her long blonde hair in messy bun, strands escaping to drape around the delicate column of her neck, wisping around her nape. There was music coming from a Bluetooth speaker next to the stove, an iPod next to it, and Aerie was dancing as she cooked, hips bopping from side to side, legs shifting and wiggling and shaking in place to Elvis Costello's "Man Out of Time", a spatula in one hand, occasionally stirring what looked like scrambled eggs. As I watched, a toaster popped, and she tossed the spatula down, grabbed two pieces of toast, and danced her way through smearing cream cheese and peanut butter on them—the way I liked my toast, something very few people knew.

I just watched.

What was she doing here?

It had been her talking to me? Feeding me pain meds and Gatorade? My heart twisted, thumped, and ached.

She turned to put the toast on a plate that was

waiting on the island, which stood between her and me. Saw me. Stopped, toast in hand. "You're up."

"Sort of."

"Just in time." She pointed at the island. "Sit."

She poured coffee from a pot into a big black mug, and set it down on the island.

"Aerie, what are you—"

She turned away from me, cutting me off. "Not yet, Cane. Just sit. Drink your coffee and shut up."

"Um. Okay."

So, I sat. I sipped coffee, and watched Aerie finish making eggs and bacon. She kept dancing, the song changing to Duran Duran, and then A-ha. Eventually, she dumped the eggs onto the plate, tonged a good half a dozen slices of bacon on and then slid it to me, handed me a fork, and took a stool next to me. I ate in silence, and Aerie just sat beside me, watching. Thinking, too.

When I was finished, I pushed the empty plate away. "Thank you."

"You're welcome."

"For the food, the coffee, and for last night, or this morning, or whatever."

"That was this morning. I got here about eight thirty."

"Eight thirty? This morning?" I glanced at the clock on the stove. "Holy shit, it's one in the afternoon."

"Yeah, you were a mess."

Silence. I had no idea what to say next, and yet a million questions zinged and seared and bounced through my head.

I heard a shuffling step behind me, and turned to see Mike and Tomas behind him. "Uh, we're gonna head out. Grab some food, kick it with some buddies."

"Mike, you don't have to—" I started.

He waved a hand. "Cane, buddy, you two need privacy to work your shit out. I got friends all over this town, okay? I can get into trouble for a day or two, no problem. Do your thing and don't worry about us."

I nodded. "Well…thanks. For everything."

He turned away, then stopped and glanced at me over his shoulder. "You remember what I said last night? About taking your shot, if you get one?"

"I remember."

"Good. Just keep it in mind." He waved again as he walked away. "See ya, buddy. Aerie, good to see you again, sweetheart."

"You too, Mike. Thanks." After another moment or two, we were alone, and Aerie smiled. "He's a great guy."

I nodded. "There's a lot of depth to him. Sort of unexpected, from a guy in that kind of band, who looks like he does."

"Yeah, well, you know what they say about

judging people on their appearances."

I nodded. "And I've known Mike for years. He's been a good friend for a long time, and I've always known he was a lot more than just a tatted-up, angry, beefy, metalhead screamer." I gestured at the grand piano that was a focal point of the living room, taking up a whole corner opposite the kitchen. "That's not just for show. He's a talented pianist, and you heard him sing when we played with him at the base."

She nodded. "I remember. I actually spent some time talking to him and Tomas today, while you were sleeping. He's actually very perceptive."

I frowned at her. "Perceptive? How do you mean?"

She kicked her foot, not looking at me. "Oh, well…I had no idea where you'd gone after you left, so I talked to Corin, who called Mike, who confirmed you were here with him, so I talked to Mike on the phone and he gave me his address so I could come find you. When I got here he showed me where you were, and after I checked in on you, gave you Tylenol and such, we sat down and talked. He told me this story, about this girl named Leah—"

"The girl he was in love with, and messed up."

"Right. He didn't go into too much detail, but he made his point pretty clearly."

"That he regrets being afraid."

Aerie nodded. "Yeah, pretty much." She sighed. "Although, I think his point was more that he regrets letting his fear get the better of him. Being afraid is natural. It happens. It's life. But…we don't have to let fear control us."

I groaned. "The food helps, the coffee helps, but I'm not sure I'm ready for this just yet, Aerie." I shot her a quick look. "I *want* to have this conversation, I swear I do. But…I'm so hungover, hearing my own heartbeat hurts right now."

She blew out a slow breath. "I haven't really slept in a few days. I could go for a nap."

I chuckled. "Wouldn't you know, all that food made me sleepy all over again."

She frowned at me, eyes narrowed. "Sleep, Canaan. By sleep, I mean *sleep*."

I nodded. "I know. I know."

"Because we are sure as fuck not *there* yet."

"I know."

"I'm so mad at you right now, I could punch you."

"I deserve it."

"Yes, you do." She stood up, heading for the stairs to the loft where my bedroom was. "Come on. I'm dead on my feet. Cooking is exhausting, and I was already exhausted."

I followed her up the stairs. And I have to admit,

in the name of honesty, that I followed a few steps below her, solely for the sake of getting to watch her butt sway as she went up the stairs.

She stopped at the top of the stairs, eying me. "You're staring at my ass, aren't you?"

I nodded. "Yes ma'am, I surely am."

She smirked. "Well, get a good look, because that's *all* you're getting."

I laughed. "Babe, if a look is all I can get, I'll take it." I stopped laughing, letting her see, hopefully, how much I meant it. "One look at you is better than the best thing with anyone else."

"Is that supposed to be a compliment?"

"Yeah."

"You're saying you'd rather look at me than hook up with anyone else?"

"That's what I'm saying. One look at your beautiful body is better than...god, Aerie, it's better than life. It's music. It's beauty itself. *You* are beauty."

She shook her head, rolling her eyes, and turned away to head into the bedroom. "God, Canaan. You can't bust out with goofy compliments and think it's going to erase anything."

I followed her into the room and slid the door closed behind us. "I'm not trying to erase anything, Aerie. I just want you to know that that's what I think, when I look at you. What I see when I look at you." I sat on the bed. "And I didn't think it was goofy."

Aerie snorted. "Maybe not goofy. Clumsy may be a better word."

"Clumsy it may have been, but it was a genuine sentiment."

She flopped onto the bed, closing her eyes. "Canaan, just lay down and shut up. I need to sleep before I can think about how to express everything I'm thinking and feeling."

I slid the blankets aside and draped them over her, and then climbed in beside her and lay down on my back, close, but not too close. There were several very long moments of tense, awkward silence. Even when things were just starting between us, the silences were never awkward, and I never felt this strange, strained reticence to get too close, this fear of touching her, this fear of…just everything.

Aerie sighed. "Canaan, I'm not going to bite you."

"But everything is fucked up." I felt a thickness in my throat. "So fucked up."

She rolled to her side, gazing at me steadily. "Yes, it is. And it's not just you. It's me, too. But this awkward silence, where you won't even let your hand accidentally touch mine? It's bullshit and I can't sleep like this. So unless you just want nothing else to do with me ever again, come closer, and let's get comfortable."

"I want *everything* to do with you." I breathed out slowly, shakily. "I just don't know where to start."

"Hold me." Her amber-green eyes found mine, held them. "Just hold me. It won't fix anything, but it's a start."

I shifted closer, extending my arm, and she nuzzled closer, lifted her head to rest it on my shoulder. We both breathed out, slow exhalations, releasing tension. She felt...right. Here in my arms, nestled against me. Even though everything was messed up and unsure, she still just...belonged.

God, that scared me.

"I can feel your mind spinning, Canaan," Aerie murmured sleepily.

"Can't seem to stop it."

She just murmured again, but I couldn't understand what she'd said because it had been mumbled as she drifted off to sleep. No such luck for me. I was honestly still exhausted, and should have been able to sleep, but I couldn't. I lay with Aerie in my arms, breathing in her scent, feeling her warmth against me, her softness and her curves, her breath on my neck. My heart was aching worse than ever, pounding, thudding, splitting.

How could I have run away from this? From her?

But then I remembered what I'd heard her say, that she was too afraid to risk actually being with me.

So far, we'd danced around the idea of togetherness. We'd never discussed what we had. We'd had great sex, and a lot of it. Incredible, life-changing chemistry. But...did chemistry and wild sex equal...*more*? No, not really. If we weren't willing to talk about what our relationship was, where it was going, how long could it last? I'm not dumb or naive enough to think a real, lasting relationship can be based on nothing but sex and chemistry.

And she's unwilling to risk her heart with me. Which, I get. Honestly. After what Lex did to her, harboring that hurt and that betrayal and that mistrust is only natural. Her father left her, and her mom shackled them to a creepy old rich businessman who they never liked, and who probably gave them more reasons to mistrust men. Then Lex comes along and takes advantage of a young, nubile, naive, starry-eyed eighteen-year-old girl, uses her, gets her pregnant, stabs her in the back, and then...god, tells her to just go get an abortion? The regret I heard in her voice, the self-loathing, and the pain of the memory. How could she ever come back from that? How could she ever believe in men, or love again?

I get it.

Doesn't mean I like it, though. For me, I mean, selfishly speaking. I want more. I really do. I may not know how to go about getting there, especially with her, but…I've watched my older brothers all find love one after another, and I've seen them transformed into different kinds of men. Bast was always gruff and closed off and aloof, more concerned with survival, keeping the bar afloat, and ensuring the rest of us had some kind of stability when he was just a young man himself. And now? He's still gruff, but he's found his sense of humor, he's become more open, more involved. The good man that was buried deep inside his rough, tattooed shell has come out, and it's all due to Dru.

I've seen the similar transformations in Zane, Brock, and Bax, and now even my own twin is finding that love, finding his place in life, and it's taking him away from me.

And goddammit, I'm jealous. Of what he's found with Tate, and also I'm jealous of Tate because she gets him, she gets my twin. It's always been the two of us, making music and doing life. Now his life is hers. And I'm jealous of that.

And I want it with Aerie.

I feel myself drifting as these thoughts spin and circle and loop back. Wanting, but being afraid.

I don't have any huge trauma in my life that's holding me back. I mean, not really. Not like Aerie has.

There was Jenna, though. I don't think about her

much, because it's past, it's over, and there's no point. But she did really do a lot to me in terms of making me wary of trusting women too far. Is that coloring the way I deal with Aerie? It's an old story, from when Corin and I first moved to LA. Could I have been more affected by Jenna that I've ever realized? Maybe.

Probably.

When Cor and I first moved down to LA, we had a great contract and a decent following. We found a shitty apartment in West Hollywood, and we played the LA rock scene, building our audience and honing our style as we worked with the label to put out our first album. With it came more success than we'd ever imagined. The audiences at our shows grew, and the size of the venues grew. The backstage experiences got more…interesting.

Girls would show up and want to have fun with us. No strings attached, no expectations, no promise of a call or even of seeing each other again. We were rock stars, and they just wanted a piece of us. Hell yeah. I was seventeen, so of course that was my dream come true. Being seventeen, having money, screaming fans, playing famous venues? Plus, the women. Hot-as-fuck chicks would just show up backstage, in our green room, and they'd strip off their tops and waggle their fine asses in their sexy little miniskirts, and they'd bang us and blow us and go on their merry way afterward without expecting jack shit in return. Who wouldn't love that?

Then I met Jenna. She was a sound tech at a club, and she wasn't impressed by me at all. She wore ripped jeans and tank tops and fitted hoodies, ball caps and sneakers. All girl and totally heterosexual, just tough, pragmatic, and no-nonsense. She painted her nails and wore rings and necklaces, watched girly romance movies and cried at the end, but if you called her on it, she'd slug you hard enough to leave bruises. She grew up with a bunch of brothers, grew up tough, grew up self-contained. Shitty home life, let's just put it that way. I asked her to coffee, asked her to dinner, asked her to shows...got told no a dozen times, but something about her kept me coming back for another rejection. Then, finally, she agreed to go out with me. Made it clear we weren't a thing. Just coffee. Told me she didn't expect me to change anything about my life just because she'd gone out with me on a date. One date became two, and by the third we were sleeping together at her apartment. She was intense, but quiet. Not a screamer, not effusive, but she was...intense. She'd shake and quaver and gasp, staring at me, and the look in her eyes would stir something inside me. She told me again and again that we weren't a thing, we were just friend with benefits. *Don't change your life for me*, she'd tell me, again and again, *don't develop feelings for me*.

I did anyway.

I stopped hooking up backstage, because it felt nasty and weird to go from nailing a groupie backstage to meeting Jenna for coffee and then going to her place and being with her. She assumed that was what was happening, and told me so in so many words. She didn't want anything real, just wanted to hang out, hook up, have the thing we had, which wasn't a thing.

I wanted more.

Jenna and I had our thing-that-wasn't-a-thing for several months, and I knew she was probably hooking up with other guys. Didn't know it for sure, but sometimes I'd call to see if she wanted to connect and she'd say she had other plans, was already out, something. Which, to me, meant she was with some other guy. Sure, okay, that's what it was for us.

I tried to keep it casual, tried to keep my emotions out of it because I knew she wasn't interested in me that way.

Eventually, curiosity and a desire for more got the better of me. After she and I had gone out and seen a movie and hooked up at her apartment, I lay in her bed with her. We were smoking a joint, still naked, Joni Mitchell playing in the background.

Are you ever going to want more than us being friends

with benefits? I had asked.

She'd blown out smoke, glanced sideways at me: *Nah, not really.*

That had hurt: *I'm not hooking up with anyone else.*

Another of those long silent sideways glances: *I am.*

Shit.

I went for broke: *I want more. I like you. I feel things for you. We could be good together.*

She took another drag, handed the roach to me: *I don't want that. It's not you, it's not that you're not a good guy. You'd be a great boyfriend. The fact that you're not hooking up with the groupies when I know for a fact how many of them are throwing themselves at you every show you play says a lot. But I'm sorry, Cane, I just don't want more. Not with you, not with anyone.*

I had lain silently, smoking, trying to contain the hurt: *There's nothing I can do or say to change your mind?*

She had shrugged, speaking through a mouthful of rolling smoke: *Not really, no. My heart is broken. In the sense that it just doesn't work right, not in the sense that someone hurt me and I'm not over it yet. I'm just broken. Love doesn't interest me. You don't interest me like that. I enjoy hanging out with you and I like fucking you, but that's all it is, and that's all it'll ever be.*

What was I supposed to say to that? There wasn't anything. Eventually I had gotten up, gotten

dressed, and got ready to leave. Jenna had stayed naked, watching me as she lounged lazily on her bed,
stoned and divorced from the fact that I was hurting.

She'd waved as I paused at the door: *If you have
feelings for me you can't get over, then it's probably best we
don't see each other again. I'd rather hurt you a little now,
like this, than let you think I'll ever change and risk hurting you more later.*

I had laughed bitterly: *Already hurts quite a bit,
Jen.*

*Yeah, well…I told you from the start what this was. I
told you not to change your life for this*—she had traipsed
naked across the apartment to stand in front of me,
perhaps intentionally teasing me with the fact that
she knew I was crazy attracted to her: *best advice I can
give you, Cane, is to lose my number and forget about me.*

So I had.

I left, deleted her number, and forgot about her.
We'd never taken pictures together, so there really was no evidence of her in my life except for my
memories. Which faded.

Except when other women came into my life,
and there were plenty of them after that. Groupies
who wanted more than one night, who presented
tempting opportunities for something more than
backstage hookups or tour bus shenanigans. I never took those opportunities, because deep down,

I remembered Jenna, and the casual, off-hand way she had dismissed me and my feelings. Why bother? Better to go for the low-hanging fruit. The easy conquests. A girl I could bang on the tour bus, smoke a bit with, drink a bit with, and then say goodbye to as I went to the next show. Eventually, that was the habit, and it was easy, and it was fun, and I stopped questioning it.

Until now.

Until Aerie.

I hadn't even thought about Jenna in years. But in the back of my mind, she was always there. Standing naked in front of me, looking up at me dispassionately, understatedly beautiful but cold and disinterested as she crushed my nascent little dream of having a relationship.

Fuck, I couldn't sleep.

I'd started to drift, but thoughts of Jenna woke me up, and now I was just…awake.

I was holding Aerie and wondering what she would say to me. What would happen next?

Why would she show up like this? Take care of me, cook for me, and then ask me to hold her? Especially if she didn't want something more…

But why would she change her mind? I ran away, and she's going to change her mind about me being worth risking her heart over? Yeah, probably not.

Eventually, I managed to quiet my mind enough to relax. Not sleep, exactly, but just…drift.

But she's there, in my arms, in my mind, in my heart, confusing me, hurting me, scaring me, worrying me. I have no answers. Does she? *Are* there any answers?

TEN

Aerie

I woke up very, very slowly. I never nap, ever. But I really hadn't slept more than a handful of hours at a time in days, and I needed the sleep.

I was disoriented, at first.

Then I remembered I was in Seattle, with Canaan.

I was in his arms. He had his arm around me, and his chest was bare under my cheek. He was breathing slowly, evenly, but somehow I didn't think he was really asleep.

There was no window in this room, so there was no sense of the time. The only light came from a naked Edison bulb hanging by a cord from the ceiling, which shed a warm orange glow, dull and soft and intimate.

"Canaan?"

"Mmm."

"I don't know why I'm here, if you want real honesty."

"Been wondering that myself."

"Why I'm here?"

"Mmm-hmmm. After the way I left, I'd think you'd want to be rid of me for good."

"Part of me does. But I also deserve more than the way you left. *You* deserve more. *We* deserve more."

"More what?"

"More…I don't know. Closure, at least."

"Closure."

I shifted to my side, levered up on my elbow, head propped in my hand. Canaan opened his eyes and stared at me sidelong. His eyes raked over me, taking in my bedhead—my hair had come loose from my bun as I slept and it was now loose and messy around my face—and my rumpled clothing. My tank top had ridden up as I slept, leaving my stomach bare, showing a hint of the bottom of my black sports bra. I'd chosen this outfit as the most comfortable, and also because it was, to me, the least sexy. It communicated, I thought, that I wasn't here to mess around, that I wasn't interested in trying to seduce him or allow us to fall back into chemistry rather than communication.

But the look in Canaan's eyes told me I had failed. He wanted me. It had been almost a week, now, since we'd last touched each other, and that was way longer than either of us had gone without sex since Tate and I had shown up in Ketchikan.

I was having trouble keeping my own libido under wraps, in all honesty. Especially when he lay there like that, shirtless, wearing nothing but tight, ripped, faded jeans, the button undone, the zipper only partway up. His abs were hard bulges and deep grooves, and his chest was firm and thick. His arms were toned and covered in sexy tattoos, and his hair was loose and messy and in his eyes, which were a deep rich chocolate brown, and wild and heated and hungry and dancing as they met mine.

"Don't look at me like that," I whispered.

"Like what?"

"Like I'm something to eat, and you're starving."

"If I'm looking at you like that, it's because it's how I'm feeling." He shifted closer to me, and his hand reached out to rest on my hip. "It's only been a few days, but it feels like an eternity since we were together in Baxter's bed." His eyes were sparkling, and his hand was roaming. "Remember?"

I breathed out shakily. "Remember? How could

I forget? You blindfolded us. You made me come so many times I thought I was going to die from orgasm overload."

"That was the goal."

"Murder via orgasm? A dastardly plan if I've ever heard one." I couldn't help the banter; it just came so naturally.

And the way he was looking at me? The way his hand was trailing down my thigh, then back up to my hip. His fingertips toyed with the waistband of my yoga pants, rolling the hem down, and then releasing it. As if he was thinking about peeling them off, but couldn't decide.

"Canaan, we should talk first."

His gaze narrowed. "We are talking."

"You know what I mean."

"Is that what you want? To talk?" He shifted closer yet, so our bodies were almost flush, but not quite. His breath was warm, and his hand warmer yet as he palmed my skin between shirt and yoga pants.

"Don't you?"

"Why would you come here just to talk? You could have called me. Did you think I was going to stay here forever? I needed some time. I needed to think." He hooked the fingertips of his index, middle, and ring fingers into the stretchy waistband of my pants. "You came here because you wanted something."

Bullshit, if I ever heard it. "Yeah, I did, but—"

His mouth trailed across my cheek, and then his lips pressed against mine, and I stopped abruptly, because his mouth has always been intoxicating, the way he kisses.

Like this.

The kiss was slow and delicate at first. A tease. A testing, a questing. Lips on mine, tongue tip sliding across my closed lips. His hand sliding up my back to the strap of my sports bra and then back down. Sticking to skin, palming my waist, then up my back again.

God, his kiss.

Why couldn't I resist his kiss?

I had things to say—I wasn't this weak.

Shit, who am I kidding? Yes, I am. For Canaan, yes, I am.

The whole notion of two people having "chemistry" together is overused, and the punch of the phrase has been lost, to a large degree. But have you had chemistry class? Have you ever set up a beaker full of a chemical and poured another chemical into it? Some chemicals react mildly together, some gasses venting and vaporizing, a little bubbling, and then nothing. Some react violently, explosively. Reactionary explosions, boiling, colors changing, instant, volcanic.

People are the same way.

Canaan and me?

It's the latter. The moment he touches me, the moment he kisses me, the reaction occurs. I can't stop it. Can't help it. Can't change it or lessen it. He kisses me, and I react; he touches me, and I react.

It's chemistry, pure and simple.

I tried to resist, I really did. There was so, so much more to me showing up here than wanting sex…but when he kissed me, it erased all that. Well, no, not erase; that's not the right word. Pushed aside. Swept away. I hadn't come here wanting sex at all, truth be told, but his kiss, his body, the ravenous, eager look in his eyes, the way he touches me…

I palmed his chest, traced the lines of his pecs, the ridges and grooves of his abs, tasting his breath—which wasn't great, but I didn't care, because his kiss was intoxicating. His tongue demanded mine, and I gave it to him. His body was hard against mine, and I wanted more. Nothing mattered in this moment, but the feel of Canaan, so familiar and strong and lean and hard and soft and warm.

I gasped into the kiss, shocked, as Canaan rolled onto his back, pulling me on top of him. He had me pinned, my arms tight against my sides, our hips flush, his hard cock a ridge against my core, his chest heaving, his arms wrapped around me. Holding me against him. His eyes pierced me, and I couldn't look away. I read him, easily. I knew what this was: distraction. Returning the favor from when I'd coyly avoided a conversation about us with sex.

I knew it, felt the awareness, and even some resentment, but then his hands were on my ass, kneading, palming, caressing, and I lost the train of thought, lost the awareness and resentment. It all boiled away in the reaction to his touch.

I arched on top of him as he played with the taut, round curve of my ass, his palms rubbing in circles, lifting and releasing. I moaned, wanting more. Wanting his skin on mine. Wanting to be bare to his touch.

How can he do this to me?

Same way I do to him: it's just chemistry. I touch, he needs; he touches, I need.

Simple.

But god, it's so easy to get swept away. Especially when he hooks his fingers into the waistband of my yoga pants and yanks them down, urging me to lift my hips so he can peel them downward, spurring me to toe them off and kick them away; no panties, just me, bare. A concession, unconsciously, perhaps, to the fact that if I came here, if I saw him, I'd end up naked, fucking him.

I'd known it all along. Counted on it. I chose yoga pants, sports bra, and tank top ostensibly because I didn't want him to think this was a purely sexual visit, but I'd forgone underwear because deep down, I think I'd known this would happen.

Is that true? I don't know.

I don't know anything except his touch. His warm, rough hand on my bare bottom, my thighs straddling his hips. His jeans were open. My arms were pinned to my sides, and I could have easily broken free and taken the touch I wanted, but I didn't. I liked this, being held like this. He wasn't kissing me, now. He was just touching.

I arched my spine, grinding my hips against his. The zipper of his jeans scraped harsh and cold against my naked core.

"Canaan…" I murmured.

He didn't answer. Instead, he gripped the lower hem of my tank and ripped it off, and then made short work of the sports bra, peeling it up, rolling it past my breasts; I lifted up enough that he could slide it free, and then he yanked it roughly over my head and threw it aside.

Leaving me utterly naked.

What was his game?

I thought he'd be inside me by now.

Instead, he gripped each of my wrists in his strong hands and held my arms wide apart, so I was lying fully on top of him. And now…*now* he kissed me again. I was helpless against the onslaught of his kiss, which wasn't slow or sweet or delicate or anything like that. It was rough. Wild. Demanding. He growled as he kissed me, and his hips pivoted, teasing me, teasing us.

I yanked my wrists free of his grip, levered myself to kneel above him. Hair loose in a wild blonde cloud, my eyes surely reflecting my burning need for him. My breasts ached. My core throbbed. I knelt above him, staring down at him, fully immersed into this. Knowing it was a delay, a distraction, repayment. Knowing, too, that neither of us were capable of stopping this, now.

Maybe we never were.

Maybe this had to happen before we could talk properly. Maybe I wasn't capable of expressing my deepest emotions and fears and needs to him until after I'd exorcised the demon of my sexual need for Canaan Badd. Maybe he was incapable of the same, until he'd released his need for me.

I yanked his zipper all the way open, tugged his jeans down, and he kicked them and away. He still had underwear on, tight blue Calvin Klein boxer briefs that were barely equal to the task of containing his massive erection. I knelt around his ankles, leaned forward, slowly slid those underwear off, baring his beautiful member, thick and veined and pink and leaking from the tip, revealing that incredible V-cut.

A momentary tableau, him beneath me, staring up. His cock flat against his belly. My breasts hanging, my hair almost, but not quite, obscuring my nipples. My core aching, needing his touch. I gazed down at him, wondering if I even wanted to know what he was thinking.

And then he sat up. Knelt on the bed, facing me. He took my face in his hands, and kissed me. It was a short, violent kiss; his teeth clacking against mine, bruising my lips. And then he slid past me, off the bed. I had no chance to think, to try to figure out his next move; I had no chance to even think about what I wanted, how I wanted him. It didn't matter. He grabbed my ankle and hauled me toward him, then pinioned my hips in his hands and tugged me off the bed, so I was standing up, facing away from him. His front was to my back, his breath on the nape of my neck as he lifted my hair in both hands, pulling it to one side, and then his lips were touching my neck, and I felt his cock against my butt. He stood flush against me, his chest at my back, nestling his cock between the globes of my ass. His palms carved over my hips and grazed my belly, and then his fingers were delving into my core; I shifted my feet apart to offer him access, and he took it. A single fingertip tracing up the seam of my pussy. Nudging into the keyhole hiding my clit, circling there until I gasped, and my knees shook. I reached up behind my head, found his hair, buried my fingers in the soft cool mass, clutching at him as he slid a finger of one hand into me, circling my clit with the other, his mouth pressed against my nape as he used both hands in synch to work me to a swift, shocking orgasm. I groaned, biting my lip, grinding against his finger.

And then he did something unexpected—with a rough, commanding shove, he pressed me forward, bending me over the bed.

"Canaan?" I queried, my voice shaky.

He gathered my hair into his fist and spread it out behind me, my cheek to the mattress, so I could see only glimpses of him behind me. His palm covered one side of my ass, pulling the cheek aside. Then his other hand gathered my other butt cheek, tugging the globes apart. What was he doing? God, god. I ached, throbbed. The orgasm had only served to whet my appetite, and now with his hands toying with my ass, pulling the cheeks apart to bare all of me for him, giving him access to every part of me, I wondered if he was going to take my asshole. I'd never been touched there, and had always secretly wanted to be. But I was afraid. I wasn't ready. If he tried to, what would I do?

Oh god, oh god. I had no idea what he was going to do, in that moment. No clue. And I liked it. God, I relished the uncertainty.

I was breathing hard, gasping in breathless anticipation.

He held my ass cheeks apart, and I craned my neck to watch as he dipped at the knees, nudging his cock against my core. Oh—oh god. Was it disappointment or relief I was feeling? Not sure. A little of both.

He said nothing, and his expression was a complicated mask, a million emotions reflected in his eyes and the set of his mouth.

"Canaan…" I breathed again.

"Yeah, babe." His voice was low, a rough growl of need.

I reached my hands across the bed and gripped the bedspread, lifted up on my toes to press myself harder against him. Urging him. Begging him silently.

He hesitated still, the firm, broad head of his cock nestled against the lips of my pussy. He released my ass, sliding his touch up my back, bending over me to press his lips against my ear.

"You want me?" he whispered.

"Yes—" I gasped it, a breathless admission.

He slid his hands up my arms, pressed his palms to the backs of my hands, and then his fingers tangled in between mine; it was an unexpected gesture of intimacy and affection, and it made my heart twist and melt, and burgeon with hope.

And then he brought my hands around, gently but firmly pulling them behind me, until my shoulder blades were pressed together. "You told me, the last time we fucked, that you wanted more craziness out of me. You told me to let go, to not be so gentle, to not be so sweet or careful." He pinioned my wrists in one hand. "You remember?"

I nodded, too breathless to speak.

"Well…here you go."

And with that, he drove into me, sudden, *hard*. His cock filled me all at once, a sharp piercing burning stretching ache, and his hips slapped against my ass, and his hand held my wrists pinned behind my back, just shy of painful. With his free hand, he gripped my hip and tugged me backward into his thrusts, which were rough and hard and demanding, taking me, using me.

My scream of surprise was loud, shrill, and hoarse. My whole body rocked forward with the force of his thrusts, and he used his grip on my wrists to yank me backward, pulling my arms upward just a little, so I was forced to lift off the bed. God, it was so…rough, the way he was fucking me. He was just *taking* me. He'd given me an orgasm, and now he was just using me for his own pleasure, giving me nothing except the rough pound of his cock.

And holy shit, was it incredible.

My heart pounded as he fucked me. Would he gentle at the end? Would he stop or slow down long enough to give me another orgasm? He usually—always, until now—made sure I came at least twice before he did.

He was grunting, holding my wrists in his strong, harsh grip; I twisted to watch him, watching the rictus of his face as he lost himself in his pleasure. His hand, the one gripping my hipbone, spasmed, releasing my hip. Palming my ass, he pushed me away as he pulled his thrust backward and then, as he drove into me, he slapped my ass with a sudden, shocking blow that stunned another scream out of me.

It wasn't a gentle, playful smack. It was a rough, hard spank that left my ass stinging and my lungs spasming and my head spinning.

"Canaan!" It was a plea, but I wasn't sure for what. To do it again? To stop?

It had *hurt,* and not just a little. But it had also sent a dark thrill through me. He slowed the pace of his fucking. Slow, deliberate. He let go of my wrists, and I clawed at the bed, arching my spine, pressing my upper torso off the bed, lifting up onto my toes. Staring over my shoulder at him. My eyes were wild, my heart crashing, pulse thundering.

Smack!

He spanked the other cheek now, just as hard.

A resounding, echoing crack of his hand across my ass, jolting me forward, the spank coming in the exact moment he slammed into me. His cock filled me and his hand spanked me in the same instant, and I screamed. I thrashed in pain and excitement and pleasure, the stinging ache on my ass cheeks morphing and throbbing through me. I felt him pulling back, felt his cock sliding out of me, and I gripped the bedsheet and arched forward to draw away, watching over my shoulder, and now he palmed both cheeks in his hands, and instead of spanking as he thrust, he met my gaze and feathered a few short shallow thrusts, teasing me, kneading my ass as he toyed with my expectations.

"Again!" I breathed, slapping my ass back into his body, filling myself with him.

"You want more? You want me to spank you again?"

I nodded. "Fuck yes."

"You want me to *really* spank you?" His eyes were dark with lust, need.

I wasn't at all sure. "That wasn't really spanking me?"

He shook his head. "That was just…a few smacks as I fuck you."

"Holy shit." I gasped as he filled me with slow, deep thrusts. "Yes. Yes, Canaan. Spank me."

He pulled out of me, left me aching and gasping and whimpering in surprise. "Stay like that. Bend over the bed. Get that beautiful ass as high as you can."

I complied, shifting forward to bend fully over the bed, presenting my ass high, feet together. "Like this?"

"Exactly." He caressed my ass. "Now I'm going to spank you."

"While you fuck me?"

He shook his head. "No. I'm going to spank you, and you're going to masturbate while I do it."

I throbbed, ached. "Oh."

"So let me see you touch yourself."

I slid one hand between my thighs, hesitantly touching my clit. Anticipating his hand cracking across my ass. Instead, he just gently caressed me, one side, the other, again and again, in slow alternating circles, soothing where he'd spanked before. My fingers found my clit and I gasped at my own touch, my clit swollen with need. His fucking had left me aching, needing, and his spanking had turned me on, and now I was left with only my own touch to alleviate the need, and I was trembling with anticipation of him spanking me again, and thus it took only a few slow circling touches to bring myself to the quaking edge of orgasm; I slowed my touch, wanting to make it last, wanting to draw it out, make it intense.

I gasped, though, aching, and then I couldn't help a whimper of ecstasy as Canaan gripped my ass in both hands again, spreading the globes apart.

"Oh—oh god," I gasped. "Why—why do you keep doing that?" I asked, as I shook, as I touched myself, as I quavered on the edge of a swelling orgasm.

"Do what?"

"Pull my ass cheeks apart like that."

He did it again. "This?"

I nodded, whimpering. "Uh-huh. Why do you do that?"

"Because your ass drives me wild. I love the feel of it. I love holding it, jiggling it—" and here, he clutched the cheeks and shook them until they jiggled like Jell-O, "and I love…I just love your ass." He let go, and then gripped them again, spreading them apart again.

"Is that…is that all?" I asked. "Is that the only reason?"

"You want another reason?" He kept one side tugged away, letting go of the other, and used his finger to trace down the crack, teasing the knot of muscle. "I want this. I want to put my finger inside you and see how loud you'll scream."

I slid my fingers inside myself, backing away from a clitoral orgasm, massaging myself inside, working toward a vaginal orgasm. Needing more.

Aching. I blinked over my shoulder, twisted a little so I could fully look at him. I said nothing, only drew my fingers out and returned my touch to my clit, gasping shrill and breathless as I neared the unavoidable edge of climax.

That was the only invitation he needed, my lack of a demurral, and the gasp, the obvious arousal in my voice, in my expression.

I watched as he brought his fingers to his mouth, letting a pool of saliva coat his fingers, which he then touched to my asshole, warm and wet and darkly thrilling.

"Oh—god, oh god—" I whimpered.

"I haven't even touched you yet."

"I'm already so close."

"I know."

I held his gaze. "Your touch, there—that's the first time for me, ever."

"For me too." He spread the saliva against the knotty tissue, and then I felt his fingertip pressing, pressing. "Talk to me, Aerie. Tell me what you're feeling."

"I'm feeling like I thought you were going to spank me, not finger my asshole."

"You complaining?"

"No."

"What if I'm planning on doing both? Spanking

you while I finger you?"

"That would be…" My eyes crossed and I trailed off as he pressed more firmly, until his fingertip pierced me, sliding in ever so slightly. "Oh god, oh fuck!"

"Good?"

I nodded, whimpering. "Weird. But good."

It was weird, too. A strange, dark, dirty intrusion into a secret place that had never felt such a touch. But it made my stomach clench, and my pussy throb, and my head spin, and my thighs quake, and my fingers flew around my clit now, and the orgasm rocked and teetered, shaking me, threatening to explode through me.

"I'm gonna come, Canaan," I breathed, as he slid his finger a little deeper yet.

"Now?"

"Almost."

I felt his other hand palm my ass cheek, and I gasped, expecting a slap. Instead, he just caressed. And his finger slid deeper. How much? Up to the first knuckle, maybe? It felt like so much inside me, so much, too much, but it was so slow, a deep stretch, a burning that throbbed in strange, explosive, expansive ways.

My hips rocked, and I felt the climax begin to break through me. "Now! Canaan, god, god, god, I'm coming, I'm coming!"

The instant the words left me, as the orgasm started to shatter, he brought his hand down on my ass, hard and sudden and sharp, and the stinging pain blazed through me and turned to a glory of ecstatic thrill, and I felt his finger inside me, more and more as I came and came, and now I heard myself screaming, and I was helpless against the bashing white-hot wave of orgasm, wave after wave, and now I felt another smack to the other side, and the orgasm shattered again, breaking apart into something more.

"Canaan!" I wanted more. I wanted him. I wanted his orgasm. I wanted his cum. "Fuck me, Canaan! Please, now! While I'm coming. Please…fuck me."

He filled me, his cock sliding deep, his cock hard and thick and warm and bare.

He fucked me.

Hard.

His hips slapped, and his finger was deep, his knuckles bumping my ass cheeks, and I was touching my clit and now my climax became another one, hard on the heels of the first, the second one making me scream so loud my throat hurt, the wrenching agony of ecstasy too much to bear as I clenched around his slamming cock, around his finger, and he slapped my ass, harder and harder, the smacks and cracks stinging and becoming deeper aches of exploding pleasure.

I felt him shuddering, slowing. Heard him growling, cursing.

"Don't come, don't come—" I gasped. "Canaan, don't—don't!"

My orgasm was a spasmodic, quavering, wracking thing, alive, shaking me to pieces, but I knew I couldn't let him come inside me like this, no matter how much I wanted him to.

As the waves of climax rocked through me, I reached behind and pushed at his wrist, and he slowly, slowly withdrew his finger. My ass stung. As his finger popped free, a fresh wave of something dark and intense slammed through me, and I nearly collapsed from it, but he was there, holding me by the hips, and his cock wasn't inside me, and I ached for the need of him. From the absence of him. I went from being full of Canaan to being empty in an instant, and it was too much, too much of not enough.

I collapsed to my knees, and then fell to my ass, turning around to sit on the floor facing Canaan, who stood over me, staring down, his expression hard and fierce and pained.

"I don't have any condoms," he said.

"Neither do I." I gazed up at him. "But...I need to feel you come the way you made me come."

"Then we have to go get some."

He turned away and went to the bureau, yanked

open a drawer, withdrew a pair of gym shorts and stepped into them, and then from another drawer he produced an oversized hoodie, which he put on over his bare chest, the bottom of the hoodie long enough to hide the evidence of his straining arousal still tenting the shorts.

He quirked an eyebrow at me. "Put on something. We're gonna go together."

I reached over and snagged my backpack, dug through it, and found what I was looking for—the loose, comfy, knee-length maxi dress I'd packed; I stood up, tugged it on, and then bent to look for underwear and a bra. Canaan grabbed my wrist and pulled me away.

"Let's go."

"I need a bra and underwear."

He pulled me to the door. "No, you don't."

"Canaan—"

"I'm one wrong move away from coming everywhere, Aerie. We'll be quick, there and back as fast as possible. Okay? So you don't need 'em. Let's go."

So I went. I walked beside him as he strode intently down the street; it was late afternoon on a Saturday, and the streets were busy, the slight drizzle not slowing down the weekend foot traffic. I felt intensely self-conscious as I tried to keep up with Canaan—my tits were bouncing and swaying, as was my ass—which was still stinging and throbbing from the spanking—and I felt the cool breeze wafting up my dress and skimming across my bare, damp core, still aching from the post-orgasm shocks that were only now beginning to fade. I felt Canaan's eyes on me, glanced at him to see that he was taking a lot of longing, aroused glances at my jouncing cleavage, which the V-neck of the dress was only barely concealing.

We reached a convenience store within a couple blocks, and Canaan prowled through the aisles to the "family planning" section, grabbed a box of condoms, and took it to the register. He had my hand in a death grip, and his breathing was ragged. As he let go of my hand to dig cash out of his wallet, I surreptitiously slid my hand to the front of his shorts and under the hoodie, trying to find out if he was still hard or if he'd lost it.

Ohhhh god; he was still hard as a rock.

He glanced at me in warning as he counted out the correct amount cash—the warning was because I had his erection in my hand through the material of his shorts, palm sliding down the thick length. The warning was obvious—keep doing that, and we'd have an embarrassing mess on our hands.

He was nearly running as we left the store, and I had to jog to keep up.

"Canaan, I'm in flats, with no bra—I can't run like this."

He slowed down. "Sorry. But it fucking hurts." He glanced at me, his gaze rife with arousal. "I need to finish inside you."

"We're almost there," I said.

But then we hit a snag—a street musician had set up at the mouth of an alley less than a block from the warehouse. He had a bass drum set up with a kick pedal, and an electric guitar in his hands; he was really, really good, and a crowd had gathered. It was nearly impossible to wade through the crowd, thick as it was, jostling to get closer to the musician as he punctuated his riffs with a thumping, pounding rhythm on the drum.

The crowd was spilling across the sidewalk, blocking the alley that led to the side door of Mike's building, where we were planning on entering. The alley was long and dark, deeply shadowed by the buildings towering on every side—it was surprisingly clean for an alley, with a dumpster full of broken-down cardboard boxes on one side, and a stack of wooden pallets on the other. The alley ended in a T at another alley that was more of a tiny side street, just barely wide enough for a car.

Canaan, somewhat rudely, pushed his way through the crowd, hauling me by the hand so we didn't get separated. Once past the bulk of the crowd, we hustled into the alley, making for the plain steel door leading into Mike's warehouse. We reached the door, and Canaan yanked it open; it squealed on protesting hinges, banged against the wall, and shuddered to a halt, partly open.

I expected Canaan to lead me up the stairs to the bedroom, but instead he stopped in the open doorway and turned around to eye me with mischievous speculation.

"Remember when we talked about fucking in public?"

"Yeah." I glanced around the side of the door at the crowd and the musician, less than fifty feet away. "Canaan, you're not thinking about—"

He had the box of condoms open, a square ripped off of the string. He tossed the box onto the floor inside and handed me the condom. "Put it on me, babe."

"Here?" I asked, hesitating.

He tugged his shorts down a few inches, revealing the straining head of his erection. "Here. Now."

"Canaan, I don't know." I did, though. My heart was pounding; my hands were trembling, excitement thrilling through me.

"Yes, you do." He sidled closer, reached for the hem of my maxi dress. "You want this."

"How do you know?" Was I playing coy? Drawing him out? Or genuinely hesitating? I wasn't sure of the answer, only that I was getting wet with arousal at the thought of doing this here, sheltered and hidden, but still in the open, in a public place.

He slid his fingers up my slit, dragging my wetness and smearing it over my clit, his smirk knowing. "You want this, Aerie. Don't act like you don't."

"Oh fuck," I whispered, as he circled my clit with his fingers, once again bringing me to the quaking edge of climax in no time at all.

He tugged down the sleeves of my dress, and then reached into the V-neck to lift out my breasts, one and then the other, caressing them as he freed them to the cool, damp Seattle evening air. His fingers kept circling as he did this, making me weak in the knees, making me gasp, making me tremble.

He pressed me backward so I was leaning against the frame of the door with the hinges at my spine, his hand under my dress, my breasts hanging in the open, and now I was toppling over the edge as Canaan bent to suckle my nipple, stretching it taut and letting it pop free before turning his attention to the other. I was biting my lip to stifle my need to cry out as the orgasm shook me, and even with my lip caught between my teeth, I still whimpered and gasped and shrieked, spasming under his touch.

He was relentless in his pursuit of my pleasure—
he curled his fingers inside me, massaging my G-spot
and rubbing his palm against my clit, tongue flicking
my nipples, pushing me to a second orgasm, and this
time I cried out even louder.

As I gasped and shuddered, breathless from the
second orgasm, Canaan grabbed me by the wrists and
pressed my hands against the front of his shorts, and
I moaned at the feel of his thick erection behind the
slippery material of his gym shorts. I slid my hand
into his shorts and wrapped my fingers around him,
stroking slowly.

He growled, leaning against me, forehead touching mine. "Need you, Aerie."

I rubbed my thumb over the tip of him, smearing
his pre-cum. "Need you too, Cane."

He took the condom from me, ripped it open,
and rolled the latex over himself. I pushed his shorts
down, and he reached up to tear off his sweatshirt.

The musician was still playing, and we could
hear the crowd, voices talking, chatting.

A light drizzle was falling, cooling the air even
further, and now my bare nipples, already hard from
arousal and orgasm, hardened further to diamond
peaks.

"I want to hear you scream, Aerie," Canaan
murmured.

And then he did something else unexpected: instead of merely pushing my dress up around my hips, he took me by the waist, spun me around to face the doorframe, and ripped my dress off of me entirely, tossing it inside to the floor, out of reach.

Leaving me utterly naked.

This was a public alley, and there was foot traffic, if infrequently. Anyone could walk by at any moment. One of the gathered crowd, so close by, could hear us and be curious and come to investigate the noises.

My pulse was thundering in my ears as Canaan slid up behind me, pressing his erection against me. I glanced over my shoulder at him. "If I'm naked, you have to be too."

He didn't miss a beat, only kicked his shorts away. He grabbed me by the hipbones and pulled me backward so I was bent forward, one hand on the doorframe, the other reaching between my thighs to guide his cock to my entrance. I fitted the thick, broad head against my slit, gasping as he slowly drove into me, a ragged groan escaping him. When he was buried as deep as he could go, Canaan palmed my ass in both hands, kneading and gripping, and then withdrew slowly. When he drove back in, he spanked me...even harder than the last time, so hard the crack echoed in the alley. A scream of surprise flew out of me, and then I had no breath left for screams, because he was spanking me and fucking me, rocking me forward with every pounding thrust, his hand smacking the left side and then the right, and then both hands clapping hard, his hips slapping against me as he drove in with raw, ragged, gasping grunts. My fingers circled and my tits swayed back and forth, and I felt him filling me, stretching me, the aching sting of being spanked translating yet again into throbbing pleasure that seared deep inside me, bringing me to an orgasm that shook me and left me breathless, and yet, as Canaan's cock slid through the clamping, spasming walls of my pussy, I couldn't help another scream, loud enough to echo, a wanton, desperate, erotic scream unmistakable for anything but the sound of a woman being good and properly fucked, and loving it.

"Oh fuck, oh fuck, oh fuck—" Canaan snarled, his driving thrusts going harder and faster, now, as he finally neared his release.

"Yes, yes, yes!" I screamed, still climaxing, my fingers flying. "Come inside me, Cane…come now!"

"Oh god, Aerie—I'm…fuck, fuck, I'm coming—"

And then I felt him come. He bent over me, cupping my breasts in both hands and using them for leverage as he thrust deep and ground against me, his forehead resting on my nape, breath on my skin, groans and grunts huffing hot on my flesh, his cock driving deeper and deeper.

We climaxed at the same time, his coming at the tail end of mine. I screamed again, and his thrust drove me against the doorframe, forcing me to slam a hand against the door to retain my balance, which slammed open to bang against the wall.

Revealing us.

The crowd had heard us, even over the musician, and when the door slammed open, all eyes went to us. To me, bent forward in the doorway, half visible, Canaan behind me, clutching my breasts, still thrusting. A stunned moment, many pairs of eyes on us, and then I reached, stretching, and snagged the doorknob, tugging the door closed. Canaan pulled away, then, bringing us into the building, and the door latched closed.

We stared at each other a moment, and we both laughed in disbelief.

"Did we really just do that?" I asked, breathless with the rush.

Canaan laughed again, reaching for my hand. "Yeah, we did."

I glanced down at his cock, still sheathed in the condom, now filled with his cum. "We just fucked in public."

"And we got caught."

I stared up at him. "You know, you also promised me dirty poetry while fucking me in public."

He palmed my hips and tugged me against him. "The sound of my hand across your ass was poetry. The way you screamed as I fucked you, the smack of my hips as I fucked you, that was poetry. The sounds we make as we fuck, that's the music."

"I literally just came, and I'm getting turned on again."

"Me too."

"Let's go upstairs," I said.

Canaan gathered the box of condoms and his shorts and hoodie, and I grabbed the empty wrapper and my dress, and we headed up the stairs to the room Canaan was temporarily staying in.

My heart was still thudding hard in my chest, and now that the rush of adrenaline was fading to a heady buzz, I realized there was a maelstrom of emotions whirling inside me.

Canaan was in the bathroom, and I heard the sink going as he washed up. I lay on my stomach on the bed, the cool air soothing my stinging butt, which I was rubbing with one hand.

The further away from the heat of the moment, the more my emotions began to take over, replacing the raging inferno of my libido.

That had been...honestly, the hottest sex of my life, Canaan fucking me from behind in an open doorway. The rough way he used me, took me, the way we'd come at the same time, and even being caught… even though nothing had come of it except some strangers getting a quick glimpse of me in a compromising position…it had been erotic and thrilling and wild, and I'd loved it.

I wanted it again.

I wanted more—more daring, more thrill, more rush of forbidden exhibitionism. I wanted to do something really crazy, really public, just for the rush of it.

But beneath that, there was a deeper, knottier thorn bush of emotions.

Canaan had used sex to distract me from the conversation we both knew we needed to have. I'd known he was doing it, and I'd let him get away with it.

Why?

Because I was still scared? Because having sex was easier than dealing with the possibility of being hurt, and the sense of betrayal and rejection?

It was all of it.

Because, no matter my emotional state, Canaan could always get my sex drive screaming hot in seconds flat, and then I just lost my head and stopped caring…

Until after.

Like now.

I heard his footsteps padding across the hall, and the bed dipped as he sat on the edge, beside me. His touch was warm and soothing, gently massaging my stinging butt. "You're all pinked up back here, babe."

I snorted a laugh. "Yeah, well, you spanked me *hard*, Canaan."

"And you loved it, admit it."

I didn't answer that. "Canaan, you can't just—" I broke off with a sigh of frustration.

How could I be mad at him for doing the same thing I'd done—avoid reality in favor of crazy sex? I couldn't.

I started over. "We can't keep doing this, Canaan."

His palm rested on one cheek, his thumb gently grazing back and forth. "Doing what?"

"Using sex as a way to avoid talking about things."

He blew out a breath. "We've both done it, more than once now."

"We've *been* doing it. Maybe even since the cabin." I rolled onto my back and sat up, but my butt still stung so bad I had to shift from side to side. "Damn, you really got me good, Cane," I said, with a wince as I wiggled side to side.

He frowned at me. "Did I actually hurt you?"

I shrugged. "It does sting a lot, still."

He took my hand and kissed the back of it. "I'm sorry, Aerie. It seemed like you liked it, and I may have gotten a little carried away." Another kiss, this one to my palm. "I didn't mean to really cause lasting pain."

I felt my tear ducts pricking, for some dumb reason. "Canaan, I—" I tugged my hand away and went back to lying on my stomach. "I can't honestly say that I didn't enjoy the hell out of it, in the moment, because I did. So...no regrets. I'm just a little sensitive, still."

He bent over me, and his lips brushed the stinging flesh of my buttocks, kissing, kissing, palms rubbing and soothing. "I'll make it all better."

God, that felt good; I groaned. "Stop, stop... Canaan, you have to stop."

He kept doing it. "Why?"

"Because that feels too good."

"That's the point."

"No...no, we have to talk."

But his lips were traveling up my spine, sending shivers racing through me, and somehow the stinging wasn't so bad now, and his breath was in my ear, and his words were dirty secrets.

"I can make you feel so good, Aerie. Kiss every inch of you, tease you, lick you, make you beg." He was murmuring, making the words almost into a chant. "Touch you everywhere, kiss your lips, kiss your thighs, make you quiver, make you plead for more. Make you plead for me."

"Canaan…"

"We make music together, Aerie. The way you sigh, the wet sounds as I slide into you. The way you beg me to come, the way your voice breaks when you come so hard you can't handle it." He was everywhere, kissing everywhere, touching everywhere, and I was trembling, aching, my skin tingling, my heart thudding all over again. "You and me, baby, the music we make together is so beautiful. I whisper your name, and it's music. You cry out and you sob as I make you feel so good, and it's poetry."

"God, Canaan…"

"Yeah, honey. That's the music. This is the poetry."

"The way our bodies slap together. The way we move so perfectly." I couldn't help getting caught up in it, and now I was on my back and he was above me, and his lips were everywhere, and his voice bathed my skin, and his words sent fire in my veins, and my own words thrummed with power, with need. "You groan as I fuck you, and it makes me crazy. I ride you, and my body moves above you and you watch me and every move and every sound is art, and poetry."

I was clutching at him, feeling him hard and hot

in my hand, and he was wedged between my thighs, and all I knew was the sound of his voice and the heat and hardness of his body, the way we fit together like pieces of a puzzle, just like this, his body against mine, filling me, hot and bare.

"Say my name," he murmured.

"Canaan."

"Tell me how this feels."

"So good. Too good."

"You make me crazy, Aerie. You make me lose all control."

"I never have any control around you. It's like you own me, like you…like you just hot-wire something inside me, with a single touch—ohhhh, oh *god*, Canaan—and I just can't control myself. I *need* you."

Movement was instinct. I *needed* this. I gave into it. There just wasn't anything else but this, like this.

We rolled and now Canaan was beneath me and I was riding him, straddling him, my hips rolling wildly, desperately, and he was staring up at me with so much need in his eyes, everything we both knew and both felt boiling just beneath the surface, everything we knew but couldn't say, didn't know how to say.

I lost my breath, staring down at him as I moved above him, taking myself there, needing no extra stimulation, just the way he filled me, just the way his shaft rubbed against me so perfectly, making me lose myself, sobbing, collapsing onto his chest, impaled by him, my hips rising and falling through my climax, and I felt him throbbing and thickening inside me, felt him tense and felt his thrusts stutter and falter.

"Aerie, I—fuck, god, I—I can't—" His voice was ragged, helpless. "You have to stop, I can't—we can't, but I—*fuck, fuck*, god, Aerie…"

I realized, then, what he was saying: he was bare inside me, and moments from exploding.

I dismounted him, pulling him out of me with a groan of loss, and slid down his body. My cheek was against his warm, hard belly and his hands were in my hair. I took him in my hands, cradling his thick length, still wet and slick from my body. Caressed him gently, tip to root. His hips pivoted, flexing him upward, and I wrapped my lips around the broad head and stroked him, tasting my own essence, tongue swirling as he growled and his hips drove up off the bed, fell, and then lifted again.

"Aerie!" He snarled my name as he exploded, filling my mouth with his tangy, salty, smoky essence.

I took it all, brought him to a cursing, gasping finish, tasting our mixed flavors in my mouth.

Tasting as well the anger at both us of us for what we just did.

I slid off him, tears starting down my face. "God*dammit*, Canaan." I backed away from him.

"Again. We did it *again*."

"Aerie, I can't help it. I can't help what you do to me."

"You have to be able to help it! So do I!" I caught up against the door, sobbing, everything too much, too much. "Dammit, Canaan. Just...*dammit*."

ELEVEN

Canaan

HER RAGGED SOBS CUT THROUGH ME LIKE A KNIFE.

"Aerie, honey—" I moved off the bed toward her. "I just—"

She held out her hands. "Don't come near me. Just...don't."

"Aerie, please."

She glared at me through tear-wet eyes. "Please what? Please *what*, Canaan? Please let you touch me again so you can keep using my own helpless, stupid body against me? Keep letting you distract me—distract *us* from getting down to what really matters?" She was loud, tormented, angry.

"No, that's not it—I just—"

"You just what? Yeah, I know, you're just as messed up and scared as I am! I know, Canaan, I know!" She quieted to a whisper. "But one of us has to be strong, and right now…it's not me."

She picked her dress up off the floor and tugged it on. Snagged a thong out of her backpack and stepped it into, wiggling her hips to get it into place—a display which definitely didn't help me in that situation. Stuffed her feet into her TOMS, and opened the door.

"Canaan, I can't keep doing this with you. What we have is…it's so much it scares me, but you won't talk about it, and I can't either, and you're scared and I'm scared—and we keep dancing around the issue, and then we have sex and we forget about it and put it off, and it all hurts even more." She backed out of the door. "This thing with us is a crazy rollercoaster, and I—I want off."

"Aerie, what are you saying?" I hurriedly stepped into my shorts and tugged a T-shirt on. "Don't leave yet. Wait for me."

She put her palms on my chest, arms out. "I know I said I wanted crazy, but this isn't what I meant." She pointed in the direction of the side door. "That? That was all the crazy I wanted, and still want." She pointed at me and then at herself. "This? This kind of crazy? This is *not* what I want."

"Me either!" I pushed closer to her.

She shoved me away. "Then fucking *do* something, Canaan!" she shouted, stabbing a finger at me.

Aerie whirled on her heel and strode angrily away, shoulders shaking.

Her words tolled in my head. *Fucking do something, Canaan!*

She was at the end of the hall, and I realized that somehow, she'd grabbed all her things, her phone, charger cord and block trailing, purse, backpack—she was leaving.

Not just walking away to get space.

Leaving.

Like I'd left her.

I heard her footsteps on the metal stairs, hand squealing on the rail.

Life is too short to waste it being afraid of getting hurt.

Fucking do something.

Let her walk away?

Lose what we had?

This wasn't about sex.

Or, it was, in a way. It was exactly about sex, because the fucking, the spanking, the exhibitionism… it was all a game, a guise, an attempt to hide beneath the eroticism of the wild, exploding, nova-hot river of love running beneath it all.

What we'd just done, just before she blew up and

walked away…

That had been love, raw and unfiltered—we just hadn't said it.

It had been obvious, though. In every move, every word, it had been obvious. The way she'd touched me at the end, the way she took me to the finish, with such love, such affection in every touch…the way she'd looked down at me?

Fuck.

Mike's words seared into my head—*if you get a chance with this girl, Cane, you take it. Take it, man. Life is too short to waste it being afraid of getting hurt. Because, trust me, regret hurts a fuckuva lot worse than heartbreak.*

I ran after her, panic blasting through me.

I caught up with her at the landing where the stairs turned a corner. I took the stairs two at a time, stopping behind her. She heard me and turned around, staring at me, waiting.

I took a step toward her, and then another. "Aerie, I—" The fucking words wouldn't come out.

I cupped her face in my hands, pressed my body against hers, and touched my lips to hers. This time, it wasn't just a kiss. This time, I wanted for her to feel everything I was having so much difficulty saying. Feel it, taste it, hear it. Know it. I kissed her slowly, softly, tenderly, and she stood there letting me kiss her. Not kissing back, not reaching for me. Nothing.

Was it too late?

God, no.

But then…I heard a thump—her backpack hitting the floor. Another thump—her purse. Then her phone, dangling by the cord, which fell from her hands last of all.

And then her hands came up, palms to my cheek, then diving into my hair. She lifted up on her toes, deepening the kiss, moaning softly in her throat. Abruptly, she tore away, backing up against the wall, shaking her head, touching her fingers to her lips.

"Canaan, you can't just kiss me and expect that—"

"I love you, Aerie." I cut in over her. "I fucking—I love you. I love you. Okay?"

She just blinked up at me, shock on her face. And then tears sprang in her eyes, trickling down her cheeks. "Don't say that."

I was rocked backward by that. "What? I don't—"

"You can't just say that. It's not—it's not that easy."

I stood in front of her, framed her body with mine. "There's nothing easy about this, Aerie. Nothing at all."

She was frozen, tears flowing. "You don't mean it. You're just saying it because you're afraid of losing me. You like the way we fuck. That's all you love.

What you said is not real. It's never been real. You're just *saying* it."

Aerie shook her head, sniffling, and then bent to gather her things, stuffing her phone and charger in her purse. She squeezed past me, continuing down the stairs.

"Where are you going, Aerie?" I asked, my voice trembling—which should have embarrassed me, but didn't.

"I need some space."

"Aerie, do you…do you understand that I have never spoken those words to anyone in my life? Not since Mom died. Mom was the only one who ever actually said she loved us. Dad *showed* us love, and we knew he loved us. The same way we all know we love each other as brothers, but we don't *say* it. I just fucking said it, Aerie. I said it to you." I moved to stand in front of her, blocking her path to the final flight of stairs. "Please, Aerie. Don't walk away from me."

"Why not, Cane? You walked away from me. Fuck that, you *ran*. Like a scared little puppy." She shrugged into her backpack and hiked her purse onto her shoulder. "I come here, *I* chase *you*, to talk to you about us, and you turn it into sex."

"More than just sex, Aerie, and you know it."

"That's not enough."

"I SAID I FUCKING LOVE YOU!" I shouted,

stepping toward her.

She got right in my face and shouted back at me. "AND MAYBE THAT'S NOT ENOUGH!" She quieted, shaking her head. "Maybe it should be—I don't know. Maybe I don't believe you. I don't know. I don't—I don't fucking know, Canaan!"

"Then what else am I supposed to do? What am I supposed to say?" I backed away, hands in my hair. "What do you want from me? Yes, I ran. It was a mistake, and I'm sorry. I was weak and scared and pathetic. I don't even have anything like what you have dealt with. But I'm still scared, and I made a mistake. Now I'm trying to make it right. And you're telling it's not enough?"

"Canaan, I—"

I shook my head, angry now. "I overheard what you said to Eva and that's why I left. *You don't know if you're willing to risk being with me. You don't know if I'm worth it. If I'm enough for you.*" I took another step backward, away from her. "Mom died, and then Dad just…he gave up. We weren't—I wasn't—enough reason for him to keep caring about life, about us. He gave up, on all of us. Then Jenna flat out told me I wasn't enough for her, that she didn't want me, she just wanted me for sex. Not for me, not for who I was. And now Corin is with Tate, and they're gonna have a baby, and—and she's—she's taking him away from me. He's all I have, all I've ever had. And she's more important to him than I am. And yeah, I fucking—I get that that's the way it is supposed to be. They're having a baby, starting a family. Great, wonderful, I get it. Still leaves me alone, out in the cold. With what? With who? *Nobody.* That's who."

I stabbed a finger in her direction. "And I'm not enough for you either. You're walking away, too. Abandoning me, just like everyone else."

"Canaan, that's not true."

I turned away and started back up the stairs. "Yeah, it is. It's fine. Fuck you."

"Canaan!"

"Just—go." I went upstairs and didn't look back. Was it a chicken-shit move? Maybe. But right now I was too strung out to think about it.

The catwalk overlooking the living room led across the width of the warehouse, to a door leading through the wall to the other side, where the studio was. I kept walking, not daring to stop, not daring to look back, agony and rage blasting through me. I went into the studio and down to where my guitars were set up. I plugged my Stratocaster into the amp, cranked the volume, and let everything I was feeling pour into the strings.

I lost track of time, of everything. I just played, letting the hate and the rage and the agony and the confusion scream through the strings in twisting, shrieking riffs, the volume cranked so loud I felt it in my bones and blood.

I played and played, for how long I don't know. I just knew that the music was taking me away.

At some point—I wasn't even sure what time it was, someone cut the power to the amp. My fingers were curled around the guitar, and I realized I'd played so long my fingertips were bleeding. I couldn't let go of the guitar.

Mike was squatting in front of me, reaching for the guitar. "Can I have this, buddy?"

I forced my hands to open, gasping in pain. The fretboard was smeared with blood.

Mike took the guitar from me, unplugged it, and snagged a rag from a counter, wiped the fretboard clean, then placed the guitar in the rack. He sat on the amp in front of me. "The fuck, Canaan?"

I couldn't look at him. "I—I told her I loved her, man." He started to speak, and I cut over him. "She told me it wasn't enough."

He stared at me in silence for a long, long time. "And you believe that?"

"How can I not? It's the second time she's said that—or something like it, at least."

"And again, you believe she's serious? That she really actually means it?"

"As opposed to what, Mike?"

He gaped at me like I was stupid. "Ummmm, as opposed to—oh, I don't know—that she's even more scared than you are, and she's pushing you away and trying to hurt you before you hurt her?"

"Bullshit." I stood up and paced away, a million thoughts and feelings banging and blazing inside me.

He stood up with me, moved to face me, to stand in front of me. He reached into his hip pocket and pulled out a folded, wadded, crumpled hundred-dollar bill. "This hundred here says you panicked and fucked it up again." He quirked an eyebrow. "She pushed, and you pushed back, because you're a dumbass and a pussy."

I turned away, something bitter eating away at me. "Fuck you. What do you know?"

Mike's voice was deadly quiet. "I'm your friend, Canaan. But don't make the mistake of thinking that just because you're my boy that I won't knock your punk-ass-bitch out. Because I will. I'm doing you a solid here, givin' you the truth. Not everyone would. A lot of other people might feed you shots and take you to get under someone else to get over her." He grabbed me by the shoulder and spun me around, and the power in his grip told me I *really* didn't want to be on the receiving end of his fist; his eyes were blazing and angry. "I ain't everyone else, Cane. So I'm givin' you the damn truth, and I don't give a fuck if you like it. You're a fuckup. She pushed, and you pushed back, instead'a manning the fuck up and seeing she was talking out of fear and giving her space and time to work through it."

Shame was a wriggling, gnawing creature, and it had control of my mouth—and my better sense. "Like I said, what do you know?"

"What do I know? What do *I* know?" Mike laughed bitterly. "A lot. About this? A fucking lot— everything. I made all the mistakes you're making right now. I made 'em, and there wasn't anyone to kick my ass about it. Wasn't anyone to give a shit that I was fucking up the best thing that ever happened to me. Wasn't anyone around who gave enough of a shit about me to knock some fuckin' sense into my thick-ass skull."

Then he took hold of my hair and rapped his knuckles against my skull. "Hello, McFly! Wake the fuck up, Cane! That girl loves your ass *hard*. But she's scared, and you're giving her every single damn reason there is to keep being scared. You're not taking care of *her*, you're covering your own ass. Guarding your own heart, instead'a hers. Call me old-fashioned, but I believe it's a man's job to take care of a woman. That don't mean keeping her in the kitchen like this is *Leave It to Beaver* or some shit—it means protecting her, body and heart and mind. I didn't do that for Leah, and I lost her. So yeah, I know about this shit, Canaan. I know, because I lived it, and I fuckin' lost her. She's got another man, a better man than me. He takes care of her. Keeps her heart safe. Wouldn't let me anywhere near her. She would'a sat down and talked to me, you know, like for closure or whatever the fuck, but he was like, nah, babe, you don't need to do that. No reason to revisit the past. Ain't gonna get you anywhere. And the shit of it is, he was right to do that. Burns my ass, but he was."

"I'm sorry you went through that, Mike, but—"

"Shut the *fuck* up, Canaan." He jabbed a finger into my chest, knocking me backward a few steps. "You fucked up twice now. Way I see it, you got one more chance to redeem this for yourself. It means you nut the fuck up, go back home and talk to her. Ask her for a chance. Be real with her. And then give her a damn minute to think it through. Chicks have to stew on shit, man. They need time to figure shit out in their hearts. Right now, her mind is tellin' her to give you the slip, to keep pushing you away. And you're just giving her more reasons to keep doing that. Yeah, she might back up a minute when you first put it out there for her, but if you give her a damn minute, she might just surprise you."

Mike stood right up against me, staring down at

me, his face hard, unforgiving. "I'm not gonna let you fuck this up, Canaan. I will drag your ass to Ketchikan by that Legolas fuckin' hair of yours if I have to. That girl loves you and you love her—so figure it out. Or I promise you, man, you'll live to regret it for the rest of your fuckin' life."

He turned on his heel and left the studio, rolling his massive shoulders like a boxer prepping for a fight. When he was gone, I sank back down onto the stool I'd been sitting on. I stared at the shredded mess that was my fingertips, thinking over Mike's words.

He was right.

The bastard was right.

I'd fucked up again. Aerie had heard me say what she'd been waiting for me to say, and when she finally heard it, she freaked out. Pushed at me, to see if I meant it. And instead of seeing that, I let myself get all butt-hurt and I lashed out.

Dammit.

I rubbed my face, groaning. I'd messed up, so, *so* bad.

The question was whether or not it was too late.

And there was only one way to find out.

I started packing my guitars.

TWELVE

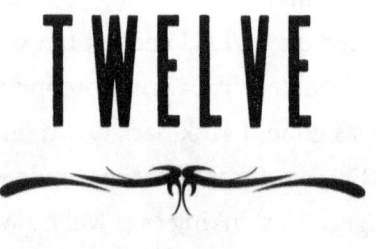

Aerie

I LOW-KEY SOBBED THE WHOLE WAY BACK TO KETCHIKAN. Several people asked if I was alright, and I just nodded and kept crying.

How could Canaan talk to me like that? How could he do that? I mean, I know I'd panicked a little, but he'd...

He had turned on me.

Abandoning him? I—I wasn't—I hadn't—

I couldn't even form coherent or complete thoughts. It hurt too much. Everything hurt.

The way he'd kissed me? The way we'd—the way we'd *loved* each other, so slowly, so beautifully? All my life, I'd cringed at the phrase *making love*. I mocked those who used it. Even if what two people shared was real, true, deep love, that phrase was just so trite and cliché and stupid and cheesy.

But he'd just…in that moment, he had been *everything*. My whole existence had been wrapped up in him, in the feel of him, the feel of *us*. These thoughts only made me sob all the harder, as I sat on the ferry from the airport to the Ketchikan docks. It was, suitably, a dull, dreary, chill, rainy day. I tugged the hood of my Helly Hanson raincoat up over my head as the ferry docked, the tail end swinging sideways to bump up against the dock, the deckhands scurrying to tie off ropes. I only had my purse and my backpack, so I was able to slip through the crowd of tourists sorting through the pile of suitcases being hauled from ferry to dock. I walked home to Grandma and Grandpa's in the rain. Head down, eyes on the sidewalk, the rain spattering against my face, mingling raindrops with teardrops.

When I entered the foyer, I spotted Mom immediately, sitting in the formal room, murmuring in low tones on her cell phone.

"I have to let you go, Bob—Aerie just came back. Yeah, love you too, sweetheart. Okay, bye." She tapped the screen to end the call and tossed the phone onto the small table beside the high-backed red velvet chair she was sitting in. She smiled at me. "Hi, honey.

How was your trip?"

I stared at her warily, hoping the rain would mask the fact that I'd been crying. "Um, okay, I guess?"

Her gaze was sharp, and knowing. "Did you figure things out with Canaan?"

"Why do you care? I thought he was just a hoodlum to you." I set my backpack and purse down, shrugged out of my coat and hung it up, and then gathered my bags as I headed for the stairs.

"Aerie, wait." Mom's voice was…quiet, something almost like desperate, if I didn't know any better. "*Please*."

I sighed, halting. "Mom, I've had…*bad* doesn't even begin to describe how terrible this day has been. I'm just not in the mood for your drama right now."

She blinked hard, sighing shakily. "Five minutes, please? Just hear me out for five minutes."

I groaned, tipping my head back. "Fine. Five minutes. But if you start shit with me, I'm walking away." I set my bags down and sat in the matching chair, angled toward hers, on the other side of the table.

"I had a long talk with Grandpa," she said, after a few moments of silence. "And I—I realize now that I've been…I haven't been very fair or loving to you and Tate."

I snorted, unable to stop myself. "Wow, you *think*?"

She gave me a hurt look. "This is very hard for me, Aerie. Do you think you can cut me some slack?"

I drew in a deep breath, held it, and let it out slowly. "Sorry. You're right, I'm not being very fair right now."

Mom toyed with her phone, spinning it in circles on the table with one finger. "Can you answer one question for me? Honestly."

I huffed a laugh. "You have to know at this point that I'm not going to mince words with you, Mom."

"The whole modeling thing. You never wanted it? Either of you?" She hesitated, looking at me and then away. "You felt I was forcing you into it?"

I didn't answer immediately. "I think this is something Tate and I may have slightly differing opinions on, in certain respects." I kicked off my TOMS and dug my toes into the thick pile of the rug underfoot. "But we do both agree that, yes, you did push us into the whole Instagram model thing. For me, personally, I did like it. It was fun. I enjoyed the attention, the modeling, the clothes, the traveling. The money has been nice, too, since I've saved enough that I'm in a pretty good position until I figure out what I'm doing next. That's beside the point, though. Your question was whether you forced us into it, and the answer is yes. You pushed us into it and we went with it because we were young, and you're our mom, and because it all just kind of kept happening. We let it happen, and we went with it. Did we want it? I mean… maybe? Sort of?"

Mom blinked hard, and kept her attention on her phone. "I just wanted you to be successful. To not feel like college was the only avenue for you. You're so beautiful, and you were just natural at it. I thought you two were…I thought it was what you wanted."

I sat forward and sighed. "Come on, Mom. Really?" I shook my head. "You had to know we weren't always thrilled with how crazy everything was. The day we graduated, you scheduled us out for weeks and months at a time, with zero downtime in between. Literally, we have done shoots or traveled or attended events nonstop since we were seventeen years old, Mom. We didn't have a normal life as teen-agers. There were good things, a *lot* of good things— so it's not like I'm saying it was horrible, or that we hated it all the time. Even Tate, who I think liked it less than me, would agree with that."

"I just—I wanted more for you than I had."

I frowned. "What are you talking about? Grandma and Grandpa may not have been loaded, but it's not like you were—"

"I'm talking about opportunities, Aerie."

My frown only deepened. "Then I'm lost."

She sighed. "How much do you know about how

your father and I met?"

I was stunned speechless. Mom never, *ever* talked about our father. Like, EVER. The last time Tate and I brought up the topic to Mom, she walked out of the room without a word, and Tate and I had just stared at each like *ooohhhhhkayyy? That was weird...*and we never brought it up again.

I hunted for something to say. "Um. Not much. Like, nothing at all, really."

"Do you know how old I am, right now?"

I frowned harder than ever. "Uhhh...ha, you think I'd know, right? Like, 43, right?"

Mom snorted, shaking her head. "I'm 40, Aerie. I turn 41 at the end of the year."

"I do know your birthday is December 10th."

"Right." She shot a glance at me. "And if you and Tate are twenty-one, how old would that make me when I had you two?"

I did some quick subtraction. "You'd have been...nineteen?" And the penny dropped. "You were nineteen?"

She nodded. "Nineteen. Eighteen when I conceived you." She sat forward, reached out, and took my hands. "I was nineteen when I gave birth to you two, honey. Can you think about that? Nineteen, and a mother."

I realized I'd never considered that, never

considered how young Mom had been when she had us. How hard it must have been. "Mom, I—"

"We got married when we discovered I was pregnant. Grandpa pretty much…I'm not going to say he forced us to, but he heavily hinted that if we wanted their help, we'd get married. So we did, and…" She sighed, heavily. "It was the wrong thing for us—for me. Grandpa saw it pretty much right away, because it was obvious. Your father, he was…he was—well, not to put too fine a point on it, but he was a piece of shit. Good looking as hell, charming, funny…and a complete loser. Selfish, narcissistic, and immature. He was incapable of thinking about anything or anyone but himself. He would try to help with you and Tate, and he'd just…he'd get frustrated and quit. Storm off and go drink with his buddies. I was honestly shocked he lasted as long as he did. It was a relief when he told me he was leaving. I mean, I'd been expecting it for so long, I was relieved it was finally happening. He had never loved me, and only barely tolerated you two. He wasn't cut out for fatherhood. Or adulthood at all, really."

She picked up her phone, unlocked it, and then relocked it again, an unconscious gesture.

"My point in all this is that I never had any opportunities. I had dreams, before I had you guys. I was going to go to New York and be an actress. I had it all planned out. I was going to do commercials and then TV, and then transition to movies. I could have done it, too. I'd actually been discovered, so to speak, in a way. I'd been in a play in high school, and a TV agent's granddaughter was in it with me. He came to see the play, saw me, and invited me to come to New York for some auditions. Mom and Dad made me finish high school first, and then I got pregnant within a month and a half of graduation. I'd been saving money, working to afford the trip and all that. Then I had you guys, and I never got to follow that dream. I don't blame you, I hope you know that. But…I never had a choice. I got my degree in accounting while I was raising you guys, thanks to Mom and Dad, and worked in accounting until I met Bob, and he changed everything for me. I know you guys don't like him, and I get it. He's not for everyone. But he's great to me, and he loves me and I love him, and he takes care of me. He made it so I could go back to school to get a management degree, so I could open my own talent agency. Working with you and Tate showed me I was good at it, and that I liked it. But it's not…it's not the dream I had. I was supposed to *be* the talent, not be the manager *for* the talent."

"Mom, I had no idea."

She sighed, smiling sadly. "I don't think many kids ever really think about their parents like that. I know I never did, until I was an adult, and older than you are now." Mom set her phone aside again. "My point in telling you all this is that I pushed you and Tate into modeling, yes, in part because I never got to follow my dreams. By watching you succeed in the world meant I could be close to it myself. But I also genuinely wanted you to succeed. I wanted you to be able to get out of Ketchikan. There's nothing wrong with living here, and I really do mean that. It's a wonderful place to grow up. But it's not a place for a young girl to learn how to chase her dreams. How to…how to have more than a quiet life in Alaska. I wanted more for you two. You're twenty-one, and you've seen the world. You have a lot of amazing connections. You have potential. Even if you never model again, the experiences will stand you and your sister in good stead. It's given you the step up in the world I never had, and a step up in the world that most people never get."

I shifted to look out the window, thinking about what she said. Eventually I turned back to face her. "You're right. We know you meant well, Mom. We've always known that. You're just…so stubborn, and just a tiny bit dramatic."

Mom laughed. "Yes, well, you and Tate come by it honestly, then, don't you?" Her expression shifted to concern. "You were crying when you came in. Don't think I didn't notice, sweetheart."

I shook my head, looking away. "Yeah, well…" I trailed off, unsure what to say beyond that.

"Care to talk about it?"

I laughed and sighed at the same time. "God, Mom. It's too much to put into words."

"Did he hurt you?"

I nodded. "Yeah, but no more than I've hurt him."

"You deserve happiness, Aerie." Mom touched my knee. "If I've learned anything from what I've been through, it's that you can't find happiness in a man, honey. He'll never fulfill you. He can make your life better, and he can be someone you can't live without, but unless you're okay in yourself, in your life, without him, he won't be able to make you happy. Because you won't *let* him."

I frowned at her. "What do you mean, I won't let him?"

"I was so…broken, I guess, by the way things happened with Vic that I just couldn't trust men. I figured they'd all be like him: selfish, immature, assholes who think only of themselves. I did date a few guys while you and Tate were young, but always when you were at school, so you'd never know. I just didn't want to ever bring anyone around you. All the guys I dated— and there weren't that many—seemed to just support the cynicism I had about men. Then I met Bob, and I realized he was different. But I still had a really, *really* hard time letting myself be happy with him, because I just...I was sabotaging myself, and us. I wasn't letting myself be happy." She squeezed my knee. "Honey, it took me thousands of dollars in therapy to figure all this out, and I'm still working on it. And you know what it is, deep down? It's not that I don't trust Bob—I do. He's proven to me that he won't hurt me, that I can trust him. I knew that from the get-go. This is stuff that my therapist had to really work hard to dig out of me, by the way.

"The real problem is that I don't trust *myself*. After Vic, I learned not to trust my own judgment. I even worry sometimes that Bob will turn on me, but I know that's just stupid, but it's all because Vic was such a huge mistake. It got me you and Tate, and you two girls—you're my—you're my greatest success. My only achievement in life. But Vic, your father? He was a huge, *huge* mistake, and I just constantly doubt myself as a result."

I blinked. "Wow, Mom." I frowned at her. "Wow. Grandpa must have really laid it out for you, huh?"

Mom chuckled. "Forty years old, and I got called into my father's office yesterday for a lecture." She smiled, though. "Once a parent, always a parent. You're never done being a parent to your kids. And your Grandpa? Well. He doesn't sit you down and talk to you about something unless it's a big deal to him, and so yeah, he laid it out for me. Pointed out that I wasn't thinking about you and Tate, that I was reacting emotionally instead of supporting my daughters. That we, as parents, may not always agree with our kids' choices, but that it's our duty and obligation as parents to support them and love them anyway. And I haven't been doing that."

"Things *are* kind of screwed up and crazy right now."

"But I just don't understand one thing."

"What's that?"

"Why didn't you and Tate just talk to me? About wanting to quit, I mean?"

I groaned. "God, Mom. You think you would have taken it any better if we had?"

She huffed. "Better than getting an email saying you were quitting, and then not being able to get hold of you, and not knowing where you were! And, oh yeah, finding out your sister is pregnant, and that you're dating those twins. They were never good influences on you."

"You don't know them, Mom."

She waved a hand. "I don't want to get into that. My point is, yes, I would have taken you and Tate quitting, or wanting a break, far better had you talked to me about it like adults, rather than vanishing on me like runaway children."

"You just don't want to talk about it because you know you're being judgmental. All the Badd brothers are wonderful men. And Canaan and Corin have been our only true friends our whole lives. And we were just as bad influences on them as they were on us!"

"Aerie, I'm just trying to protect you!"

"No, Mom. I'm not going to sit here and let you talk bad about them. *Any* of them, but especially not Canaan."

She eyed me carefully. "I haven't said anything about Canaan. Corin is the one who got your sister pregnant. Canaan has…well, I don't know. Hurt you, at the very least." Her expression went speculative. "But I find it interesting that you were so quick to defend him."

"Things are messed up right now."

"Let's get back to you and Tate vanishing."

I rolled my eyes. "Mom, honestly. You would have lost your ever-loving mind if we had told you beforehand. You would have yelled and screamed and coerced and manipulated us into staying with it. The one time we tried to suggest a vacation, you went mental."

"I did not go mental, Aerie."

I stared at her. "You don't remember yelling at us for thirty minutes straight about work ethic and relevancy and how fast we'd lose any shot at Hollywood if we took a vacation?"

"I didn't yell, and it wasn't thirty minutes."

I snorted. "Mom, we were in a hotel, and you got us a noise complaint."

"You wanted to go to Tahiti!"

"For a week! To relax! We'd just wrapped that huge shoot for Modality Swimwear, which was eight days on a beach, sweating our asses off from dawn to dusk. And before that, a three-day festival in Bern, and before that a shoot in Manhattan, and a shoot in Vegas before *that*, and before that, I don't even remember. The only downtime we ever got was while traveling, and that's not exactly relaxing! We just wanted to take literally a week to catch our breath, and you weren't having it."

Mom sighed. "If I ever pushed you it was only ever—"

"I *know*, Mom. *For our own good. In our best interests*. We know." I pinned her with a hard glare. "The problem with that is Tate and I are adults. We have our own ideas now about what's in our best interests. And it feels to us like you're still operating under the impression that we're teenagers who would be lost without your guidance."

She gestured angrily. "And would I be wrong? Tate is *pregnant*!" Her breath caught. "Exactly the thing I wanted to prevent. All the talks about being safe, and trying to impress on the two of you the importance of protection, of *not* getting pregnant, and Tate *still* ends up pregnant. History is repeating itself."

"Except Corin isn't our father. He's nothing like him. He genuinely loves Tate. He's not going to abandon her. They're going to have a family. They're going to be okay, Mom. It's not the same as your experience."

"But what is she going to *do*?"

I shrugged. "That's her decision. Maybe she *wants* to be a stay-at-home mom. That's not your choice— it's *hers*. If she wants to stay in Ketchikan and be a mom and a wife and never go back out into the career field ever again, that's her choice. Not mine, and not yours. It's not what *I* want, but that's *me*. We're identical twins, and we've been on the same life path up until now, but we *are* separate people, not a single unit. Tate has her own life to live, her own decisions to make, and we have to love her and respect those decisions and support her no matter what."

Mom had no answer to that. Eventually, she met my gaze. "Aerie, honey, what's going on with you?"

I shook my head. "I'm not ready to talk about it. And I don't mean just with you, I mean with anyone. It's mine to deal with, and I just can't handle talking about it right now."

"Will you be okay?"

I shrugged. "Yeah, I guess. Eventually?"

A nod from Mom. "Meaning you're not, but you're determined to figure it out yourself."

"I'm not okay right now, no, but I will be, somehow, someday. I just don't know how that's going to look, or how I'm going to get there."

"Well, if you ever want to talk about it, you can talk to me. I know I haven't always been the confidante sort of mom for you girls, but I want to be. Because you *are* adults, and the days of me trying to help mold and guide your lives are over. Now I just have to accept that you're not kids anymore and I will try to be there for you however I can."

I sighed. I wasn't sure what to say to that. But then something did occur to me. "There is one thing…you said you had to learn how to let Bob love you."

She nodded. "We've been together for five years, and I'm just now starting to figure it out." She sighed. "I've put Bob through a lot in the meantime."

"How do you do that? How do you learn to let someone love you?"

Mom took time to think before answering. "It's hard. I won't lie, sweetheart, it's really, really hard. It's scary. It means stepping out in faith and trust and accepting the fact that you may end up getting hurt, and there's no way to be one hundred percent sure he won't let you down or hurt you. It means letting yourself be vulnerable when everything inside you is just absolutely *screaming* at you to protect yourself." Mom's gaze was knowing. "Something tells me you know exactly what I'm talking about."

I nodded slowly. "Yes," I whispered.

She leaned over and took my hands in hers. "Oh, honey. Who hurt you so badly?"

I shook my head. "I can't—I can't talk about that, Mom. I just managed to stop crying. If I get into that, I'll start all over again, and I'm sick of crying."

"It wasn't Canaan, was it?"

I shook my head. "This is different." I stood up and bent over to hug Mom. "I love you. We probably should have handled this whole hiatus thing differently, and I'm sorry for hurting or scaring you. It just felt to us like it was the only way to really make a clean break and get the time we needed to figure things out."

"I love you, too, sweetheart."

"How long are you in Ketchikan for?" I asked.

She shrugged. "I don't know. Tate being pregnant changes everything. I honestly don't know what I'm going to do."

I stared at her. "Are you—you aren't thinking of staying here, are you?"

She shrugged one shoulder. "It has crossed my

mind as a possibility, yes. Bob can telecommute for just about everything he needs to do—he might need to fly into Manhattan once in a while, but that's it. As for me? I enjoy the talent agency work, but…I don't love it. Not as much as I thought I would. I don't know. I have to talk to Bob, and think through my options."

"Mom, what would you even *do* here?"

She laughed. "I don't know. I honestly don't."

"You got out of here as fast as you could. The minute you and Bob decided you were serious, you up and moved to New York. Now you're thinking of moving back?"

Mom shrugged. "Yeah, I know, I know. But things are different now." She sniffed. "I'm about to be a grandmother, Aerie. I…how can I live in New York when my daughter and my grandbaby are here?"

"Wow. I mean, that makes sense. I just…"

Mom's eyes cut to mine, her gaze sharp. "Why do I feel like you're surprised by the idea that I'd want to be near you and your sister, and eventually, my grandchild?"

I sighed. "That's not what's surprising." I hesitated. "What *is* surprising, I guess, is that you'd even consider coming back to Ketchikan. I just always assumed that once you got out of here, you'd never come back."

Mom laughed. "I've always assumed the same

thing, actually." She blew out a breath. "But I mean, I've only known Tate is pregnant for a matter of days, and I feel like everything has changed so much already. So by the time she's ready to have the baby? Who knows?"

I rubbed my face with both hands. "You're absolutely right about that." I leaned over again to hug Mom. "I love you."

She didn't let go of the hug immediately. "Aerie, baby—I hope you know, like really *know* that you can talk to me. You know that, right? I really do just want you and Tate to be happy. You're—it's just that you're my little baby girls, and it's hard to let go. It's hard to accept that you're not babies anymore and that you're going to do things I may not understand or agree with. But I really do want you two to be happy, and I promise to be better at supporting you."

I sniffled, tears starting in my eyes. "Mom—god. You don't know how bad I needed to hear that. Seriously."

She brushed away her own tears as she stood up. "I haven't been a very good mom, have I?"

"You've been a great mom. The best ever. Things just got a little crazy. They're still a little crazy, but… well…they're getting better." I let out a breath and wiped my eyes. "I think you should probably tell Tate what you said to me. She probably needs to hear it even more than I did."

"I will."

I got to the stairs before Mom stopped me yet again. "Aerie? One last thing."

I laughed and stopped on the stairs, turning around to glance at her. "For real, the last thing. I'm exhausted."

"Just a quick piece of advice I'd like to offer, as unsolicited as it may be.'

"What's that?"

"Men are stupid."

I laughed. "That's not exactly a newsflash, Mom."

"No, but you have to keep that in mind. They do dumb things. They react without thinking, and then when we get pissed off, they're like *what'd I do*?" Here, she deepened her voice to a mocking parody of a dumb male. "And then they're all panicked because they realize they messed up, and expect us to just be like, oh honey, it's fine. What I'm saying is, if Canaan did something to hurt you, he's probably just now realizing it. So if he shows up, just…try to give him a chance."

I walked upstairs and thought about what Mom had just said.

Will he show up?

That's the burning question.

If—*IF*—Canaan shows up, I'll not only give him

a chance, I'll be the first to apologize for freaking out on him. But he has to show up. I'm not going to chase him again. If he wants this, if he wants me…he has to prove it to me. It'd be better if I could just stop myself from being in love with him. Because…I was. I knew that much. I couldn't deny it any longer and saw no point in trying. But what would loving Canaan get me, except heartache?

I collapsed into bed fully clothed, pulled the blankets over my head, and fell into a restless, troubled sleep, filled with dreams of Canaan cursing at me, walking away from me, dreams of growing old alone, dreams of Canaan looking right into my eyes and telling me he never loved me and never will.

THIRTEEN

Canaan

MY FIRST INSTINCT WAS TO BARGE INTO THE KINGSLEY'S B and B when I got back to Ketchikan. I knew I had to get some shit straightened for myself before I tried to work things out with Aerie. My worry was that she'd decide to leave Ketchikan before I got a chance to talk to her and ask for another shot at us. I knew I had to sort myself out so my life could be in a place where a relationship was a possibility.

And right now, things with my twin were a fucked-up mess, and I had no idea what to do with my future. That had to get fixed first.

So I after my plane landed and I took the ferry across the channel, I dropped my guitars off at the

studio and went looking for Corin. I found him with
Tate, in what used to be Corin's and my bedroom—
they'd gotten rid of the bunk beds and replaced them
with a single king bed. Corin was on his back on the
bed and Tate was lying on her back between his legs,
her head on his stomach; she was listening as he read
out loud from a paperback copy of a book for new
parents.

They looked up as I leaned against the doorway.

Corin set the book facedown on his chest. "The
prodigal returns."

Tate's eyes narrowed at me. "Or are you here just
to grab the rest of your shit so you can move permanently to Seattle, like the great big pussy you are?"

Corin frowned down at her. "Really, babe? How
is that helpful?"

"Who said I was trying to be helpful? My sister
came home today and locked herself in our room at
Grandma and Grandpa's, and she hasn't come out
since. She's been crying for hours. So...yeah, not exactly feeling *helpful* at the moment." She got up and
left the room, intentionally bumping her shoulder
against mine on the way past. "I'll leave you two to
talk."

When she was gone, I sat down on the edge of
the bed, and Corin scooted up to sit cross-legged beside me.

"She has every right to be pissed at me," I said. "Everyone does. Running away like I did was a dick move."

"Yes, it was."

"Everything is just…hard and confusing right now, though."

Corin laughed bitterly. "Trust me, bro, I know what you mean."

"Yeah, I guess you would, wouldn't you?"

He slugged me on the shoulder. "Why'd you run, Cane? That's not how we do shit around here. We don't run from our troubles in this family, man—we face our shit head-on."

"I know, I know." I sighed, and moved to lean my back against the wall, feet hanging off the side of the bed. "I just…I couldn't handle everything."

"Handle what?"

"Everything! You, and this whole pregnancy thing, and Aerie, and…just everything."

He pulled his hair out of the ponytail, ran his fingers through it, and then retied it. "Okay, well let's start with me, and this whole pregnant thing. I don't get why you're so upset about it, honestly. You're not the one about to be a father."

"You honestly have no idea why I might be upset?" I asked. Corin shook his head, and I huffed a laugh. "Wow. Okay. Well, here it is, then. Tate being pregnant, and really even your whole relationship with her, but especially the pregnancy—it takes you away from me."

"That's fucking stupid, Cane. I'll always be your twin."

"No shit. That's not what I mean."

He fiddled with the bedspread. "Then what do you mean?"

"Our whole lives, we had one direction. Our lives, from the time we were old enough to play with toy guitars and bang on Mom's pots and pans with wooden spoons, has been about music. Starting a band. Booking gigs. Getting signed. Getting national and international tours. Moving here to Ketchikan was meant to be a...an interlude, or something, I don't know. Spend time with our brothers, start our own label, make our music our way. That was what we were doing, and we've always done it together."

"Why does that have to change?"

I snorted. "Come on, Cor. Never bullshit a bull-shitter. You're done touring. You never loved it, not the way I do. I'm not sure you'd have wanted to go back to it even if Tate wasn't pregnant, but now, with that? Yeah, we'll always be brothers, always be twins. But now you've got your life sort of...on a different path than mine, I guess. And I just...I don't know where that leaves me."

Corin sighed, a long, deep, thoughtful exhalation. "Ah."

"Ah? That's all you have to say?"

He frowned at me. "So me getting Tate pregnant
messes up *your* life?"

"Don't make it out like I'm being selfish here,
Cor," I said. "It *does* affect me though, yes. I know
it affects you more, and I get that, I really do. But it
changes my life, it changes what I'm going to do. Like,
you're here, now. You're gonna be Daddy, and Tate's
husband or whatever, and you're gonna…I don't
know what you're gonna do, but it won't be going
back on tour with me. It won't be us working on our
label. Maybe that'll happen in the future, but immediately? Your life will be here with Tate and your baby."

"And your life is out there, on tour?"

I shrugged. "Maybe. I don't know, anymore."

"So, you and Aerie?"

I scrubbed my face with both hands, groaning.
"It's messed up. *I'm* messed up, she's messed up, we're
messed up."

He laughed. "So what you're saying is, things are
messed up?"

I laughed with him. "A little, yeah."

"How so?"

"Everything. The whole reason I ran away is because I'd finally gotten to a place where I was able to

admit how I feel about her, and when I went to talk to her about it, I overheard her telling Eva that she didn't think she'd ever be willing to risk even finding out if I'm worth being with. That, plus you and the whole pregnancy thing? I just freaked out. I needed to get away. I needed to…I just couldn't handle it all. Being here was just…it was all too much. I didn't know what to do about Aerie, or about you and me and my life, so I just took off to Seattle, stayed with Mike for a few days, worked on an album with him, got wasted and didn't think about any of this shit."

Corin stared at me. "Dude, really? You're serious-ly having trouble with *how you feel* about Aerie?" He used air quotes around the emphasized words. "How is this not obvious to you?"

"Just because you and Tate fell in love and had no issue jumping right into it doesn't mean it's going to be that easy for me and Aerie."

"It may not be *easy*, but it's pretty fucking simple from where I'm sitting."

"How do you mean?"

"Well like I said, it may not be *easy*, but it's as simple as falling off a stool. Either you're in love with her, or you're not. And trust me on this one, Cane, if you're in love, you *know*. If you have to ask yourself if you're in love with her, if you have to, like, *think* about it? You're not." He eyed me. "So…Canaan, are you in love with Aerie?"

"Yeah," I said.

He laughed. "Why do you sound so miserable, like I'm dragging some dark and ugly admission out of you?"

I glanced up at him, frowning. "This whole thing is just…hard."

He shook his head. "Then you're an idiot, bro."

"Helpful."

"No, for real." He twisted on the bed to face me. "You're scared, is that it?"

I shrugged. "Yeah, I guess."

"Why? I mean, after the story about Lex Landon, I can see why *she's* afraid. She got fucked over and heartbroken by an asshole who should have known better. But what's your deal, Canaan? Unless you went through something I don't know about, what do you have to be so afraid of? I know about that thing with what's her name—the sound tech chick in LA— but you can't tell me you were legit *in love* with her. I mean, maybe you could have been, or wanted to be, or thought you were—"

I sighed. "Nah, none of that. I thought we could have had something, but it wasn't anything like love."

"Right, exactly. So…unless there's something I don't know about…"

"No, not really."

"Then you're just an idiot." He spoke over my protestations. "I'm your twin brother and I'm allowed to tell you when you're being an idiot, and you're being an idiot, Cane—so shut the fuck up. You *are!*"

I growled in anger and sprang off the bed, pacing back and forth. "How am I being such an idiot?"

"Because you love her and she loves you! You know her. You've been friends with her your whole fucking life. You know you have insane sexual chemistry. You know her secrets. I'm guessing you've told her yours, not that you really have any secrets to speak of unless you're keeping them from me. So what's left? Fear? Of what? Getting hurt? It not working out? Shit, man, yeah—that's scary. When you love someone, it's scary. I love Tate, and I feel the fear. But what, you're gonna miss out on loving an amazing woman, and letting that amazing woman love you just because you're *afraid* of it not working out? What the fuck, man? Since when are you such a pussy? You think a woman like Aerie Kingsley is *ever* going to come around again? You think you'll ever, fucking *ever* find someone who gets you like she does? You miss out on this because you're afraid, Canaan…" he hissed, too pissed to even speak. "Seriously. You're the dumbest asshole on the planet if you let her slip through your fingers."

"You make it seem so obvious."

"BECAUSE IT IS!" he shouted. "She went after

you! You ran away, vanished on her, on all of us, and she went after you! That says she loves you. What more do you want? How much clearer can she make it? She's the one with a very, *very* good reason to not trust you, to be afraid of love, of giving her heart to anyone, and she still went after your stupid ass. And you still fucked it up."

Rage, self-hatred, panic…which one was stronger inside me, right then? It was a toss-up. "Corin—"

He shook his head, sliding off the bed to his feet. Knotted both fists in my shirt and slammed me up against the door, putting his face in mine. "Canaan, man the fuck up!" He let me go and turned away, then spun back to face me once more, but from a foot or so away. "Being vulnerable with a woman who loves you is scary, yes, and I get that. But it makes you *stronger* to do that. It makes you a real man. It makes life make sense. What will you do with your life? I don't know. Yes, you'll have to figure that out on your own, and yes, it probably won't include me the way it used to. Life happens, man. Change happens. Get with the program, bro. You wanna go be a rock star, live on a tour bus, bang groupies and drink yourself stupid, go for it. That's not the life I want."

"I'm not saying that's the life I want either—"

"Also, for what it's worth, being in a committed relationship with Aerie doesn't mean you have to have babies and get married and settle down—either right now or ever. You do realize that, right? That letting yourself be in love with her and all that doesn't mean she's, like, going to somehow automatically demand you suddenly settle down? From what I can tell, I don't think that's what she wants any more than you do."

I felt his words smack into me like so many bullets.

Realization after realization, epiphany after epiphany, slammed into me.

He was right. Top to bottom, he was right. So was Mike.

What did I have to be afraid of? Getting hurt? It made me feel stupid, when he put it like that, like it was the most obvious and simple thing on the planet.

God, I'm an idiot.

I shot to my feet. "I have to go."

Corin grabbed my arm and pulled me in for a hug as I opened the bedroom door. "Cane, brother—we're the baddest twins on the planet, okay? We always will be. No matter what."

I hugged him back. "Damn right."

He shoved me out the door. "Go. A woman like Aerie isn't going to wait long."

I took his advice and literally ran to find the woman I loved.

FOURTEEN

Aerie

I WOKE UP AND THE FIRST THOUGHT I HAD WAS *FUCK IT*.

Fuck him.

Fuck this.

I have a life to live. I'm not going to sit around waiting for Canaan Badd to get his head out of his ass. I may not ever love anyone the way I love Canaan, but...

Shit, that line of thought doesn't take me anywhere good.

It doesn't matter. I don't need him. I don't want love—I never wanted to be in love. Neither did he.

So fuck it, right?

He ran, so now it's my turn. I went after him, and

he freaked out on me. Didn't even give me a chance. Pushed me away before I could hurt him when all I needed was time to absorb what he'd said.

Which was that he loved me.

Shit.

He's not coming back. Who am I kidding?

I started packing. I didn't bother folding anything, I just tore skirts and dresses and shirts off the hangers and started shoving them into a suitcase as fast as I could. For some reason, it was hard to see the clothes, though. They were all blurry, and my eyes stung.

Which was stupid, because it felt like I was crying—*again*—and I'd only just managed to stop.

Why did he have to be so stupid? I never abandoned him. I wasn't—I just needed time to process, and he couldn't give that to me. What was I supposed to do, pop out with "I love you" when even hearing him say it at all had shocked me to my core, had shaken me so badly I couldn't think?

I found myself on the floor, sobbing all over again. How had everything gotten so messed up? Why did love have to suck so bad? Why did it always have to hurt? Books and movies always make it seem like if you just take the leap, things will always pay off. The guy would always show up at the last second, proclaiming his love. Probably all wet from a rainstorm, wearing a thin white shirt.

It wasn't over…it still isn't over!

Except this is not *The Notebook,* and I'm not Allie, and he's not Noah.

He's not going to show up, because this isn't a romance novel. This is life, and people suck, and they let you down and they don't show up and they're not going to love you. They're just going to hurt you.

I pushed myself to my feet, wiped my eyes, and tried to stop crying. Tried to tell myself to stop being stupid. I'd survived Lex and everything he did to me, which was just about everything a man could do to hurt a woman. I'd survived Lex, and I would survive Canaan.

Only…I never loved Lex. Not like I loved Canaan.

But that didn't matter, did it?

I went back to packing.

I jumped out of my skin when I heard a knock on the door. My heart pounding, I unlocked it and pulled it open.

Canaan. Standing there in faded, ripped jeans. Combat boots. Plain white V-neck T-shirt, soaked to the skin, his tattoos bright in the dim light of the hallway. Eyes wild and wide, chest heaving from exertion. Hands fisted at his sides.

His deep, rich brown eyes searched me. Saw the tears. His eyes flicked past my face to the open suitcase on the bed.

He shook his head. His hand lifted, slid underneath my loose blonde hair to cup the back of my neck. He pulled me closer. I resisted, shaking my head, tears trickling down my cheeks. Instead of pulling me closer, then, Canaan moved up against me, staring down at me, brushing my tears away with his thumb.

"I'm an idiot," he murmured, his lips half an inch from mine.

I laughed through my tears. "So am I."

"It should have been the most obvious thing in the world, but I'm such an idiot." He cradled me against his chest instead of kissing me like I thought he would.

Right then, holding me was both the best and worst thing he could have done: the best, because it was what I needed more than anything in the whole world, to just be hugged by Canaan, and the worst, because what I needed more than anything in the whole world was to just be hugged by Canaan. It meant more tears. But they were tears of relief.

"God, Canaan."

"I know."

"You hurt me by leaving, and then you pushed me away when I panicked."

"I know. I'm sorry."

"I'm sorry, too. I should have done a better job of just saying that I just needed time to absorb what you'd said."

"And I shouldn't have freaked out. There's no excuse for the way I reacted." He pulled away just enough to touch my chin with his fingertip, gazing down at me. "I want to be able to say I'm not scared of loving you, but I can't."

Fresh panic sizzled through me. "Canaan, what are you—"

He smiled down at me. "What I can say is that I love you. I'm giving that to you. Putting myself out there, even though I know I have no way of knowing if it'll work out. I know I want *us*. I want *you*. I don't know what our future will look like, but—"

I sobbed, laughing, and reached up to put my fingers over his lips. "Canaan? Shut up a second, baby." He went silent, blinking at me in confusion. "I know all that. I know you love me. I know you're still scared of...everything. I know I haven't given you a lot of reasons to trust me, to trust that I'm willing to love you back, especially because you heard me saying I doubted I could. I know all that."

"You have every reason to doubt it, to doubt me, to be scared of loving me."

"Canaan, what I'm trying to say is that I love you. I do. We don't have to have our whole lives figured out. We're only twenty-one and we don't have to have it all figured out. If you love me, and I love you, then we can commit to figuring it out together."

His lips framed mine, and his hands cupped my cheeks, and his body was hard against mine. My tears didn't stop, but I didn't care, because these were tears of joy, of relief, of love. I lifted up on my toes and kissed him back, tearing his hair free of the wet top-knot, letting the damp locks drape around his shoulders. He stepped forward into the room and kicked the door closed and pressed the lock, and then we were moving together toward the bed. I felt him push the suitcase aside, and I heard it *thunk* heavily to the floor, clothes scattering everywhere. He sat down, and I stood between his thighs; it was my turn to grasp his face in both hands, our kiss pausing as our eyes locked.

"This is different, Aerie," he murmured.

"What is?"

He lifted my dress, the same one I'd put on back in Seattle the last time I'd seen him, over twenty-four hours ago; I'd slept in it, never took it off. "This. It's not a distraction."

I shook my head, and took the dress off and then yanked off my thong. He already had his shirt off, so I helped him out of his jeans and found him hot and hard and waiting.

"It's different," I agreed.

He had a condom in his hand, and I took it from him, opened it, rolled it onto him. "I love you, Aerie." He hesitated. "I want you in my life. Whatever it ends up looking like, I want *us*."

I climbed onto the bed and lay down, reaching up to grasp his shoulders as he moved above me. I gazed up at him as he positioned himself over me, and I gasped as he nudged against me, and then I groaned as he slid into me.

"I love you, too, Canaan. I love you." He filled me, and I whimpered, eyes closing. "I love you so fucking much."

"Look at me, honey," he whispered, and I opened my eyes, meeting his gaze. "This is love. You and me, forever. Okay? No matter what."

I moved my hips, then, meeting his, and we groaned in unison as our bodies met in perfect rhythm. Our eyes remained locked on each other, and we moved together, gliding and grinding, gasping and murmuring *I love you*, over and over and over.

It was slow and delicate, and then it was fast and desperate. His hands found mine as I fell into climax, our fingers tangling as I wept with the sweet, wrack-ing bliss, which I reached at the exact same moment as Canaan, and he was crushing me with his beautiful weight and he was slamming into me and my heels were hooked around his backside and his face was buried between my breasts and I heard him chanting my name, chanting that he loved me, and I heard my own voice screaming or singing or keening, a high wailing sound that may have been words, but which I knew he understood as an expression of love. And then, when I was capable of speech, long moments of aching gasping rapture later, I nibbled on his earlobe and whispered to him that I loved him, over and over and over and over, as he gasped above me, shuddering, still hard and throbbing inside me, and my hands caressed him, petting his hair and the firm muscles of his back.

And I knew, then, that I'd never understood love: you can only truly understand it after you've totally given yourself over to it and trusted it and let it take you over and fill you and complete you: it is sweet and it is strong; it is deep and it is wide; it is endless and it is permanent and it cannot be fathomed, only embraced despite the mystery of it, despite the terror of how completely it transforms you, if you let it.

I understood, finally, as I lay in Canaan's arms, that *this* was love—knowing despite everything, that Canaan was mine and I was his, and nothing could ever change that.

It was early the following morning when we finally stirred from the room, taking separate showers and dressing in comfortable silence and walking in the damp gray morning to a nearby breakfast cafe. We sat on the same side of the booth and sipped coffee together, and said nothing except to order food.

A thought had been percolating inside me, which I finally found the words to express. "Canaan? I want us to do music together."

He set his mug down and eyed me thoughtfully. "Beyond just jamming for fun, or playing at the bar once in a while, you mean?"

I nodded. "We're good, Cane. Together, I mean, as musicians—we're really, *really* good. We can write our own music, and we could even start touring. We could be a boyfriend-girlfriend music duo, like Johnnyswim."

"You want that? To tour, to record, all that?"

I nodded eagerly. "More than anything. I love making music with you. I love traveling. To be able to travel and make music with the man I love? What could be better?"

He tapped the tabletop with the spoon he'd used to stir his coffee, a smile spreading across his face. "I think…I think that sounds like the best thing in the world."

I giddily bounced up and down in the booth.

"This is going to be so fun!"

"What should we call ourselves?" Canaan asked.

The waitress came by then and topped our coffees, and we both sat in silence, thinking.

"Canaan and Aerie?" I suggested. "Not exactly original, but…"

He shook his head. "Too much to say." He stirred cream into his coffee. "Cane 'n Aerie?"

"Cane 'n Aerie…" I mused, an idea swirling in my head, taking shape. "Cane 'n Aerie…"

He just watched me in silence.

Then it hit me. "Cane 'n Aerie—" I turned in the booth, my grin brilliant. "Canary!"

"Canary, like the bird?"

"The most famous songbird in the world, and it sounds like Cane 'n Aerie." I waited for it to really hit him.

When it did, his face lit up. "Holy shitballs! That's brilliant!"

He flagged down a passing waitress and borrowed a pen and a sheet of paper from her order book, and began feverishly sketching. Within a minute or two, he had a rough outline of a canary, sitting on a branch, mouth open to sing, with the lettering of the name beneath the branch in curling calligraphy.

"We can get Eva to fancy this up for us," he said, "but this a decent rough idea for a logo."

I grabbed his arm and shook it, laughing out loud. "Cane, it's brilliant. We are gonna take this world by storm, baby! We need to get into the studio and start working on our setlist, start coming up with some original songs."

He got a clean paper napkin and started scrawling song titles as they came to him, songs which our sound would do justice to. Within an hour, we had a couple dozen songs listed, which we either both knew or one of us did.

After a while, Canaan sat back, twirling the pen around his fingers. "This is the most obvious thing in the world, isn't it? I mean, why does this seem like such a shockingly brilliant idea to us, when it's just… duh? Right? I mean, we played together in Anchorage for Mike and the guys, and it was even more instant chemistry than our physical connection. Every time we sit down to play together, it's just…perfect."

I sighed. "I think because we were still denying other how we really felt, that us being in love had already happened. Until we had that figured out, I don't think we could have conceptualized what it would be like to live together, be together, make music together, tour together. That much closeness, all the time? We couldn't do it and not be *together* together."

"So it was always there and we knew it deep down, but until we got this figured out—" and here

he gestured between us, "we couldn't allow ourselves
to think about doing music together."

I nuzzled up against him. "We should go make
some music together right now."

He chuckled. "We just spent twenty-four hours
making music, sweetheart."

I playfully slapped his chest. "I meant actual music, with instruments." I gazed up at him, a coy smirk
on my lips. "But if we can nail down at least three
new songs, you might be able to convince me to reward us both with a nice long blowjob."

"If we nail down three new songs, I'll tie you up
and sixty-nine you on the couch in the studio."

"Tied up *and* blindfolded?"

"You have a deal."

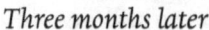

Three months later

We started slow and simple. We played as Canary at
Badd's on the weekends, and the response was over-
whelming. We had so much demand for some kind
of buyable or downloadable music, we started video
recording our practice sessions and uploading them
to YouTube. We put up an Instagram page and posted
short videos of song clips and stills of us practicing,

usually taken by Eva. Our YouTube channel exploded, as did our Insta follower count. We booked gigs in Anchorage and Fairbanks, and then in Seattle, Portland, and Vancouver. At the Vancouver show, which was a two-hour slot at a bustling rooftop bar, we were approached by a major record label exec who offered us a contract on the spot.

We turned it down.

In between gigs, practicing, and working at the bar, Canaan and Corin got to work on developing C&C Records, of which Canary was the first and only artist. Corin took over the brunt of that work, acting as the manager and producer for Canary. Tate had begun practicing with the cello again, and every once in a while the four of us would play at Badd's. We called our foursome CaCoTae, a mash-up of the first two letters of the boys' names, plus T-A-E—T-A from Tate's name and A-E from mine. Our CaCoTae music, and the videos we ended up recording and posting to our YouTube channel, became almost as popular as Canary, and so for a while Tate was still able to travel, and she and Corin would go to shows with Cane and me and the four of us would do surprise sets.

Things at the bar were changing, though. The year stipulation from Mr. Badd's will had come and gone, and the monies had been distributed...

But none of the brothers left town.

Even as Canary's following grew, and we started booking gigs farther and farther afield, Canaan and I still returned home to Ketchikan as much as possible.

Mom and Bob moved back to Ketchikan and Bob was able to work from home almost exclusively managing their talent agency, and Mom, surprisingly, ended up being C&C's first employee, as head of marketing and promotions. She was, technically, a paid employee, but she didn't do it for the money. She liked the work; it turned out putting together ads, or contacting tour managers to get Canary opening gigs were things she loved to do, and she was really good at it.

And then, on a slow Wednesday afternoon at the bar, Bax swaggered in, with Eva's hand in his. The whole gang was in the bar at once, a rarity these days. Bast, Lucian, and Brock were all behind the bar, Dru and Claire were sitting at the bar chatting, Mara was in the family booth with Jax in her arms, feeding him from a bottle of formula, with Zane on the other side of the booth, doing something with his laptop. Xavier was beside Zane, also with his laptop out, posting videos and photos of his latest crop of robots to his website. Canaan and Corin were arguing about a hook for a song they were writing, I was sitting on a stool with my ukulele, tinkering with a melody I had running through my head, and Tate had her new camera out, snapping photos of everything and everyone—after weeks and months of using her phone for photography, Corin had bought her a professional quality Nikon DSLR and a set of lenses, and had told her to stop fucking around and start getting serious about it, since she was freakishly talented with a camera.

Bax had retired from underground fighting and had opened a gym, where he acted as personal trainer and boxing coach, having gotten his personal trainer certification. Bax and Eva had leased an apartment a few blocks from the bar, a two-bedroom place, and Eva had turned the extra room into an art studio, where she spent almost every waking hour. The walls of Badd's now featured her artwork, which was for sale—she'd seen steady sales and had plans, once she could afford it, to rent out a dedicated studio space where she could work and sell.

They strolled into the bar, big grins on their faces, both of them positively beaming. As a matter of fact, and no matter how jovial Baxter may be, he wasn't the type to *beam*, no matter how good his mood, so this meant something was up.

I also noticed that as he entered, Canaan and Corin suddenly quit arguing and gave each other meaningful glances.

Tate noticed it too, and shot me a quizzical look, which I returned with a shrug and a face that said *I have no idea.*

Bax and Eva stopped in the middle of the bar, glanced at each other, and then Bax cleared his throat. "Hey, everybody. Can I get your attention real quick?"

Corin laughed. "No. No attention for you."

"Shut up, twink." Bax grinned at Eva again, and then swept his attention over the room. "So, Eva and I are engaged." There were whistles from Canaan and Corin, and a lot of clapping from everyone else, but Bax wasn't done. "And, since she and I don't really do anything the normal or easy way, we're getting married here, this weekend. And we've invited her parents. No answer from them yet, and we don't expect one, but if a stuffy old fucker and a snooty old bitch show up looking like they just bit into a lemon, you'll know it's them."

"This weekend?" Claire asked. "Why so soon?"

Eva answered. "We love each other, and we see no reason to not be married, but we also see no reason to make a big deal about it. We're just going to have a pastor come and marry us, like Bast and Dru did, and then have a party. Simple, easy, and fun."

"Um, if you want, I could call Dad and see if he can pop up here and do the ceremony for you," Dru said. "After he did ours, he actually went and got licensed to do weddings, and he's actually really good at them, now. He's doing it as a post-retirement thing."

"That would be amazing!" I said, clapping.

So, Dru called right then and there, and her father happily agreed to head from Seattle immediately.

Bax glanced meaningfully at Canaan and Corin, and then cleared his throat. "So, um…there is one other thing—"

"Eva is pregnant?" Mara piped up from the booth.

"Nope." Baxter hesitated, and then smirked. "The wedding this weekend is actually going to be a triple wedding."

There was a stunned silence.

"A…triple wedding?" Brock asked, as confused as the rest of us. "Who else is getting married?"

All eyes went to Canaan, Corin, Tate, and me.

The twins nodded in unison, stood up off of their stools, reached into their hip pockets—all of this in rehearsed synchronization—produced identical black ring boxes, and knelt in front Aerie and me. Tate had let her camera hang from the strap and was standing beside me where I sat on the stool with my ukulele.

They knelt in identical positions, one knee up, both hands cupping the rings boxes, which were extended up to us.

"Tate—"

"Aerie—"

This, in unison.

"Will you marry me?"

I looked in shock from Canaan, to Corin, and then to my sister. "I—"

"Marry you…on *Saturday*? Like…in three days?" Tate asked.

"Yes. Marry us on Saturday, in three days," Canaan answered.

"In a triple wedding, with Bax and Eva," Corin clarified.

"Mom and Bob already know, and Mom has given us her blessing to marry you," Canaan said. "In fact, I think she's already got dresses picked out for you."

"That's why she wanted to go shopping with us last week," Tate said. "To get our dress sizes."

"Sneaky sneaky," I said.

"So? Will you marry us?" the boys asked, once again in perfect synch.

Tate tapped her mouth, feigning having to think. "I mean…I *am* having your baby in less than six months. So, I guess I should probably just go ahead and marry you." She held her left hand out to Corin who, laughing, slid the ring onto her ring finger, and then stood up to kiss her.

In the meantime, I was just staring down at Canaan, still shocked. "Really?" I whispered. "We've only been together three months."

He stood up, removed the ring from the box, and took my left hand in his. "But I've known you my whole life, and us being together is the most perfect thing in the world. This is just…making us *us* forever." He kissed the knuckle of my ring finger. "Be mine, forever. Say yes, Aerie."

I blinked back tears and nodded. "I'm already yours forever, Canaan."

Canaan fitted the ring onto my finger, and then his mouth was on mine and I was kissing him as if my life depended on it, and there was more applause, more whistles and cheers from the brothers and their women—my brothers, my sisters.

"Whooooo-hooo! Triple Badd wedding, baby!" Baxter shouted. "We're gonna tear this shit up, son!"

Eva whacked him on the arm. "Baxter Badd! This is a *wedding*, not a kegger at Penn State."

Bax just laughed. "Sweetness, you clearly ain't been to a Badd wedding."

Zane and Mara both cackled.

"That's how we met, actually," Mara said. "Bax drank a whole bottle of whiskey, Zane shoved him, and they landed on broken glass, Bax ended up with a giant shard of glass in his thigh, which I had to deal with."

"And we ended up screwing each other's brains out until the small hours of dawn," Zane said. "In fact, I don't think you ever actually left, after that, did you?"

"Not for lack of trying, my dear. I was about to get away, but then you went and knocked me up."

"Indeed I did. And I plan to do so again at the first possible opportunity."

"My poor hoo-ha isn't ready for that again just yet, babe," Mara said. "Give it a year or so, and we'll talk."

Excited conversation bubbled around us, but I tuned it out. My focus was on Canaan, who was gazing down at me, those signature Badd brown eyes hot enough to melt me.

"What if I'd said I wasn't ready?" I whispered to him.

He shrugged. "You're ready. I knew you were."

"How?"

He grinned. "The other day, I casually mentioned something we'd do after we're married. Buy a house or something, I don't remember what exactly. I mentioned it just to see how you'd react, and you didn't even bat an eye at the idea of us being married. Which was how I knew you were ready."

"But...in three days?"

He quirked an eyebrow at me. "You'd rather a big church wedding with a billion roses and 'Here Comes the Bride' and a fancy reception, and everyone we've ever met?"

I tried to picture that, and I couldn't; I shook my head. "No, you're right, that'd be awful. A small, simple, fun ceremony with our family, here at the bar, with all the regulars and tourists and a band...that sounds perfect."

"Exactly. Bax, Corin, and I all talked about this a lot and figured that's what you girls would want."

"I'm surprised Eva doesn't want the big traditional wedding, though."

Canaan waved the idea off. "Nah. She had that, with what's his nuts, the rich fuckhead she walked away from. She hated it. The triple wedding with a party at the bar...it was all her idea. She asked us when we were planning to marry you guys, and we said we didn't know, and then the next day Bax popped the question to her, during sex, I believe, and she suggested this plan, where we propose to you at their engagement announcement."

"I'm glad you didn't propose during sex."

"Yeah, it's not exactly romantic, is it?"

I snorted. "The opposite, actually. I'd have cried so hard I wouldn't have been able to orgasm."

He laughed at that. "Babe, have you *ever* not come during sex?"

"No."

"Exactly. That'll never happen."

I rested my head on his chest, holding out my hand to admire my ring—a princess cut diamond, three-quarter carat, with two smaller diamonds on either side, which I took to symbolize Corin and Tate, the other two pieces of this puzzle that is the four of us. "You know, the other night we were falling asleep in the hotel room in Vancouver and we'd just had incredible sex and I was so deliriously happy that it almost scared me, and I remember thinking to myself *I absolutely cannot possibly be any happier*, and now you go and ask me to marry you, and I get to be your wife forever and ever, and now I'm even happier than I was then, which just shouldn't be possible, but it is."

"You know what's funny?" Canaan said, tipping my chin up so our lips met. "I think the same thing pretty much every day."

EPILOGUE

Joss

"I REALLY CAN'T JUST LEAVE YOU HERE, SWEETHEART." The truck driver was a big, burly, bearded man of fifty or so, wearing a red flannel shirt and a puffy black NorthFace vest. "Ain't exactly real friendly country for someone on foot, especially…you know, someone in your situation, eh?"

I sat with the door of the semi half-open. "My situation?"

He shrugged, struggling for the right words. "Young, female, alone…and, ah…in between permanent situations."

I decided to let him off the hook. "Homeless is the word you're looking for, Mark. I am homeless."

He shrugged again, rubbing the back of his neck. "Yeah, well…yeah."

"I'll be fine. But thanks for the concern."

"I'd sure feel a hell of a lot better taking you all the way to Prince Rupert, Joss. Look around you." He gestured at the thick forest on either side of the Yellowhead highway in western British Columbia.

We were on the side of the Trans-Canada Highway, called the Yellowhead in some places, such as here, just a mile or so south of where it crossed north from the mainland to Kaien Island. It was a lonely, quiet, wild, barren place. It was December, and it was cold. Three below zero, Celsius. Which meant… like, twenty-six Fahrenheit, if I was doing the conversion right. Snow blew in thin, gusting swirls of small, hard flakes. The sky was a leaden ceiling, low, angry. In truth, I really didn't want to get out of the warm, toasty cab of the semi, but I'd learned the hard way about letting truckers drop me off in towns, or close to them. People see me get out of a semi, nothing but a backpack on my back, and they assume. They ask questions. They want to *help*, or just pass judgment. No. The best way is to get out away from towns and walk in, try to blend in, find somewhere warm to park my ass, try to find some temporary cash work so I can, maybe even find a room for the night.

I tried to smile at Mark, but I'm not much for

social niceties such as smiling and shit, so it probably looked more like a constipated grimace. "I promise, I'm fine. It's only, what, ten, twelve kilometers into town?"

He shrugged. "Eleven or so from the bridge itself." He gestured again at the forest, and the snow. "It's cold and it's snowing and it'll be dark soon, and it's a good two and a half, three-hour walk from here. Let me take you closer. To the Butze Rapids Trail area, at least. Please. It really ain't safe, Joss."

I held my breath, thinking hard. I looked out at the swirling snow, feeling the cold biting my cheek just from the open door of the cab, and thought about spending the next two or three hours walking in that weather. It was late afternoon already, which meant I'd be walking well into evening, and it got dark awful early this time of year. The cab was warm, and Mark was kind, and not at all creepy, and he played decent music, too—Elvis, The Beatles, Zepplin, that kind of stuff.

I sighed and climbed back in. "The trail area, then."

Mark nodded and shifted the truck into gear, and with a groaning and roaring of the engine, we ground and rumbled onto the highway. "Where you headed, anyway? Long term, I mean. You never said."

I buckled the seatbelt across myself and picked

up the atlas from the seat bench between us, and went back to examining it. "Not sure. Alaska, maybe?"

"Alaska, huh? How are you gonna get there? Can be kinda tricky, what with all the islands and such." He glanced at me, obviously fishing for information.

I rolled my eyes at him. "I said I'm not sure. No real plans. I'm just…drifting."

Mark leaned forward to watch the snow skirl. "Awful remote area to be drifting through."

"Better than being stuck in one place." I studied the map rather than meeting Mark's gaze. "If I don't have anywhere to be, I might as well be wherever I end up."

Mark scratched his beard. "Not sure if that's smart or stupid." He steered with one hand and pulled a thick binder out from under the bench and set it on the bench, opened it, and flipped through it until he found what he was looking for, a booklet listing ferry times, destinations, and prices. "Here. Keep it. You wanna get out of Prince Rupert and into Alaska, that'll get you there."

"Thanks, Mark."

He shrugged again, and tugged on his beard. "I got a daughter a few years younger than you. I couldn't live with m'self if I left you on the side of the road in the middle of nowhere. That ain't right, eh? Hadda do something."

"Well, I appreciate it."

He nodded, and we drove in silence for a few miles, until we came to an area where the highway split off downhill to the right to a much smaller side road. A sign announced, "Welcome to the City of Prince Rupert," and it was down this road that Mark angled his tractor-trailer. We trundled to a stop a few hundred feet in. There were cars parked on one side, with concrete barriers on the other, and the forest beyond. A few people walked in pairs and small groups, bundled against the cold, some with walking sticks, others with cameras. I prepared to get out, hitching my backpack onto my back.

"I know I probably don't gotta tell you this, but be careful accepting rides from truckers, eh? Not all of 'em are like me. Some can be a bit rough around the edges, if you know what I mean. So just…be careful. Somethin' don't feel right, don't get in."

I nodded. "Yes, I've learned that. Thanks."

He stared at me, somewhat wistfully, clearly wishing there was something else he could do for me, so I waited, because he was kind and I didn't want him worrying about me.

"Ah, I got it," he said, and put the gear into park. Climbing into the back, he rummaged around for a minute, grunting and muttering, until he came out with a huge, thick, puffy baby-blue parka, from

Columbia. A knit hat. A pair of mittens.

I started shaking my head. "No way, Mark. I'm not taking your stuff."

He shoved it at me. "It ain't mine. I happened across a resale thing a while back, and found this stuff. It's girl stuff, good stuff, new. Got it for my daughter, but you need it more. She's got enough winter gear to last her 'til she's thirty, I just picked this stuff up because I can't pass up a good deal. Take it."

I glanced down at my own coat, a tattered, thin, too-small fleece that wasn't at all up to snuff for the winter up here. "Dammit, Mark, I hate taking charity."

"Ain't charity," he groused. "It's simple kindness and human decency." He shoved his hand in his pocket and pulled out a wad of cash, mixed US and Canadian currency, and tossed the folded wad into my hands. "That there is charity. I ain't been to church in a few months, which means I ain't done my tithing. Take it and no questions. It's enough to get you to Alaska. And if you wanna pay me back, find yourself a good place with good people, and live a good life. No more of the drifting."

I felt my hand closing over the money, even though I hated accepting charity. I thought about tossing it back at him, but something stopped me. The cold, beyond the cab? The thought of hunting for work in the cold, sleeping somewhere outside in an alley? I had enough cash for a meal, but not enough to pay the ferry fee, or get me a room anywhere, and the cash Mark was offering would keep me from going hungry, walking through the night and sleeping in libraries or bus stations during the day. I knew I'd need it. Working for cash with no questions asked… it was hard to find.

"I've never taken a dollar from anyone," I said. "I may be homeless, but I'm not a beggar."

"You still ain't. You didn't ask—I gave it, because it's the right and Christian thing to do."

I shoved it into my pocket, half expecting him to ask me for a *favor* in return, but I knew he wouldn't. Not a man like Mark. "Well, thanks. And if you're a Christian, you might ask God, next time you pray, why he hates me so much."

"He don't hate you, sweetheart—"

I shrugged the coat on over the one I was wearing, grasped the hat and mittens in one hand and climbed down from the cab. "Thanks again, Mark. For everything."

I closed the cab door before he could say anything else, and walked away. I tugged the hat on over my dreadlocked black hair, which hung down almost to my waist, and then pulled the mittens onto my hands. As I walked through the cold of early evening, I found myself intensely grateful to Mark for the winter stuff, because the air blew cold, and the snow stung my eyes and face, and I knew without the coat and everything else, I'd have certainly gotten sick, if not frostbitten.

I found a twenty-four-hour fast-food place, got a meal, ate it slowly, savoring every bite. I managed to kill a few hours there before the management started getting suspicious, so I found a twenty-four Tim Hortons and bought a large coffee and a couple of donuts, and took my time with them. I had a paperback in my backpack, so I got it out and spent a few hours reading, until I got sleepy and started nodding off.

I was startled awake by someone sliding into the booth opposite me—a young girl about my age, pierced and tattooed.

"I'm not supposed to let people sleep here," she said.

I sighed. "I know, I know."

She handed me a coffee. "But I happen to know the cameras don't record, and I'm the only one here 'til five. So, if you happen to lie down for a few hours, I wouldn't care. But I'll have to kick you out before my shift relief gets here at five."

I could have cried with relief, but I didn't, because I never cry. But I could have, in an imaginary world, where that would be okay. "Thanks."

She just nodded, got up, and left, disappearing

into the back of the kitchen.

I lay down on the bench and, hard and too short as it was, I curled up and managed to drift off to sleep instantly.

I was woken by the same girl, the sky still dark outside. She had a paper bag in her hands, and a cup of coffee, both of which she handed to me. "Manager is going to be here soon." She toyed with a lip piercing. "I spent six months being homeless. I know how it is."

I didn't even try to deny it, or refuse the food she was offering. "Thanks."

Another of those terse nods, and then I left with the bag and the coffee. I made my way to the ferry terminal, eating the sandwich on the way so it wouldn't get cold. It was lightening up outside when I arrived, but the ferry terminal was still closed, even though there were people coming and going beyond the terminal, getting the ferries ready.

I stood outside, shivering, hat tugged low, bouncing on my toes, sipping the black coffee until the terminal doors were opened.

The woman behind the counter eyed me with a dull, uninterested expression. "Need a ticket?"

I nodded. "First ferry out of here to Alaska."

She tapped at her keyboard, staring at the screen. "That's going to Ketchikan. Leaves at seven.

Seventy dollars."

"That's fine. Thanks." I counted out the money, stuffing the remainder—eleven dollars—in my pocket, accepted the ticket, and followed her directions to the correct ferry.

I took a seat, sipped the last of my coffee, and waited for the ferry to load. It only reached half-capacity, and then departed.

Ketchikan, Alaska. I wondered, idly, what it would be like.

I'd been drifting steadily westward for a long, long time. I'd started in Yarmouth, Nova Scotia… when was that? Two years ago? Three? Three, I think. I'd been stranded there, alone, after—

I mentally stopped myself from going down that path.

I'd started in Yarmouth, Nova Scotia, three years ago, and had slowly made my way across the entire continent, walking a lot of the way, taking rides as I could get them. Once, I even splurged all of my cash on a train ride across part of Saskatchewan, simply because I hadn't had the heart to walk across all that flatness. But then I'd been stuck, and had paid for my splurge in weeks of walking, begging for a day's work here and there from farmers and highway cafe and gas station owners. I'd wait on tables for tips, clean bathrooms for change from the till drawers, anything that anyone would pay me a few bucks cash to do. Anything that meant I could keep eating without having to strip, hook, or beg, all three of which I refused to do.

The ferry ride to Ketchikan was long as hell, but it was beautiful. I finished my one paperback, and spent the last hour watching the waves ripple and crash and crest out the window, and I even saw some orcas porpoising together.

When I arrived, it was blizzarding. Like, snowing so hard I couldn't see my hand in front of my face.

Welcome to Ketchikan, I guess. I'd heard it wasn't supposed to get as cold here as most people expected, which is part of the reason why I'd been drawn to Ketchikan. It wasn't tropical, but it certainly wasn't the Arctic. So either they'd lied, or this was an unusual snowstorm.

I sighed, pulled up my hood, tugged my hat lower, zipped the coat up all the way, and trudged out into the blizzard, totally unsure as to where I was going, just following the sidewalk, with the docks and the sound on my left, buildings on my right. It was something like noon, almost one in the afternoon, but perhaps because of the blizzard most of the stores and shops I passed were closed.

I needed to get out of this snow. It was getting colder by the minute, and even with the winter gear

Mark had given me, I was starting feel the cold in my bones.

Honestly, I'm not sure what happened next. Maybe it was the fact that I'd only managed a handful of hours of sleep at a time in the last week, and was exhausted. Maybe it was the blinding snow obscuring my path, making it so I only thought I was walking in a straight line, following the sidewalk. Maybe I just wandered in the wrong direction. I don't know.

I just know one second I was walking, stumbling in the snow, my teeth chattering, cursing the snow, desperately hoping to come across somewhere open that was warm where I could wait out the storm. The next second, I was toppling airborne, my foot hitting air, and then I was weightless. I hit the water and went under, flailing in shock, so cold it hurt, so cold it burned. So cold I couldn't breathe, couldn't move, couldn't swim, could only pull helplessly at the water as I sank, weighted down by my coat and my backpack.

And then...I don't know what happened.

I just don't.

I don't remember a thing. Just the cold and the darkness and the ache and burn, and then nothingness, and then I was waking up, bobbing up and down rapidly. In someone's arms? I saw sky, through a break in the snow, a hard, dark gray sky. A face. Thin, sharp

features. Hard planes, high cheekbones. Elven, is
the word that came to mind. Dark eyes. Chocolate
brown, piercing.

He was wet.

Snow was coating his features, and ice was forming on his face, frozen by the cold, knifing wind.

I felt him tugging open a door. The wind vanished, the sky vanished. Warmth, or so I imagined it
to be, but I could only feel it as at the absence of cold.
I was shaking, shivering, having trouble breathing. I
heard voices, male and female, asking questions. The
man carrying me didn't answer, and I felt him going
up stairs. Felt him set me on my feet and then kick a
door closed.

I couldn't stand, and he caught me.

"Gotta get you out of these wet clothes." He
wasn't asking, he was telling.

I shook my head. "No…no."

"You'll die of hypothermia."

I let him take my backpack, and watched him set
it on the floor—that backpack had everything I own
in it. I was numb, now. Aching. Beyond shivering or
chattering, I was so cold I was almost hot. Bleary.
Dizzy.

I felt him strip off my coat, kneel to take my
shoes, gently helping me to sit down on the floor, because I couldn't stand on my own. Layer by layer he

stripped me, his eyes always on mine, until I was down to bra and underwear, and I was too cold to care. His eyes stayed on mine as he got those last wet things off me, and then he wrapped a thick towel around me and used it to dry me, rubbing vigorously, then helping me to sit on the edge of a bed. When I was dry, he wrapped a furry, fleece-lined blanket around me, the fur tickling my nose.

My hair was still damp.

It hurt.

But his eyes were…I want to say kind, but that wasn't quite the right word.

Cutting.

Piercing.

Intense.

Wild.

Deep.

He'd seen me naked, and hadn't so much as glanced away from my eyes for even a split second.

I've got Mom's body—medium height, narrow in the waist and wide in the hips, thick in the thighs and heavy at the chest. My point is, men look. Even homeless and wandering, men look.

This man didn't.

But not because he didn't want to—I could see his gaze flitting back and forth, as if forcing himself to keep his eyes focused on mine.

He was gorgeous. I didn't miss that, now that I was dry and wrapped in a thick blanket, and was warming up. He was…a god; I couldn't look away.

"I'm Lucian Badd," he said, in a voice like the black silk of midnight, quiet, strong, smooth, dark.

"J-j-j-Joss." I tried again. "I'm Joss Mackenzie."

He got up and moved to the door. Something inside me twisted, cracked. Broke.

"D-d-don't leave me alone," I heard myself say. "P-p-please."

He gazed at me steadily, his expression unreadable. "I have to change. I'm wet too."

"Did you—did you j-j-jump in after me?'

He nodded. "Couldn't let you drown. In that water, you would have been gone in another few seconds."

He didn't leave though. He just peeled off a thick sweater, a t-shirt, then kicked off his boots.

My heart thundered.

Lucian Badd was beautiful, and I was delirious. Or crazy.

I don't know.

I just knew I didn't want him to leave me alone.

Jasinda Wilder

Visit me at my website: **www.jasindawilder.com**
Email me: **jasindawilder@gmail.com**

If you enjoyed this book, you can help others enjoy it as well by recommending it to friends and family, or by mentioning it in reading and discussion groups and online forums. You can also review it on the site from which you purchased it. But, whether you recommend it to anyone else or not, thank you *so much* for taking the time to read my book! Your support means the world to me!

My other titles:

The Preacher's Son:
Unbound
Unleashed
Unbroken

Biker Billionaire:
Wild Ride

Big Girls Do It:
Better (#1), Wetter (#2), Wilder (#3), On Top (#4)
Married (#5)
On Christmas (#5.5)
Pregnant (#6)
Boxed Set

Rock Stars Do It:
Harder
Dirty
Forever
Boxed Set

From the world of *Big Girls* and *Rock Stars*:
Big Love Abroad

Delilah's Diary:
A Sexy Journey
La Vita Sexy
A Sexy Surrender

The Falling Series:
Falling Into You
Falling Into Us
Falling Under
Falling Away

The Madame X Series:
Madame X
Exposed
Exiled

The One Series
The Long Way Home
Where the Heart Is

Badd Brothers:
Badd Motherf*cker
Badd Ass
Bass to the Bone
Good Girl Gone Bad
Badd Luck

The Black Room
(With Jade London):
Door One
Door Two
Door Three
Door Four
Door Five
Door Six
Door Seven
Door Eight
Deleted Door

Standalone titles:
Yours

Non-Fiction titles:
Big Girls Do It Running
Big Girls Do It Stronger

Jack Wilder Titles:
The Missionary

To be informed of new releases and special offers,
sign up for
Jasinda's email newsletter.